SILENT

INVITATION

PROLOGUE

Something was wrong with the quiet.

It pressed too close. Thicker than night. Heavier than silence should be. Not the kind that lulled you to sleep, but the kind that held its breath beside your ear—waiting.

Katherine didn't know how long she'd been awake. The clock on her nightstand had died days ago, the batteries rolled under her dresser, forgotten.

Outside, the trees creaked. *Normal sounds*, she told herself. *Wind in the eaves.* A branch tapping the glass. She stared at the ceiling anyway, pulse shallow beneath her skin.

Something had shifted. Not tonight—before. Before she had words for dread. Before she knew you could grieve the living. Before she understood that fear could wear your own face.

The air felt wrong.

Not colder. Not warmer. Just… displaced. Like something had stepped through her life, leaving a faint imprint.

Later, she would learn to follow that feeling. To trust the prickles on the back of her neck. *To listen when the world went still in all the wrong ways.* But tonight, she only knew to hold her breath. To wait.

And in that waiting, something inside her changed.

It would be years before the knock on the door. Before the first case. Before the briefcase. But this moment—this stillness—would become the thread she followed through everything that came after.

Because the quiet wasn't empty. It was a message.

She just hadn't learned how to read it yet.

Do Not Disturb (Please, Universe)

Katherine

A long stretch, arms overhead, toes curling into the sheets. The wall clock came into focus. Then again—rubbed the sleep from my eyes. *No way.*

Afternoon.

Had I really slept through the night... and the entire morning?

A slow smile tugged at my lips. I couldn't even remember the last time I'd slept like that. *Not without jolting awake from a nightmare or a buzzing phone or just... tension.* Every part of me felt heavier, in the best way. Rested.

This. This was exactly how a long-overdue day off should start.

No guilt. No rushing. No people. Just pajamas, junk food, and a full season of my latest Netflix obsession.

The fridge was mostly empty except for the essentials and a couple things I'd been saving for a day like this. An hour later, and the kitchen was warm and alive with smells that made my mouth water.

Steak hissing on the indoor grill, juices searing in just right. Onions caramelized in my favorite cast iron skillet—rich and golden and sweet. Potato had just finished baking, wrapped tight in foil and puffed full of steam when I unwrapped it. I leaned into it like a hungry animal, eyes half-lidded, nose inhaling the buttery, earthy scent.

This beat the hell out of microwaved leftovers and gas station coffee.

The steak rested on the plate, perfectly cooked—*medium rare, just how I liked it.* I set the table.

One plate. One fork. One knife. *Always just one—Better that way.*

The first bite was heaven—tender, juicy, better than half the restaurants in town. *The moment it touched my lips—*

Ping.

My phone. A text.

Of course.

Do Not Disturb was on. Always was. Everyone knew the rule—if it wasn't a life-or-death emergency, don't call. Don't text.

Phone buzzed on the table by the front door, something cold crawled up my spine.

My stomach growled for my steak—a deep, hollow reminder I hadn't eaten in... *who even knew?*

But then the phone buzzed again—louder this time, a cold, insistent vibration that cut through the quiet like a knife.

I looked over again at it, not wanting to respond.

Charging cord tugged loose as I snatched it up. One text. Four words.

WE NEED YOU NOW!!!

Four Years Gone

Katherine

12 P.M.– Her Apartment, Manhattan
The air seemed thinner. Like the walls were pressing in.

I called the station, already reaching for my boots. *Crime scene. Homicide.* My throat tightened like a hand was wrapped around it.

My stomach dropped. One name clawed its way to the front of my mind before I could stop it.

No. No way.

He was gone.

Had to be.

There it is. The wrongness in the air.

Still, the thought slithered in deeper.

Two years in, and they handed me his case. I thought I was ready, but I wasn't. His name still crawled under my skin.

What he did to those women...

What he did to me.

Every clue felt carved for me.

He knew me. Studied me. Mocked me in silence, in symbols. It was never about just getting away—it was about watching me break while he did.

And I did.

Had to take a leave. Couldn't even look in a mirror without hearing his laughter in my bones. He vanished. Cold trail. No trace. No closure. *Just fourteen women and fourteen hollow spaces in their families.*

Four years gone. *If this was him, rest wouldn't exist.*

This time, I wouldn't just chase him.

I'd catch him. And I wouldn't let go.

Room 412

Bride (Unidentified)

10:03 P.M.–Midtown Hilton, Room 412
The zipper stuck halfway up her back again.

She huffed, twisting in front of the mirror, her fingers fumbling with the slick satin. "Betray me now, and I swear I'll go naked down the aisle,"

Her reflection stared back in soft ivory. The seam across her hips hugged tighter than last week. Stress-snacking was real, no matter how many carrot sticks she'd choked down.

She turned sideways, smoothed the bodice, and held her breath to zip the last inch. Victory—but the win felt hollow. The lighting was wrong—too yellow and flat. Candlelight and laughter would fix that.

She peeled out of the gown and hung it on the hook, slipping into her robe with a sigh.

A knock startled her.

She checked the peephole. A man in a gray suit stood there with a clipboard and a smile.

"Apologies, Miss. Wrong room," he said when she cracked the door a few inches. "Congratulations, though. Big day tomorrow?"

Her eyes flicked to the dress behind her, visible in the mirror.

"Yeah," she said softly. "Thanks."

She shut the door, bolted it, then slid the chain into place.

Her fingers lingered too long.

She crossed the room, dropped into the desk chair, and tugged the notepad toward her. Her phone sat beside her, screen still dark.

Then it buzzed.

A single red heart.

9:16 P.M.

Weird—it was almost ten-thirty now.

Maybe the signal lagged. Concrete walls, or maybe the universe held it back until her nerves needed a soft place to land.

Just a heart. After they'd agreed on no texting the night before.

She wasn't sure if it was sweet or if he was spiraling too.

She liked the idea of both falling apart in tandem. That felt romantic. Honest.

The city glimmered through the crack in the curtains. Headlights blurred at the intersection. A man walked a golden retriever with balloons tied to its collar. She smiled.

Then wrote.

"I vow to learn what your silences mean…"

A few more lines followed, about choosing each other when the coffee burns and life gets too heavy.

By the time she folded the paper and tucked it into her jewelry bag, it was nearly midnight.

She yawned, stretched, and decided to grab ice for her water. The machine was just down the hall. She didn't even bother putting shoes on—just slippers and her robe.

The hallway was quiet. The vending machine buzzed like a tired bee. She waved at a man exiting the elevator but didn't notice if he waved back.

Back in the room, she kicked the door shut behind her. Didn't lock it.

She curled up in bed, robe still on, hair still damp from earlier. One hand under her pillow.

The AC clicked on. The curtain lifted, then settled again. A musty smell lingered.

And just before she drifted off, a chill passed through her—

as if someone out there already knew which room was hers.

And that the door never really latched behind her after all—its faint click swallowed by the hum of the AC, so soft she never even heard it.

Where the Air Dies

Katherine

12:36 P.M.–Service Alley Behind to Thai For
Flashing lights bounced off slick surfaces, and the blur of reflective vests moved like ghosts through the drizzle.

Homicide—*and the kind of staging that always made my phone ring.*

The door groaned open. The stench hit me first—rotting garbage, clinging to everything. Rain didn't wash it away. It made it worse, like the air itself had gone sour.

For a half-second, the stink hooked into a memory I didn't want—four years ago, different city, same sick weight in the air.

I missed West Virginia. Clean air, pine needles, damp soil. Not this choking rot coating the inside of my nose.

My chest tightened, the memory of home curling around me, locking my boots in place. I couldn't move, couldn't think past the scent.

Wind shifted. The full brunt of the stench hit hard, like a slap across the face.

Gag reflex flared. Acid crawled up the back of my throat. *Swallow it down. Do not contaminate the scene. Do not lose it.*

Didn't matter how many of these I'd been to—never got easier. The smells always found new ways to invade.

A young officer stood nearby, trying to look useful.

"You never forget that smell. Burning flesh. Who found it?"

He flinched, throat bobbing. "First on the scene."

The tremble in his voice gave him away.

He held out the clipboard, fingers twitching. I scrawled my name across the security log, eyes scanning the list—who had already been through.

"First one?"

"Yes, Ma'am." Rigid posture. Stiff as rebar.

He'd break down in the car after. Or in the shower. Somewhere he thought no one would hear him.

"Wish I could tell you it gets easier. But if it ever does," I handed back the pen. "That's your sign to get out."

He nodded once, eyes distant. Probably already filing this moment into some locked box in the back of his brain.

"The body..." His voice dropped. "I think she was placed here. It looks like the perp tried to stage it—like she climbed in on her own."

Clever.

"Ma'am, we haven't touched anything but what we had to. Just walked the perimeter. I'll take you through the scene."

Evidence would come later. First came the story—the one the scene was already trying to whisper.

The alley reeked—old grease, wet cardboard, and something sour buried deeper beneath it all. Narrow, slick, boxed in by dumpsters and the backs of restaurants that hadn't cleaned their bins in weeks.

A metallic clatter echoed down the brick walls—trash cans shifting. Too soft and quick to be human. Cat, probably. Or something chasing one.

Voices tangled around me, overlapping. Theories tossed out like dice—blood loss, overdose, maybe dumped postmortem. No one had the full picture yet, but that didn't stop the guessing.

Barricades lined the edge of the scene; officers posted every few feet to keep the crowd from pressing in. The perimeter was locked down tight—no hazards, no lingering suspect.

Movement caught my eye—an officer speaking to a man in a stained apron.

To Thai For.

He stood stiff, arms crossed like a man trying to hold himself together with tension alone.

The caller. Had to be. The one who found her.

The Scene Speaks

Katherine

The dumpster loomed ahead—faded blue, streaked with rust. Rain from earlier still beaded along the rim, sliding down in slow trails.

Boots crunched on wet gravel. Footprints crisscrossed in every direction. Too many to sort by sight. Forensics would handle that.

Check security log. Print everyone's shoes. Rule out who didn't belong.

Scrawled it into my notebook, flicked the pen.

Peeled on the gloves—*snap, stretch, seal.* A barrier between skin and what waited.

The dumpster lid stood open, heavy.

The scent hit—stale rainwater, rust, something sharper underneath. Burned hair. Blood.

Inside, the shadows took shape.

Left side—cardboard, sticks, arranged like a makeshift fire pit. Desperate.

Right side—

She sat slumped in the corner. Knees drawn to her chest. Arms wrapped around them. Her posture was so human, so normal, it took a second for the rest to register.

Skin split in thin, deliberate slices. Blood dried in layers across her limbs. Charred patches trailed along her torso— half-burned, like the killer lost patience halfway through.

Mid-twenties, maybe.

She'd been arranged—no doubt about it. Someone wanted her to look like a vagrant, hiding out from the rain. Just trying to stay warm.

If that employee hadn't come out for a smoke, she'd have burned unnoticed. Written off as an accident.

No autopsy. No justice.

The cuts—so shallow, so precise—would've been missed beneath the scorched skin. The pose would've told the wrong story.

But now—the truth showed through the cracks.

It was a message.

The killer knew this place. The alley. The trash schedule. When the kitchens went dark and the cooks stepped out for air.

This took time. Planning. Patience.

The victim wasn't dumped—she was arranged. The killer waited for the perfect window, when no one would be watching.

The faint yellow dust coating her skin caught my eye. Not soot. Powder.

Fire extinguisher residue. Class ABC. Monoammonium phosphate—pale yellow, clings to everything.

Flipped through the eyewitness notes—no mention of using one. Why leave that out?

Scribbled a note: *Ask why. ABC residue=intentional?*

The closer I leaned in, the harder my stomach turned.

Half her hair burned away. Charred tufts clung to her scalp. *Even from here, I could see the way the charred strands fractured at the slightest stir of air.* The left side of her face...melted. Cracked skin peeling back over bone.

Her head hung low, chin on knees. Clothes—rags, torn, soiled, reeking of smoke. Dressed to look homeless.

But the blood told the truth. Or the lack of it. Nothing pooled beneath her. No spray, no drag marks.

She didn't die here.

That knot twisted deep in my gut. Heavy. Hot.

Him.

Walked around the dumpster. Stepped over glass. Shined my flashlight down on her arms—still wrapped tight around her knees like she was freezing.

The beam sliced through shadow.

Nails. French tips. Clean. Precise.

Not a vagrant. She'd been chosen.

Eyes tracked her knuckles, slow.

There. The left hand—bone jagged where her ring finger should've been. Skin torn just right.

Cigar cutter. His signature.

Didn't matter that someone almost caught him. Didn't
matter a new hire wandered outside at the wrong time.

He wanted her found.

And he wanted me to find her.

Reentry Wounds

Katherine

The weight slammed back before I could stop it—every insecurity, every crack I thought time had sealed.

His case.

The past punched through, dragging me under before I had a chance to brace.

My desk. Mail spread across it, meaningless envelopes blurring together—except one. Handwritten. My name.

Katherine Poe.

No return address. Just that name in a neat, scrawl.

My stomach dropped before I even touched it.

The flap peeled back, and then the words—

Hello there, the game has begun...

Heart in my throat. Sweat on my palms. Nausea curled deep.

An artist gets better with time. I will get better with each one.

I hadn't caught him.

And somehow, I'd convinced myself he was done. That he'd burned out. That four years of silence meant closure.

But it was a lie. A soft, dangerous lie I let myself believe just to sleep again.

Now—his silence shattered, and the echo of that first letter screamed louder than the crime scene around me.

Why now? What had shifted after all this time?

This wasn't a return. It was a continuation.

Cat and mouse. Still his favorite game. Still feeding on attention, the choreography, the ritual of it all.

But this time, I was different. Stronger.

Years buried in his files—his language, his tone, the twitch behind his phrasing. Every nuance cataloged. Every detail burned into me. The slant of his handwriting under stress, the manic energy behind his staging.

Fingernails bit into my palms. Couldn't stop clenching. Couldn't release.

This time, there was no escape. No bowing out.

I would end this.

Notebook out. Every move practiced. Sketched the layout—sharp, precise. Every angle, every object marked."

If someone else had to finish it, they'd have enough to build from.

Cold crawled down my spine. The last time I handed off a case like this...

His threat had nearly broken me. Had broken others.

But that was then.

This was now.

Deep breath. Focus.

I motioned the photographer over. "Full video sweep. Then stills. Every angle."

Voice steady. No tremble. Not this time.

The phone was already in my hand before I realized I'd moved.

"Bella." No preamble.

"We've got a homicide. I need you here."

A breath. Then that tone—clipped, coiled steel. "Text me the address. I'm on my way."

Dr. Bella Vine. Medical Examiner, Manhattan. She'd outlasted three mayors and half the force. Sharp as a scalpel, steady as stone. She'd stood with me over every bride in New York—gloved hands, leveled voice, never blinked.

Just the facts and a flashlight.

The call ended. Phone slid back into my coat.

I walked to the kid on the stoop—pale, shaking, one breath away from collapse.

He looked steadier now, like someone trying to convince himself he felt fine. Hands twitching. Guilty of something—just not this.

"Katherine Poe. Lead Investigator."

He nodded too fast. "Okay."

"Clarify a few things. You said you came out for a smoke?"

"Yeah." He swallowed. "Came out back, saw the dumpster lid up. That's not supposed to happen..."

"We're told to keep it shut—people, animals, looking for food. I thought—"

"Homeless," I finished for him. "That's what you told patrol."

"Right. I walked over, and I saw her. Just… sitting in there." His eyes flicked to the alley. "I didn't touch anything. I swear."

"You didn't try to put the fire out?" I asked.

"What?" His head jerked back. "No. There wasn't a fire."

"There was," I said quietly. "Burned down one side of her body, clean and controlled. The other half was dusted in dry chemical. Like what's in your wall-mounted extinguishers."

He blinked like I'd spoken another language. "I didn't do that. I swear. I just saw her, puked, and ran inside."

He gestured toward a damp patch of concrete.

"Right there."

I signaled the forensic team. They converged fast, quiet. Cameras clicked. Notes scribbled.

The smell of bile still hung in the air.

I studied him. "You didn't mention the yellow powder."

"I didn't see powder," he insisted, but the lie was too honest to be intentional. "I—I just panicked. She looked… melted."

His throat worked.

She had been. One half charred. The other scrubbed like someone had started a fire, then changed their mind halfway through.

Not to save her.

To preserve what was left.

Back at the dumpster.

Everything marked. Sketch done. Photos taken. Now came the real work.

One leg over the edge, boots scraping against cold metal. The stench hit harder inside—burnt flesh, rain-soaked trash, blood.

She sat curled, unmoving. Waiting.

The shadows swallowed detail, but I didn't need much light to feel the chill settle under my skin.

A dark stain by her side. Dried blood—or rust. Hard to tell in this light.

"Camera," I said. The photographer climbed halfway up, aimed. Flash lit up the walls, the body, the stain.

Luminol hissed against the surface, the blue glow unmistakable. Blood.

Kneeling, I popped open the tool kit. Fingers found the vial of distilled water, unscrewed the cap one-handed while the other grabbed a sterile cotton swab.

Dip. Shake. Swab. Six times until every cotton tip ran dark. Each one clipped to dry, logged, and bagged with the same relentless rhythm. Even the control sample—clean—got the full treatment.

Every move mechanical. Precise.

Footprint in the corner. The angle caught the tread just right—deep grooves, partial toe. Size nine boot. Not fresh but not worn out either.

Lifted with adhesive. Transferred clean. Logged. Sealed.

Still that pressure in my gut. Tight. Unshifting.

Too clean. Too familiar.

Nothing that wasn't meant to be found.

Teeth clenched hard. He was meticulous. Always had been. Left just enough to make us think we were close.

And yet—I couldn't stop. Wouldn't. He slipped once. He'd slip again. One hair. One fiber. That's all it took.

I breathed slow. Refocused. Body first. Evidence second.

Flashlight swept over her. Wrists—bruised, raw. Ankles too. Rope burns. Bound.

She hadn't climbed in herself.

He set the fire. Then used the extinguisher. Covered his own tracks, left the performance intact.

Costume still intact—rags burned into her skin, like he needed her to look disposable.

A glint caught in the beam.

No mistakes. No rushing.

He'd led us here.

But this time—I wasn't following.

I was hunting.

The Postmortem Hour

Katherine

Dr. Vine emerged from the rain—tall, straight-backed, trench coat snapping like a war banner.

The streetlight caught the silver threaded through her dark hair, twisted into a no-nonsense bun at the nape of her neck. Fine lines bracketed her mouth and eyes, but there was nothing soft about them—just years of unsparing truth. Her presence didn't announce itself. It pressed in. Calm, composed, clinical.

I'd seen her work enough scenes to know—when she stepped forward, time seemed to hush.

Her hands pulled on a fresh pair as she approached the body without hesitation. She nodded to me once—sharp, surgical.

"Let's move her," she said, voice low and cool as the rain soaking through my collar.

Gloves on. Breath held.

Her body settled into our arms—light, fragile.

The body bag lay open on the gurney, waiting. We eased her in, every limb a final pose. A breath of silence before the zipper.

Dr. Vine crouched beside her, quick but careful. Her fingers moved with the kind of familiarity of years of seeing the worst.

"Strangulation," she murmured. "Time of death—10 a.m."

So recent.

She slid paper bags over the girl's hands, sealing in whatever she might have fought to keep.

Something caught—

Her eye. Left lid gone—peeled back or burned away. Green, glassy. Right eye shut. Eyebrow intact. Brunette.

Something tightened at the base of my skull.

I swallowed hard. Wrote it down. Didn't say it out loud.

Gone.

Another one ripped out of the world too early.

I swallowed hard, throat raw. Couldn't go there. Not now.

She disappeared behind the zipper.

The team wheeled her out, careful steps echoing off metal.

I crouched where she'd been.

Water pooled in rusted dents. Rain from the cracked lid dripping a slow rhythm. Nothing else. No trace.

Like she'd just appeared. Like he'd conjured her from nothing.

Outside, canvassers were already moving. Knocking on doors. Asking the same questions.

Had anyone seen anything?

No. Nothing. No CCTV flashes, no delivery van, no stolen car. Just a void where a girl used to be.

He was a ghost again.

We bagged it all—open containers, cigarette butts, shattered Styrofoam, torn plastic lids. Garbage. All of it.

Garbage could speak. Garbage could bleed.

If even one molecule of him lingered—skin cell, print, a breath sealed in plastic—

We'd find it.

And when we did, I'd be waiting.

Move Seven

Katherine

By midnight, all we had was garbage—and ghosts.

11:56 p.m. My pulse lagged. We were getting nowhere, the walls of the office pressing tighter with every dead-end lead.

I told the team to go home—lie if they had to, pretend the world wasn't crumbling. We'd pick it up in the morning.

The air outside assaulted me as soon as the door shut behind me—humid, electric, humming with something I couldn't name. I wrapped my coat tighter around me and headed to my car.

Then I saw it—an envelope tucked beneath my wiper, tugged by the wind. My stomach dropped. Hand trembling, I pulled it free, scanning the shadows. No one. But he'd been here.

I didn't even open it right away—just stared at it, heat rising from my chest into my throat. That sick bastard had walked right up to me. Brazen. Mocking. I was so tired of being the mouse in his game of cat and...

Artist.

Feeling the weight of it, I braced for impact. I tore it open, jaw tight—and a motel key slid out, clattering against the hood of my car. The metallic sound felt deafening. I picked it up with numb fingers, flipping it over. No number, just a tarnished brass tag.

The letter inside was handwritten—slanted, elegant, menacing.

You've disappointed me, Katie.

My grip crushed the paper, fury rising.

The name punched the air from my lungs, skin crawled.

No one had the right to use it. Not him. Never him.

You should've found the first clue by now. No worries—I'm advancing you. The map leads to the motel this key belongs to. You must go alone. If I see anyone else with you, my model is dead.

My mouth went dry.

I'm giving you what you want more than anything—your chance to save her.

No signature, but it didn't need one.

I could feel him in every flourish of ink.

I stared at the key for too long, my hand still trembling. No blood on it. No hair. No obvious sign that this was another of his riddles laced in gore. But the real weight wasn't physical.

It was time.

He was pushing the clock forward. Advancing the game.

He was watching to see how I'd move.

I spun on my heel and headed back inside. My boots echoed through the empty hallway like a warning. This wasn't protocol. This wasn't procedure. This was obsession.

He had a weakness. One glaring, bleeding weak spot.

Me.

He needed my attention the way an addict needs a fix. That meant he would eventually screw up. And when he did, I'd be right there.

I expanded the motel search to surrounding boroughs, zooming out and out until something clicked—A match.

Heart pounding, I hesitated for half a second. Just one.

Brandon's number hovered under my thumb.

Then I remembered her. The model. The ticking clock.

She dies if you bring anyone.

I swallowed the urge for backup and closed the file.

Another message. Another performance. But this time, I wasn't just his audience—I was his actor, too.

This was my move.

And I was going in alone.

Where The Light Doesn't Reach

Katherine

The Lynbrook Motor Inn came into view, its neon sign flickering like it was as exhausted as I felt. My stomach twisted. I gripped the wheel, trying to steady myself.

I parked under the buzz of a broken streetlamp. My pulse thundered in my ears as I climbed the stairs, each step heavier than the last. Room 142 loomed ahead, its metal door dull and unassuming—except I knew better.

My fingers hovered over the key like it might burn me.

What if he was in there?

What if this was the end of the chase?

I drew my weapon, holding my breath as I slid the key into the lock and pushed the door open with the barrel of my gun. One inch at a time.

Silence.

The room smelled like bleach and mildew. I swept the corners, checked the bathroom, the closet, under the bed. Nothing. Just my thunderous heartbeat.

I locked the door behind me, double-checked it, then pulled on my gloves.

The briefcase sat on the bed, waiting. I stared at it. The combination lock taunted me with its sealed numbers.

I tore the place apart—drawers, cushions, mirror—frustration mounting like a ticking bomb.

Then, inside the nightstand, etched into the wood—929. I entered it.

The lock clicked. The lid creaked open.

I angled my flashlight inside, the beam shaking just slightly from the tension coiled in my wrist.

There inside was a map fragment, ripped from a larger map.

A chess piece. The black queen. My throat tightened.

A lock of brown hair, streaks of blonde tied delicately with a bright blue ribbon.

Not the silky kind, tied in a bow. This one, the edges frayed, suggesting it had been carried, not worn.

My stomach knotted. Elisabeth used to braid a ribbon into my hair before school.

My fingers twitched—muscle memory—before I caught myself.

Not like this one, but still—the color hit like a sucker punch.

But this wasn't about her.

I sealed it in an evidence bag, tried to move on—but my fingers twitched, wanting to smooth it back into place. I didn't know why it felt so intimate.

Then the glint of something polished—an emerald paperweight. No, not real. Too light.

Next to it, my eyes narrowed as I spotted a bulge in the fabric beneath it.

Something sewn in.

I pulled my pocketknife out with a trembling hand and carefully sliced the stitching. My fingers closed around cold metal.

Gold. Circular. Etched with wear.

Coal mine scrip. West Virginia. My chest constricted.

I cradled the scrip in my palm, the weight of it almost unbearable—not from the metal, but from everything it meant.

He was sending me a message.

Somewhere in the back of my mind, I knew—I wasn't chasing him through the streets anymore.

I was following him into the dark.

Into the places where the light doesn't reach.

I packed everything carefully back into the case, every motion deliberate, controlled. The urge to scream was locked tight behind my ribs.

***

I dropped it in the lab queue when I returned, forcing myself to walk like I hadn't just unraveled.

He could've chosen anything—any object, any clue. But he chose that. A currency that only meant something to someone from where I'm from.

It wasn't a breadcrumb. It was a trigger.

He wanted me to feel it. The pull of home. That ache of memory. The blue ribbon. The scrip.

Cold Instincts

Katherine

By dawn, I'd shoved the nightmare—briefcase and all—into an evidence locker, the key biting through my palm. The chain-of-custody slip fluttered, still damp with motel bleach. Nobody asked where it came from. They didn't have to. The frantic scrawl across the label—*For Poe*—screamed louder than any answer I could've given.

By noon, I'm back in the task force conference room, clutching a cold mug of coffee. The projector ticks like a migraine in my skull. On screen: a burned woman, sitting curled in on herself, ring finger gone, blackened flesh peeling like old wallpaper. Even flattened on the wall, she smells like smoke and funeral homes.

"Trauma or timeline?" Brandon mutters, voice rough. He's propped against the table, eyes rimmed red from another sleepless night. Early forties, tall, thick-shouldered, built like he never stopped lifting. Close-cut curls glint with a hint of gray at the temples. But it's his eyes that always get me—dark, unblinking, honest to a fault. He has the kind of gaze that makes you want to tell the truth, even when it burns on the way out.

Trauma, always trauma. Let the pain tell the story first.

Brandon points: third-degree burn, wire garrote, severed finger, no soot in the lungs. Controlled. Clean. He didn't just kill her. He curated her."

"No DNA," Kali adds. "Nails scrubbed clean. Like she was embalmed before the fire." Kali in her mid-thirties, sharp in both mind and presence. Dark chestnut hair, straight and neatly tucked back, framed a face that gave little away. Her gray eyes were steady, clinical, always watching without haste. She didn't waste words, didn't waste energy.

My pulse stutters. *Too perfect. Too careful.*

The word slips out before I can cage it. "Staged."

Heads turn. Cheryl Maddox raises a single brow.

She stands near the screen, arms folded across a slate-gray blouse, the color of dry storm clouds. Early forties, hair a halo of auburn curls pulled back in a no-nonsense twist. Her eyes are green-gray stone—cool, calculating, but not unkind. When she speaks, it's deliberate. When she listens, it's lethal.

I set my mug down. Porcelain clicks against the table, a sharp staccato. "This wasn't disposal. This was exhibition. He wanted us to see it. All of it."

He. No proof yet. Just the ache in my bones and the pulse of memory telling me the Artist is back on the canvas.

Brandon doesn't flinch. "Feel familiar?" he asks, low.

I hold his gaze. He knows that look—I wore it the last time the bodies started stacking. "Not enough to swear to," I lie. The pattern's forming but saying it aloud makes it real. And I'm not ready to give him that yet.

Kali had the timeline queued up already, but it was Cheryl who spoke first.

"Watch this."

I leaned over the desk, elbow digging into the edge, heart doing its usual dance against my ribs.

"11:57 p.m.," Cheryl said, hitting play.

The hallway lit up in black and white. Hotel carpet, walls like a waiting room. Then—there she was. The bride. Robe tied, slippers, ice bucket tucked under one arm.

She looked relaxed. Half-asleep maybe.

"She waved at someone," I said, pointing to the figure stepping out of the elevator in the distance. "But…"

The man didn't wave back.

Didn't even pause.

Just kept walking.

"Watch," Cheryl said. "That's key."

The bride turned the corner, out of frame.

And that's when it happened.

Not a knock. Not hesitation. Just a shadow—low, hunched, moving fast. A man, all in black, hood drawn low. He didn't glance around. He didn't fumble.

He had a key.

He slipped into her room like he'd always belonged there.

I straightened, throat tight.

Cheryl rewound it. Played it again. Slower this time.

No defining features. No limp. No swagger. Nothing you could use to describe him. *That was the point.*

The bride came back on-screen twenty-three seconds later. Still humming to herself. The ice clinked.

She nudged the door closed behind her.

Didn't even look at the lock.

And then—thirty minutes passed. Nothing unusual. No motion in the hallway.

Until 12:31:08.

Just a blink.

The screen skipped—a digital twitch, like a scratched DVD. 'Was that--?' I asked. 'Yeah,' Cheryl said. 'Watch again."

12:31:07. Clean.

12:31:08. A hiccup.

12:31:09. Clean again.

"That's not a gap. That's a splice," Cheryl muttered. "Like a loop was patched in."

"But why wait until after she was back inside?" I asked.

"Because this isn't when he went in." Her eyes never left the screen. "This is when he took her out."

I felt it in my chest like a dropped stone.

"He erased the exit."

"Looped the hallway feed," she said. "Just long enough to cover the abduction."

"But everything else looks normal," I whispered.

She nodded. "That's what makes it good."

I reached for my pen and circled the timestamp anyway.

12:31:08

"The moment she disappeared—and no one knew to look.

Circle back later, pull the footage from victim thirteen's building. If he'd scrubbed her too, then he wasn't just slipping past locks. He was rewriting the truth.

They move on—dumpster logistics, pickup routes, missing fiancé—but it's static in my skull. I hear the motel key ticking in my coat pocket. West Virginia coal. New York ash. *He's drawing a line only I'm meant to follow.*

Cheryl finally dismisses the team, but I stay rooted. The screen is dark now, but I can still see her. That missing ring finger. That ritual-level care.

"You want back in?" Cheryl asks quietly.

I never left. "I already am."

She studies my face like she's searching for the fractures beneath the surface. Then nods once. "Then let's prove it."

Ash on the Wind

Katherine

Katherine stepped out into the daylight and winced—too bright; too open.

The city hummed around her with a kind of unbothered urgency—cars crawling past, someone laughing across the street. Ordinary chaos. Indifferent.

She stood there for a beat on the sidewalk, her hands buried in the pockets of her coat like she might anchor herself through sheer pressure. The door clicked shut behind her. It should've felt like relief. Instead, it felt like exile.

"Take the morning off," Cheryl had said.

As if time still worked the same after a body like Glenna's.

She walked.

No destination. No rhythm. Just movement. Like if her legs stopped, her brain would catch up—and she didn't want that. Didn't want to replay the image of Glenna curled in on herself like she was trying to hide from life. Katherine knew that feeling too well.

The air carried the scent of roasted peanuts and wet concrete. A street vendor was setting up near the park entrance. She almost smiled at the normalcy of it. *Almost.*

She found herself at a bench near the fountain—not the one from her dreams. Not the fountain from the woman with whispering eyes. This one was cracked and shallow, water speckled with leaves and pennies. Still, she hesitated before sitting. Water didn't feel neutral anymore.

A pigeon landed on the armrest beside her, twitching its head like it was judging her thoughts. She stared at it, then looked away. *Even the damn bird had better boundaries.*

She pulled her phone from her coat and checked it. No new messages. She almost wanted one. Something unrelated. A wrong number. A reminder about her auto's warranty about to expire. Anything that didn't involve bodies or burnt flesh or ring fingers gone missing.

A breeze kicked up. Cold. She tugged her coat tighter and leaned forward, elbows on knees, gaze falling to the concrete. Someone had scrawled *Forgive yourself* in blue chalk near the bench.

Her breath caught.

She didn't know if it was an order or a dare.

Her phone buzzed.

Not a message. Just a calendar reminder: *Therapy at 4 p.m.*

She stared at it like it belonged to someone else.

She wouldn't cancel. But she wouldn't go in ready, either.

She drew a slow breath, let the cold burn down her throat, and exhaled like she could exorcise something with it.

Then she stood.

Time to get moving. Again.

The Longest Hour

Katherine

4:03 p.m.

I was late when the elevator sighed open on the tenth floor of the Midtown medical co-op—a beige hive that smelled faintly of antiseptic and paper coffee cups.

The fluorescents buzzed in sync with my pulse. Every second asked a question: *still here? still breathing?*

Therapy. Right. The bureau shrink thought one hour in a padded chair could keep me from breaking when the next bride turned up missing a finger. Cheryl called it maintenance. Brandon called it bullshit. I called it optional—until the chief made it mandatory.

Mandatory doesn't feel like help. It feels like surveillance. Every minute here is a debt not being repaid.

The door read *Dr. C. Delaney, Psy.D.* in pewter letters trying not to matter. I signed in with a pen taped to a daisy.

A soft chime—Dr. Delaney herself, cardigan sleeves pushed up, flats whispering across the carpet…

4:10 p.m.

Soft voice. Softer office. A window spilled afternoon light across two chairs angled toward each other.

I chose the one nearest the exit.

She clicked on a small recorder. "Just for accuracy."

"Rough week?" she asked gently.

"Rough year."

She didn't reply. That silence worked better than questions.

"He's back," I said. "Same mutilation. New staging. I thought we had him, Cass."

First time I used her name. She didn't flinch.

"Describe what that realization felt like." she prompted, calm and steady.

"Tight." I curled my fists. "Here." My chest.

"Still now?" she asked, tilting her head slightly.

I nodded.

"Can we breathe with it?" she encouraged, voice low.

I wanted to scoff. *Breathing doesn't unburn bodies.* But I did it—box breathing, in for four, hold, out for six. Something I taught rookies after their first child homicide. Easier taught than practiced.

"Better?" She asked.

"Quieter," I admitted.

"Let's talk about the ring finger." she continued. "You connected that mutilation to earlier victims?"

"He takes what people use to feel complete. A finger you promise with. A future you build on. He leaves them unfinished. Like they didn't deserve to be whole."

She jotted something down. *Wholeness*

"Does that word mirror something in you?" she asked.

"You mean survivors' guilt." I flexed my fingers—ten. "I got out. She didn't."

"Elisabeth," she said softly.

I nodded. "Every case file's a debt. I pay it with time, with blood, with sleep."

"Debts imply repayment," she observed. "What does repaying look like?"

"Stopping him. Making sure no one else's mother imagines what color flowers her daughter would've carried."

"And if catching him never happens?" she asked.

I looked out the window. A ship drifted past on the river—slow, deliberate.

"Then the debt compounds."

4:27 p.m.

She flipped to a clean page. "What memory keeps resurfacing?" she asked.

"Dad, Mom, Elisabeth, and me sitting around the fireplace"

"You'd forgotten it?" she asked gently.

"Until this week. Now I can't shake it."

"If it returned, it matters." she said, more certain than I felt.

- 29 -

I hesitated, then nodded. "It came back like it never left."

"How does that affect your process?"

"It destabilizes it. Makes everything porous. I start wondering if I missed something. Or if I'm making things up to fill the gaps."

"Does that scare you?" she asked quietly.

"It should. But I'm too tired for scared. It's like chasing a shadow that edits itself mid-step."

"And where does that leave you?" she asked.

"Alone." I looked down. Ink on my thumb. I hadn't noticed picking up a pen.

"Are you?" she asked, gentler now.

Brandon's tired smile flickered in my mind. Cheryl's steady presence. Dani's laugh.

"I shouldn't be. But you can't bring autopsy photos to brunch."

"Isolation as tactic?" she asked.

"Survival."

She nodded slowly. "Where's your safe place? Not strategic. Not guarded. Just... safe."

I didn't have one. Not my apartment—haunted by files. Not the precinct—neon purgatory. Not my parents' house—just ghosts there.

"Let's build one," she said. "Not physical. Memory. Ritual. What grounded you before the job?"

I searched the past: pine needles under bare feet, creek water so cold it stole breath, Elisabeth humming Fleetwood Mac while braiding wildflowers into my hair.

"The woods," I said. "Back home."

"Can you anchor to that?" she asked.

"It feels far away."

"Then bring it closer." She handed me a small river stone from her desk. "Texture is memory. Scent is memory. You need talismans, Katherine—not trophies."

I rolled the stone in my palms. It smelled faintly of moss. Maybe real. Maybe not.

4:42 p.m.

The recorder clicked off.

"Homework," she said gently. "Bring one tangible reminder of the woods next session. And maybe… call your mother. Family isn't a debt."

I slipped the stone into my pocket. "What if he follows the talisman?"

"Then you'll know he's still behind you," she said quietly, "Better than wondering if he's ahead."

I didn't argue. But it chilled me anyway.

She walked me to the door. "Text me if the panic widens. We'll tighten it together."

I nodded.

4:58 p.m.

The August heat smothered me as I stepped outside, but the stone stayed cool in my hand.

I breathed—deep and slow.

The city smelled the same: diesel, seawater, roasted nuts. But the stone in my pocket pulsed against denim like a heartbeat from another life.

Maybe that was enough. For now.

The world steadied—barely.

The debt still waited. And so did he.

The Quiet Collector

The Lonely Heart Murderer

I have seen the Poe girls a thousand ways.

Katherine laughing, head thrown back beside a rust-stained creek in Bluefield.

Their mother's hands—calloused from the garden—cupping cracked China mugs while smoke curled from a woodstove that never quite warmed the corners of that sagging house.

Those memories do not belong to me, all in photographs inside her parents' home, yet I wear them like borrowed skin. Slide inside, practice the angles, fix what time has blurred. Rehearsal is survival. I replay them until they feel real.

It started with a newspaper clipping, yellowed and damp: *LOCAL GIRL MIRACULOUSLY ESCAPES ABDUCTOR.*

The ink bled in the rain, but the photograph endured—Katherine at twenty, blanket around her shoulders, eyes hollow and blazing. I wanted to crawl into that photograph, peel it open like a seed pod, see what rot or gold lived behind those eyes.

Rule One: Know Your River

A life's current leaves debris: report cards, Facebook posts, property records, a father's forgotten VA loan. I drifted the edges first: courthouse archives, the obituary of a grandmother who canned peaches and taught Sunday-school hymns.

The internet supplies what nostalgia edits. With enough usernames and patience, you can resurrect a childhood you never lived. People digitize everything eventually, even ghosts.

When a detail snapped into focus—Grandpa's coal scrip carried like a lucky coin—I catalogued it. Not a relic; an artery. Hold the right artery and you feel another person's heartbeat.

Rule Two: Speak Their Dialect

Observation is only half the hunt; mimicry seals the trap. I practiced West Virginia cadence in motel mirrors. One word could open or close a door. I knew she preferred her birthday candles arranged so no two colors touched. That was enough to believe I'd been there.

Almost…

Rule Three: Rewrite the Origin

They say a hunter should not love his prey. Folklore. Love is the finest snare—invisible, pliant, irreversible.

But love needs a story, and stories need beginnings. The truth—how we really met—wrong for many, so I wrote us something keener. Childhood neighbors across barbed-wire fences. The boy she never noticed, who memorized the clack of her bicycle spokes. The lanky teenager she loaned a pencil to on the first day of Chemistry. Lies taste better if they curl against something plausible. I rehearsed variants until I could recite them without a pulse jump. In one version I carried her books when her wrist was sprained; in another I listened from the shadows while her father yelled about curfews. Detail is adhesive: people doubt broad strokes but cling to the grain pattern on the door.

One day—soon, if she tracks the breadcrumb trail—I will offer a version like a confession. She will test it against her fractured recollections, find room where it might fit, and the hook will set.

Tonight, I stand in the dark across from her apartment— five floors up. She's inside, pacing, phone pressed to her ear but not dialing. Even from here her shoulders curve inward like parentheses—whole sentences trapped between.

Poor Katherine, collecting clues like splinters under skin, never suspecting how long I have sifted through her refuse—digital and literal. *(She shreds her mail now. Good habit. Too late.)*

The streetlight hummed above me. For a moment, I thought of the way my mother used to hum while mending shirts, thread catching the light.

I pulled a copy of a Polaroid from my coat: Elisabeth and her on the roof during the summer. Sunlight, fearless grins. I stole the original from a photo album.

I imagined the sound she made when it arrived, postage from a town long forgotten.

Did she think *family* then? Or *ghost*?

Either would do. Missteps keep the dance alive.

Rule Four: Stay Ordinary

Real monsters don't lurk; they commute. I pay rent on time, exchange mild laughter in office hallways, forget coworkers' birthdays like a normal man. Human camouflage is laundry left unfolded on the couch, a half-eaten burrito in the fridge.

Katherine sees patterns in ashes and smoke, but the glue of everyday life bores her. That is where I live—in the dull glue. She'll never sniff there until the last move, and by then the board flips. *Queen takes king—game resets.*

I love giving her riddles that rot into answers.

Rule Five: Memory Is the Only Weapon

She thinks survival makes her stronger. It makes her readable. Trauma etches grooves; water follows the easiest channel. Pour fear here, anger there—it will obey physics.

I don't need to be her brother or neighbor or childhood shadow to know how the creek behind their house sounded after June storms. I have recordings. A geologist's survey lists decibel ranges for runoff over shale. I loop it at night to lull myself, to rehearse.

Data becomes memory, memory becomes history, and history is heritage.

Across the street her lamp snaps off.

I press two fingertips to the Polaroid, sealing an imaginary kiss on a thirty-year-old image, then slide it back into its sleeve.

Good night, Katherine... Tomorrow, we move one piece closer.

When Silence Doesn't Hurt

Katherine

Twelve hours off.

No crime scene tape. No briefing room. Just time—unstructured, unwelcome.

She hadn't asked for it. Wouldn't have. But the Chief had seen it in her eyes—how tightly she clung to the case already.

"You won't take a single day off after this," He'd said. "Not even your regulars. Take these twelve."

It felt like exile-like being benched in the middle of a collapse.

She didn't know what to do with the stillness. Twelve hours without a morgue tag. Without evidence bags or cause-of-death guesses whispered over coffee.

Maybe it wasn't him. Maybe Glenna didn't fit the pattern. Maybe this wasn't the start.

But she knew better.

Still, the silence pressed in. And all she could think was: *what if she missed the next one while she was off the board?*

The apartment windows breathed cold air against her spine as she leaned against the sill, watching a man below sell soft pretzels from a steaming cart. His hands moved with certainty, like they'd done this same ritual on this same corner for decades. She envied that kind of rhythm. There was nothing rhythmic about what she did.

The mug in her hands was too hot, but she didn't let go.

It was the first time in weeks she wasn't dressed for war.

No blazer. No badge digging into her hip. Just sweatpants with a stretched-out waistband, a tank top with a crusted coffee ring near the hem, and sleep-tangled hair she hadn't bothered to fix.

The city moved outside her window, loud and alive, utterly indifferent to the fact that she was off duty—against her will.

She stepped back from the window, crossing the apartment in socked feet, everything too quiet, too soft beneath her. She sat at the edge of the bed, unmade since yesterday, maybe the day before. Her fingers gripped the edge of the mattress, grounding herself in the sag of it.

No radios. No morgue call. No briefing buzz.

Just the hiss of the radiator. Her own breath, shallow and disobedient.

The silence pressed in like a sealed room. It didn't feel peaceful.

It felt staged, like something important had just been scrubbed away.

It felt like the space between a heartbeat and a scream.

She rubbed the heel of her hand into her chest, trying to press the weight out. Maybe she could convince her body it wasn't always under siege. She tipped backward onto the mattress, the ceiling coming into focus.

There were water stains in the corner she hadn't noticed before.

Her phone was face down on the nightstand. She didn't touch it. Not yet. She wasn't ready to see another message from Brandon asking for a status update, or another headline with words like *mystery or pattern or ritualistic.* No pattern. Just losses. Each body took more of her. Less of her left to find the next.

The phone was right there. Her mom's voice would be soft. Steady. But the lie would catch in her throat before she even said *I'm okay.*

Instead, she stared at the cracked ceiling and wondered if it had always looked like that—or if she'd just stopped looking up.

Her tea was cold when she finally got back to it.

She poured it down the sink.

Twelve hours.

She could try.

Later, she showered longer than necessary, letting the water beat down on the back of her neck until her thoughts stopped pulsing so loud. Then came jeans. A black tee. Her hair pulled back. Civilian Katherine, not Investigator Poe. Just a woman headed into the city to see a friend.

Dani had chosen the brunch spot—some fusion joint tucked between a florist and a record shop in SoHo. The kind of place that served overpriced coffee and lavender pancakes. Katherine didn't care. She liked Dani's laugh. She liked the way she never asked about the bodies or the man they still hadn't caught.

Over lemon scones and iced espresso, Katherine smiled. A real one. Not forced. Not shaped like a weapon.

"You're glowing," Dani said, leaning over her cup. "Did you finally go on a date?"

Katherine rolled her eyes. "No. I just slept."

"What? Two hours?"

"Five. Uninterrupted."

Dani placed a hand over her heart. "My God. She lives."

They laughed. Loud. Whole-hearted. A woman at the next table side-eyed them. Dani flipped her off without missing a beat, which made Katherine laugh harder.

But underneath it all—beneath the ease, the warmth, the city pulsing with life—Glenna stayed threaded into the back of her mind.

Katherine stirred the ice in her glass. "I think he's escalating."

Dani sobered instantly. "Same guy?"

She nodded. "He's building something. I don't know what, but every move feels more… deliberate."

"You'll find him."

"I must. This one is not going to be the last if I don't."

The air shifted. Dani didn't speak for a moment, then reached across the table and squeezed her hand.

They didn't talk about it after that. They finished their meal, browsed the record shop, argued over a Stevie Nicks vinyl, and hugged goodbye with promises to meet again soon.

The scent of cinnamon and clove curled through Katherine's apartment, thick and warm. She hadn't meant to bake—the plan was just to make tea, but her hands had itched for something tactile. Something with clear instructions. Whisk, pour, stir, knead. There was comfort in the math of it, the quiet science of heat and sugar.

Her windows fogged at the corners from the oven's breath. Outside, the city blurred. Lights smeared across slick pavement. But in here, her world had shrunk to four walls, the hum of jazz from the record player, and the quiet tap of her spoon against the ceramic mug.

She sat cross-legged on her couch, in leggings and a hoodie, hair tied up in a sloppy bun. No makeup. No case files. No murder boards.

Just her.

And, remarkably, that was enough.

Her phone buzzed, but she didn't look. It could wait. Everything could wait.

She stretched out, letting her head fall back against the cushion. Her fingers still smelled like nutmeg.

Tonight, she allowed herself to be human.

The scones were cooling on the counter. Cinnamon orange with a hint of vanilla. She'd bring some to Brandon tomorrow. Maybe share a few with the rookie in forensics who always forgot to eat.

The smallest smile tugged at the corner of her mouth. *This—this was what she was fighting for.* The soft, fragile normalcy of real life. A night without sirens. Without headlines. Without monsters pressing up against the glass.

She carried her tea to the window and leaned her forehead against the cool pane. Below, people moved like shadows between streetlamps. A couple laughed as they ran through the rain. A taxi honked. Life kept going.

She let the warmth of the tea seep into her palms.

She breathed.

Tomorrow would come. It always did.

But tonight, she was whole.

Missed Call

Katherine

Morning had crept in, light dull across the kitchen tiles, indifferent to her sleeplessness.

Her thumb hovered over *Mom* in her recent calls.

Don't. Not yet.

She looked at the message from last night. "*We love you, Muches.*" Light. Simple. Safe.

She never wrote back.

Katherine had planned to call the other day—her first day off in forever. They were supposed to talk about that Netflix series they'd been watching in sync, one episode at a time. That had been the deal. Her mom hated waiting but promised not to move ahead without her. Katherine could practically hear the playful impatience in her voice, the "*Well, I guess I'll just rewatch season two again while you get your life together*" sigh.

But the call never happened.

Life didn't wait.

Somewhere between *I'll call her after dinner* and *just one more minute of quiet*, the world cracked open. And now nothing felt simple. Not even a phone call.

Her phone screen dimmed. Her reflection ghosted in the black glass. Her thumb retreated like the number might burn her.

The coffee in her mug had long gone cold. It sat untouched on the counter. She leaned against the counter's edge, trying to will herself into calling—just a quick check-in. Say something upbeat. Pretend everything was normal. Lie.

But her throat tightened.

She wasn't ready to lie to her mother yet.

The worst part was they were supposed to visit next weekend.

That was before the dumpster. Before Glenna's body hit her like a punch below the ribs—burned, posed, too quiet.

Before she stood beside a victim, unraveling in real time, watching her world collapse in a single breath.

Before the air reeked of cooked flesh and something older, more final.

Before the case came screaming back, like it had just been holding its breath beneath the surface, waiting for the right moment to lunge.

Now she couldn't imagine them coming. Not here. Not to this space where everything felt haunted and half-lit. She didn't want her mother anywhere near the version of herself that came alive when bodies hit cold metal. The version that saw blood patterns instead of carpet stains, that read smiles like codes to be cracked.

She opened a text thread. Her fingers hovered over the keyboard.

Hey, I might need to reschedule next weekend—something's come up.

No. Too vague.

I've got a work emergency. Might need to push the visit a bit.

She frowned. *Push* implied delay. Temporary. Hope.

That felt like a lie too.

Backspace.

She typed again.

Hey, I know you were planning something, and I was really looking forward to it...

No, she wasn't. She was dreading it. But she had wanted it. Craved it, even. A chance to feel normal. To hear her mom complain about the traffic and fuss about nothing and everything. To sit across a dinner table and eat something with texture without imagining the crime lab file underneath it.

She swallowed hard and forced herself to finish the sentence.

...but things at work have gotten heavy. I'll explain more later. I love you. I promise I'm okay.

She stared at the message for what felt like an hour before pressing send.

Three dots appeared almost instantly. Then disappeared.

Came back. Vanished again.

She could picture it—her mom holding the phone, rereading, trying not to overreact, pacing the hallway of their log cabin in the mountains of West Virginia, probably calling for her dad in the next room. "*Paul, she says she's fine but it's that tone, you know the tone…*"

Katherine set her phone facedown. She couldn't handle the reply just yet.

Instead, she walked to the living room and sank into the couch, wrapping a throw blanket around her legs like armor. She hadn't turned on the lights, and the gray of early dawn smeared across the windows, bleeding into the floorboards.

The silence buzzed. It didn't feel restful. It felt like something lurking.

A memory crept in—her mom, curled on this same couch last Christmas, knitting half a scarf while Katherine worked a cold case on her laptop nearby. They hadn't talked much, but it had been enough. Just being there.

"You need better lighting in here," her mom had said. "It's like you're living in a cave."

Katherine had mumbled something about mood lighting. She liked the dark. It helped her think.

But now, the dark only reminded her of what she hadn't said.

That the job made her feel like a ghost sometimes. That she missed them more than she knew how to say. That she couldn't sleep without triple-checking the locks and memorizing the creak patterns in her hallway floor.

That her sister's absence still echoed in her bones.

Her phone buzzed once. Then twice.

She reached for it, already bracing herself.

We love you too, baby. Call when you can. We're here.

Simple. Safe.

Katherine's throat caught.

She pulled the blanket higher, up to her chin, and tried to breathe through the ache in her chest.

They'd want to come anyway, she knew. Her mom would offer to cook, clean, talk about anything but work. Her dad would bring that stupid book of logic puzzles he always tried to get her to do with him. It would be awkward. And good. And hard.

But not now.

Not yet.

She stood again. Restless. Pacing.

At some point, she drifted toward the hall closet—her pulse quickened, though she couldn't say why—opened the door. Inside sat a small box, unmarked, plain. She hadn't touched it in years. But her fingers moved on their own.

She knelt and dragged it out, setting it on the rug like it might detonate.

Inside were old photographs. Printed ones. Her mom had mailed them years ago, back when she still believed in scrapbooks and holiday letters.

She flipped through them slowly.

Elisabeth's face stared back at her in nearly all of them. Sometimes blurred mid-motion. One photo made us look almost identical. Same wild hair tumbling over our shoulders—her eyes brighter, mine darker—but both carrying that flick of sunfire around the pupil, like we'd caught a piece of summer and kept it. Elisabeth's smile broke wide, mine was still shy at the edges. It hit me then how much of her I still carried in my own face, no matter how many years had passed, no matter what I'd tried to scrub away.

In one, we sat on the roof of our childhood home, legs dangling over the edge like nothing could ever break them. Elisabeth's eyes were closed; chin tilted to the sky.

Katherine had always envied that—how easily Elisabeth could surrender to joy.

A note slipped from the back of the photo. She caught it mid-fall.

Her mother's handwriting.

Found this while organizing old boxes. Remember this day? You two made Dad climb up there with you. He was terrified. I think this was the last time I saw you both just... still.

Still.

That word lingered too long.

Katherine set the note aside.

Her phone buzzed again.

Also—tell me when you're ready for season three. I've been good, I swear. Not even a sneak peek.

Katherine smiled despite herself. A small one. The kind you feel more than show.

Hey Mom. I was going through that small box of photos you mailed a couple years back for the scrapbook and found this one of me and Elisabeth on the roof. It made me remember that day. Thanks for sending it.

She sent it quickly, but her thumb lingered, the cold weight of the photo growing heavier. Her mom responded immediately.

Sweetie, that's not one of the photos I sent. It went missing from the photo album years ago. I must've put it somewhere and lost track of it. I'll look for it next time I visit.

Katherine frowned, a tug of doubt in her gut. She quickly typed again:

Are you sure? I know it came around the same time. I think it was in a separate envelope—maybe you mailed it later when you found it.

She stared at the screen, waiting. When the reply came, it was quick, certain.

No, it disappeared at least 10 years ago. I was so upset when it went missing. I promise, it's not one I sent.

Katherine felt the breath leave her lungs. Her mother's certainty sat heavy in her chest. She stared at the phone, the edges of the photo blurring in her hands, wondering why she couldn't shake the cold feeling that lingered in the room.

She typed back:

I'll be ready for Season 3—soon. I promise.

Then she shut the box. Tucked the photos back into the dark.

Some griefs weren't meant for daylight.

Some truths had to wait.

But not forever.

Blueprint of An Obsession

The Lonely Heart Murderer

He wiped the blade with a cloth soaked in vodka—not because it needed cleaning but because he liked the gleam.

Clarity. That was the word. Everything before her had been noise—messy, rushed, ordinary. But Katherine Poe? She demanded curation.

Stepping back from the table, he surveyed the rows of bridal props lined in meticulous precision: lace gloves. Pressed veils. Shoes dyed ivory and arranged toe-to-heel. In the center, a mannequin draped in white satin—unfinished, armless.

His hands hovered above the bodice. It needed movement— ripple, tension. Something human. He examined the hem, then reached for the pinned swatches taped beside it: tulle, raw silk, beaded chiffon.

Nothing felt right.

He turned to the display board, flipping to the next Polaroid. Katherine—walking along the sidewalk, hair tucked under a beanie, coffee still steaming. The tilt of her head. The deliberate stillness in her shoulders. Always ready to bolt.

He pinned the photo beside the mannequin.

"Your lines are too stiff," he told it. "She folds tension like origami. You're flat. You're lazy."

He moved to the shelving unit along the far wall—each drawer labeled with tight, unforgiving block print:

Photos-Preserved
Fabrics-Organza, Tulle, Leather
Personal Effects-(Unreturned)

Facial Studies-Angled Profiles
K.P.-Evolution

He slid open the bottom drawer.

Sketches—each version of Katherine in charcoal and ink—stacked with obsessive care. One with her mouth parted like she was about to speak. One with her spine arched, caught mid-turn. Another with her eyes shut; head tilted toward his imagined voice.

Not captured. Not posed. Summoned.

He traced the line of her cheekbone on one drawing.

Turning back to the canvas, he noticed the mannequin's neck looked wrong.

He fetched a scarf from another drawer, draped it around the base like a garrote in reverse—soft, not brutal. Still wrong.

He stood there a long while, arms crossed.

Eventually he whispered,

"Frame by frame... stitch by stitch... she'll flinch at the ninth."

The room echoed with the hum of fluorescent lights and the low whirr of the dehumidifier, which kept his collection from rotting too soon.

The Space Grief Left

Katherine

Pacing. Always pacing. The floors at the station practically memorized the soles of my boots. Lead after lead, call after call—every dead end only wound the tension tighter in my chest.

Still nothing from Dr. Vine. Still no report. Every tick of the clock dragged behind my ribs like barbed wire.

By the time the silence stretched past midnight, the words stuck in my throat. *"Call it for the night."* It wasn't rest we were walking into—just a new kind of waiting.

***

The apartment was too quiet.

Routine kicked in. One room at a time. Every closet. Every door. Checked the locks.

Three times.

Still didn't feel safe.

Not with him out there.

That old knot twisted deep, like it never left. How long before he reached out? How long before the next letter, the next game?

Here we go again.

Sleep? Not likely.

I fought it—kept my mind from drifting where it always went. Tried to pull it back with logic, with planning, with anything but that.

But my mind didn't listen. It drifted anyway.

***

I was back there again.

Back in the days after I came home. After I escaped.

And she didn't.

We'd already finished a year of college by the time everything shattered. I didn't go back. Couldn't imagine walking those halls without Elisabeth beside me—nudging my shoulder, whisper-laughing at professors, scribbling notes that made no sense to anyone but us.

Everything we planned—grad school, internships—it all went dark.

I stayed.

Didn't eat. Barely slept. I didn't want anything but her.

But no one said her name.

They circled around me like I might shatter. Whispered around corners. *Don't upset Katie. Don't bring it up.*

They meant well.

But I couldn't breathe in that house.

I got out. Two years later. Stronger. Colder. I changed everything.

Dyed my hair midnight black. Blue contacts. The girl in the mirror was a stranger, and that was the point.

I got a job at the library. Quiet days. Endless nights. Time to search.

Search him out. The man who tore through my life like it was paper.

Eventually, I drove there. Back to the place we were taken. And the road where the trooper found me.

Nothing clicked.

They said it was GHB.

Fifteen minutes. From injection to blackout.

They scoured every building, every mile I could have walked in that window of time.

Nothing.

No more hiding.

I lived—*for Elisabeth*. Because she couldn't.

Went back to college.

Criminal Justice.

Became an investigator.

Turned my grief into something that could hunt monsters.

I asked the department if I could help. Started combing through cold case articles, missing girls, buried headlines. What if he'd taken someone else? What if he'd already started again?

He promised us he would.

When he was done with us, he'd find another girl to play with.

We found 22 of them. Alive.

Runaways. Trafficked. Missing for years. But breathing.

Fourteen of them in a rundown warehouse.

I couldn't look at it and not see her. Not see me.

Same smell. Same terror. Same silence.

What if it was him?

But the girls talked. An older man. Three other men working with him. Patterns. Details. *Not him.*

Still—it mattered.

We'd ended a ring. Saved girls before they disappeared for good.

And even if it wasn't him—we made sure he never would be.

One day, I'll find him.

But until then? I'll keep doing what I was born to do: stop predators before they taste blood.

My body finally gave in somewhere around 1 a.m.

Crime scene photos across the bed. Notes scribbled up the margins. A half-drunk cup of cold coffee on the nightstand.

Signal Noise

Katherine

4 a.m.

The heater kicked again. A metallic bang like a pipe splitting open. I didn't flinch, but my shoulders locked.

Across the table, the coffee had gone cold hours ago—thick sheen rippling with every vibration through the floor. I didn't bother reheating it. *I just stared at it like it owed me something.*

Glenna's file was still open in front of me. The top page warped at the corner where I'd touched it too many times—burn patterns, staging attempts, finger bone on the left ring.

The theories had started the moment they found her body. Everyone guessing where he'd been hiding, why he came back.

But I knew.

He never left.

The case hadn't gone cold—it had gone quiet. Like something lying in the grass, waiting.

My phone vibrated.

BLOCKED CALLER.

Second one this week.

Not unusual. Not alarming. But the timing cut through me, sideways. No message. No trace. *Just absence left behind.*

It rang long enough for my hand to hover—then the screen went dark.

No voicemail.

I turned it facedown and pressed my palm flat against it like that could stop the echo of it.

Tires peeled somewhere below. A siren passed two blocks over, not close enough to register direction. The city was still asleep, but I wasn't. *Couldn't.* Every time I blinked, her face snapped back behind my eyes—Glenna, huddled like trash in a dumpster that should've never been touched.

I reached for the mug.

Cold. Bitter.

Like everything else in the night.

I set it back down and pinched the bridge of my nose.

Across the room, the windowpane offered a warped reflection—The glass showed the stranger I'd built for this—wrong eyes, wrong face. That was the point.

Checked the front door—deadbolt, chain, hinge—window latch, fire escape, vent. Each tested, each holding. Not fear—just proof.

I wasn't scared. I just... needed to be sure.

When I sat back down, the stack of evidence looked like a mountain I could never climb—photos, autopsy notes, press statements, Brandon's rough field sketch of the alley layout. The time stamp on my laptop blinked:

4:19 A.M.

Still no update from Vine. Still no leads from the canvas.

And that silence? Louder than anything else.

The phone lit again.

Brandon: ME bumped to 10. Get sleep. Seriously.

I didn't reply. Just closed my eyes and let my hand fall away from the phone.

Ten meant four hours to crash, reset, and lie to myself that I wasn't unraveling.

I stood again, walked the lights off one by one until the room folded into shadow. Gun in the drawer. Doors locked. Coffee untouched.

I dropped onto the mattress, arms heavy, boots still on. The sheets were cold, the air colder. But I didn't bother warming them.

Sleep came the way it always did—sharp, fast, and full of ghosts.

Flashpoint

Katherine

✦

It's always the same.

Elisabeth—barefoot in white, sunlit and safe—drifts just out of reach. My hand lifts, but she's already gone.

And I'm back.

Back in the room.

Duct tape rips at my skin, wrapped tight around my mouth. The scent of sweat and stale metal clings to my face. My wrists, numb and pulsing, bound too tight to move.

Left ankle—shackled. Always the left. The cuff digs deep into torn skin, cold iron bolted to the wall, rusting. The chain long enough to pee in the corner, but not long enough to matter.

Same wall. Same mattress. Same quiet waiting for the door.

I yank at the cuff. Always yank. Even though I know.

Flesh splits open. Old wounds tear wider. New ones bloom like heat under the skin.

The door unlocks.

That sound—metal dragging against metal—roots straight into my spine.

He's here.

He steps in.

I close my eyes.

I freeze.

Every time, I think *this is it*. This is when it happens.

He grabs me. Pushes me down onto the mattress. My stomach clenches. The scream behind the duct tape chokes me.

But he doesn't.

Never does.

His eyes scan the bruises, the cuts, the cracked skin.

He exhales, annoyed. Like I'm the inconvenience.

He leaves.

Comes back with a first aid kit. Bandages. Antiseptic. Tape.

Patch, patch, patch.

Why? Why fix what he's destroying? *Why pretend it matters?*

He plays with me like a child pulling wings off a fly, then bandaging it back up.

Mind games. That's what this is.

He wants me broken in a different way.

"Where is Elisabeth?"

I scream it through my tears. The tape is gone now—I never feel him take it off, it just disappears, like the rules are shifting.

"What did you do to her?" My throat cracks. "Please, if she's still alive… let her go. I'll stay. I'll do whatever you want. Just… please."

Then it changes.

Elisabeth again.

White dress soaked in blood. Her arms outstretched, face twisted in pain, skin pale and sunken, lips tinged blue. Eyes dead. Empty.

"You left me,"

No—

"Do you know what he's done to me, Katie?"

Her voice rips through me like teeth.

I reach for her, sobbing, begging.

But she turns away.

Darkness swallows her whole.

I snap awake.

Breath ragged.

My heart slams against my ribs, shaking everything loose inside me.

Sweat clings to my skin like ice. Arms locked around my knees, pulled to my chest, holding myself together so I don't splinter apart. I can't breathe. Can't think.

Wake-Up Call

Katherine

04:47 A.M.—Apartment

My scream yanked me out of the dark, the echo still clawing the walls when the phone lit up beside the bed.

BRANDON CALLING.

I fumbled, tangled in sweat-sticky sheets. "Yeah."

"Vine's prelim is in early. Tox screen found Succinylcholine in Glenna's system. She's bumping autopsy to seven, not ten."

Seven. Two hours from now.

I swung my legs off the mattress, boots half-laced, heart still jack-hammering from the dream. "I'll be there."

"You, okay?" he asked, voice low like he already knew the answer.

"I'm vertical."

"That's not what I asked."

Silence. I could still feel the cuff on my ankle, the stale metal air. "Send me the report. I'll read it on the way."

He sighed—the kind of sigh that said I'll let it slide because time is bleeding. "Check your e-mail. And Katherine?"

"Yeah?"

"Lock up."

Click.

The apartment was too bright now—streetlamp glow washing through the blinds, turning dust mites into tiny ghosts. I pushed off the bed, checked the deadbolt, the chain, the hinge lock—again—then pressed my palm against the door until the tremor in my wrist settled.

The phone chimed: *1 attachment from Dr. Vine.*

I didn't open it. Not yet. Instead, I grabbed my go-bag, tossed in fresh gloves, a new notebook, and grabbed the cold coffee from the counter—still bitter enough to burn thought into muscle memory.

Outside, a taxi's horn blared downstairs. The sound punched straight into memory: Elisabeth yanked backward by an unseen hand, her gasp swallowed.

Not now.

I shoved the image aside, pocketed the keys, and killed the lights. The hallway smelled of someone else's burnt toast—harmless, ordinary, real. I let that anchor me while the elevator rattled up to collect the pieces of me still shaking.

Present first. Past later. That was the deal I made with myself when I took the badge.

The past didn't always keep its end of the bargain.

Phantom Pain

Katherine

The elevator's stale air jolts a memory I never invited—suddenly I was twenty-two again, shoulder to cinder block, praying a sticky note wasn't the whole future.

Dorm hallway, 2 A.M.-Huntington, WV.

Cinder-block chill bleeding through a faded hoodie.

Sticky note on the desk: Support Group — 7 PM, Fine Arts 101.

Lemon spray. Microwaved ramen. Ceiling vent rattling. Pulse misfiring.

I remember clicking *Send* on Charleston P.D.'s internship acceptance, thinking, *If the past wants me so bad, I'll hunt it on my own terms.*

I packed the newspaper clipping—*LOCAL GIRL ESCAPES ABDUCTOR*—because Elisabeth's name deserved more than third-line print.

I didn't know what I'd find in Charleston—answers, closure, maybe more silence. But standing over Glenna's crime scene years later, I realized this: I wasn't just chasing shadows anymore.

I was chasing someone real.

The elevator dings. Present snaps back.

Manhattan air slaps my face when the lobby doors hiss open.

I march toward the curb, dorm corridors still echoing in my skull, and tell myself the same lie that got me this far:

Keep moving and the past can't shoot you in the back.

Before Vows, After Death

Katherine

The taxi braked hard outside the precinct, just as my phone lit up—*WHERE ARE YOU?*

No time at home to shower. No time to rinse the night off my skin. Up the back stairs. Down the service corridor.

Locker-room showers scalding. I stood there too long, skin raw, scrubbing like I could wash the memory of the nightmare off my hands.

Skin scrubbed until it stung. Red. Raw.

Still didn't feel clean.

Almost human, maybe. Almost.

Dried. Dressed. And joined the others in the conference room.

Crime scene photos splayed out across the table. Paperwork bleeding ink under my fingertips. I stared at the images until they blurred.

We had answers.

ME's report.

Glenna Rogers. Age 20. Staten Island.

Pronounced dead at the scene.

Time of death confirmed: Between 9:00 A.M. and 10:00 A.M.

Strangled—wire garrote, tight, deliberate. Clean. Efficient.

No defensive wounds. Nothing under her nails.

He'd scraped them or he didn't allow her to fight back. Didn't want a trace.

The cuts—postmortem. Jagged, deliberate.

Not sexual. Not random.

All planned.

Fibers, hairs—inconclusive.

Of course they were.

He never left anything that would lead us to him.

Every detail of that scene was part of the performance. The placement, the pose—it was never an accident.

That boot print. Useless. Common tread. Size 9. Could be anyone.

But the blood—on the floor of the dumpster—it was Glenna's.

Glenna wasn't just a victim.

She had a name. A life. She was getting married.

The day before we found her.

She never made it to the altar.

Just like the others.

He still followed the same pattern. Brides-to-be. Taken right before their weddings. Left behind like a cruel joke—no note, no ransom. Just an empty aisle and a ruined man waiting.

And Glenna—

Calling her by name made it harder. But it also made it real.

Made me dig deeper.

Fight harder.

She deserved that. They all did.

We'd profiled him before—mid-to-late 30s, white, lives alone. Charming, forgettable. Probably volunteered somewhere. Smiled at neighbors. Held doors open.

The kind you never suspect.

Intelligent. Precise. Always watching long before he made a move.

He knew their routines. Their wedding dates. Their dress sizes. The color of their flowers.

He didn't just kill them. He erased them.

And the finger—he always took the left ring finger.

Symbolic. Personal. Ritualistic.

Jilted groom, maybe. Heartbroken. Humiliated.

And now he wanted the world to feel it with him—especially the ones left standing at the altar.

And maybe most of all—*me*.

Charleston Shadows, Manhattan

Silence

Katherine

I walked outside for some fresh air and maybe some lunch

The sandwich sat half-eaten in my lap. Bread soggy. Coffee cold.

The hum of the engine, the low murmur of the city beyond the windshield—none of it reached me.

Something about the air today—damp, metallic, too quiet—dragged me back.

Charleston, West Virginia

That year, God, that year.

I was twenty-nine, younger than most Lead Analysts. Fresh into the role, only two years in, my first lead case carrying the weight of nightmares.

Dayna Cookson.

Her name still hit like a bruise.

We pulled up to the Capitol Building—where life once felt simple. Safe.

And there she stood.

No—posed.

Like some grotesque masterpiece ripped from Michaelangelo's marble, twisted into something obscene.

Brown hair, glossy and long, draped over her chest like a veil. Eyes wide, green and glassy.

She looked alive. That was the worst part. Like she might blink any second.

Arms gone. One at the shoulder. The other mid-bicep.

Postmortem.

At least there was that.

Upper half bare—bruised, bloodless, drained of anything that once was alive. Below the waist, the sheet clung to her limbs, her flesh cold but still soft, a subtle warmth lingering, her body couldn't decide to surrender or hold on.

But her arms—

Under the sheet.

Tucked beneath, like they'd just slipped free.

Left ring finger missing. Not torn. Not hacked.

Cut.

Precise, intentional.

We didn't know it then, but it was always the cigar cutter. Clean. Ritual made blade.

And he didn't stop there. He filleted it down to the bone.

Tiny cuts scattered across her body, postmortem too. A scalpel's touch.

He took her finger. And the ring.

Trophy.

Her fiancé confirmed it. The ring was custom—couldn't be pawned or sold without notice.

He didn't take it to hide her identity.

He took it to *own* her.

Eight months. Seven victims. Charleston, Huntington, Parkersburg, Morgantown—each one marked with his touch. His M.O. had been clear, unyielding. Then…nothing. Just silence.

The CID's air felt suffocating now. The clock's tick grew louder, each second echoing in my chest like a countdown I couldn't stop. His presence pressed in on me, tighter, squeezing the breath out of my lungs.

Then my phone rang.

The voice on the other end was calm. Too calm. "Miss Poe, I think we have a case that'll interest you immensely."

My stomach dropped before I even heard the rest.

"It's the finger," he said. "It's gone. Filleted down to the bone. That's what brought your name to mind."

The phone clattered on the desk—slipping from my hand.

I was already moving before he finished.

NYPD

A flight booked. Three weeks in New York City.

Two weeks in and he'd killed Victim 9; we were no closer to catching him—

Then poof. No new brides, no notes, no games. Nothing. The waiting gnawed at me.

I didn't unpack. Half-ready to go home, half-ready for war. But the killer—like in West Virginia—vanished.

The city was too big to feel real, but his presence followed me everywhere—on the subway with the girl clutching white orchids, in the diner with the waitress wearing a silver bangle, outside the hospital with the crying nurse.

At night, I caught myself wishing for him to strike again—just to move, just to stop waiting. The thought made me sick. I burned it from the page in the hotel sink. Still the silence pressed on.

Then the phone rang again. No voicemail. Just the echo of something watching.

Charleston

A month later, I was back in Charleston. But the silence here was just as suffocating. The city, my apartment, the CID—all the same, but I wasn't.

Then the call came.

He had left another body. Victim ten.

Third in New York.

I took a leave of absence, indefinite.

Rented a tiny apartment in the city, accepted the liaison role with the NYPD.

I couldn't keep dancing with him like that.

Four months. Gifts, bouquets, letters—sick twisted Artist/Muse dance.

I stopped playing. I stepped away.

The call.

"Has Poe called in sick?" Male voice not altered but muffled.

I stood listening.

"If she's not on the case, I'll make a point. Think bus. Think children. Think the American Museum of Natural History."

"Okay. I'm here. I'm back on. Just…why me?"

Click.

Within the hour, the call was traced to a payphone outside a hotel. CCTV led us to an old garage. We went in hard—S.W.A.T., air support overhead—but the place was a ghost. Undisturbed. No recent footprints. No trapdoor. No escape hatch. No killer.

He was smoke.

He resurfaced for another six months.

Four more women died.

The he vanished again. Four years of silence.

But I didn't return to Charleston. The city had dug its hooks in me. I stayed. I moved into my apartment in Manhattan, away from the ghosts of the past.

***

Brandon knocked on my window.

I blinked, dragging myself up from the undertow of memory.

"You good?"

My mouth opened—nothing came out.

"Yeah," I lied, voice raspy. "Just thinking."

He gave me that look. The one that knew better. "I've been out here for longer than five minutes. You were staring right through me."

I exhaled slowly. "We need to pull every file. Every note. Everything we ever had on him."

Brandon nodded. "Way ahead of you."

And just like that, the memory folded back into the quiet. But it never really went away.

"Let's go."

I followed him. Not because I was ready, but because sitting still meant thinking.

Filed, but Not Forgotten

Katherine

Gathered around the tables in the glass-walled conference room, we reviewed every lead, every piece of evidence—but the silence lingered, a living thing—waiting, suffocating, until it became impossible to ignore.

I used to tell rookies the worst kind of silence is the moment before the phone rings. Turns out I was wrong. The worst silence is the one that smothers you after the ringing stops—for a week, then a month—when you're sure the next shrill burst is only a breath away, but it never comes.

Victim Eleven:

The first after I unpacked the last box in my Manhattan shoebox): Harper Singh, twenty-three, a pastry chef. He left her posed in the window of her own bakery at dawn; white tiered wedding cake balanced on her lap like an offering. Blood soaked the fondant roses; the smell of buttercream still clung to her hair. Busloads of commuters saw her before the first beat cop did.

Ring finger gone, of course.

That morning tasted like burnt espresso in the back of my throat. I remember scrubbing frosting crystals from under my nails hours later and thinking they looked like snow.

Victim Twelve:

Three weeks later—Lydia Cho, Columbia doctoral candidate, found in the Rose Main Reading Room of the NYPL. He'd sealed her eyelids with library glue, posed her upright in a Windsor chair, bridal gown hem fanned like paper petals across the marble.

I can still hear the echo of the security guard's vomit splattering between the stacks.

By then sleep was rationed in thirty-minute rations. Every siren outside my apartment cracked me open.

I taped butcher paper to the walls and charted his timestamps: interval, method of access, postmortem window. Nothing lined up except the certainty he was choreographing this for me—a brutal waltz, each victim a downbeat.

Victim Thirteen:

Zara Benítez, fashion buyer, age twenty-nine—should've been impossible. Midtown penthouse, twenty-four-hour doorman, five digital locks.

He laid her on the bare parquet floor like a final swatch sample.

The doorman swore no one came or left. Cameras corroborated.

I started double-locking my own door after that, even though I knew locks were a polite suggestion to someone like him.

Victim Fourteen:

Detonated something inside me. Joelle Cunningham, thirty-five, dancer—bronze skin, freckles, the kind of laugh that cracked ceilings.

He displayed her beneath the suspended blue whale at the American Museum of Natural History, fluorescent exit signs tinting her dress sea-green.

Children on a field trip were the first to notice the missing finger. Their teacher fainted.

I didn't. I never faint.

I calcified.

Four women in six months. Four different boroughs, four different security profiles, one identical savagery.

The hum of the fluorescent lights above the conference room buzzed in my teeth, the pen biting into my finger until a crescent ridge formed in my skin.

I started tasting copper whenever my phone buzzed—

Bruise-Purple Sky

Katherine

The meeting had dragged on longer than I expected.

I needed air.

The elevator cables hummed like taut nerves all the way to the roof. Each jolt turned my pulse into Morse code: *still here / still hiding / still breaking.*

I stepped onto tar paper slick with rain and industrial grit. The skyline wore bruise-purple clouds; Manhattan looked punched in the jaw.

Wind knifed through my coat and reminded me why the city never apologizes for anything. Fall was in the air.

Somewhere below, Glenna's fiancé was still answering questions none of us could soften. *Will you release the body? Do you still want the dress?*

Questions, gut punches.

My boots thudded toward the parapet. I flattened chilled palms on rough stone, let concrete drag skin the way I wanted to scream.

Last week, Bella said I had to give my spirals structure— *"Name the fear, box the fear, move the box."*

Box #1: Another woman is already dead, and we haven't found her yet.

Box #2: I'll miss the next clue. *Again.*

Box #3: I'm not enough. Not fast enough. Not *him*-proof.

Wind tore the boxes apart.

A door banged behind me. I flinched, Brandon's silhouette, shoulders hunched against rain.

"Figured I'd find you on a roof," he said.

"If I jump, you'll have to write the report."

"Then please don't." he pleaded. "Paperwork's murder."

He joined me, elbows on stone. We watched city lights stutter like failing pulse-ox monitors.

"Our tech guys traced Glenna's RSVP site," he said. "Someone logged in, edited her guest list. Deleted family e-mails. Added himself under a fake name, Dusty. We ran it nothing popped, another dead end."

Not just digital clutter—her lifelines, cut.

The image crawled under my skin. He hadn't wanted to stop her plans. He'd wanted to unmake her. Erase the people who would've been waiting, searching, calling her name.

Another layer of dread settled in. He wasn't only taking bodies. He was stripping away their witnesses, their anchors. Leaving them his, and only his.

The killer was scaling up, modernizing. Keeping pace with me.

Brandon's voice softened. "You slept yet?"

"Two hours."

"Eat?" he asked.

"Coffee counts."

He offered silence, the nicest thing.

A siren echoed off high-rises. My scalp prickled; adrenaline never asks permission. I straightened.

"Go home," Brandon said. "Both of us. Four hours, then we hit this fresh."

"Four," I said, *meaning two*.

Phantom Pulse

Katherine

The first real quiet moment came in mid-November. A Sunday. No scheduled shifts.

My apartment smelled faintly like cinnamon candles I hadn't bothered to light.

Downstairs, I passed St. Patrick's Cathedral. Candles glowed behind security barricades—Glenna's vigil, hastily relocated from the park because of rain.

I hadn't planned to stop. But a mother in a plastic poncho pressed a white rose into my hand.

"You're the one chasing him, right?"

I nodded.

"Then stand with us."

The crowd parted, eyes tracking me—some hopeful, others angry. A volunteer thrust a microphone at me. The priest whispered, "Say something hopeful."

Waiting for Applause flashed through my mind—Cheryl's joke that press conferences are just theatre. But these faces weren't a reporter's blank stares; they were wreckage.

"I can't promise quick justice," I said, my voice thick with the weight of it. "But I can promise obsession. The man who did this thinks he's directing a masterpiece. So did every coward before him. We wrote their names in indictments, not art history. He'll join the list."

Silence cracked into soft claps—no applause break, just shared pulse.

That was enough.

I set a rose among twenty others, one for each victim he'd promised.

Glenna's fiancé caught my sleeve. "Bring her ring home," he whispered.

"I'll try."

The truth tasted like blood.

Tethered Souls, Torn Threads

Katherine

Therapy. God, I hated needing it.

But I went. Sat there on that stiff couch week after week, trying to peel the guilt off my bones like it wasn't fused there.

Survivor's guilt, they called it. Slapping a label on it didn't make it easier to breathe.

I couldn't save her. I should've.

That truth stalked me, even in my dreams.

Elisabeth wasn't just my sister. She was the other half of me—the steadier heartbeat, the louder laugh. Without her, I'd always felt... *unfinished.*

Growing up, we refused to be "those twins." No matching outfits. No mirror games. We carved our own lives, even if our souls stayed tethered.

She was sugar and satin. Nail polish that smelled like candy.

Me? Grease under my nails. Dirt on my jeans. Climbing trees and crawling under the truck with Dad to fix whatever the hell was rattling.

I wore bruises like medals.

She collected perfume samples and boys' phone numbers like souvenirs.

She flirted like breathing but always kept the line clear— hand-holding, maybe a kiss. That was enough for her. She said she liked feeling wanted, but she was saving herself for something big.

"That kind of love that makes you forget how to breathe," she used to say, her voice dreamy, eyes glazed. "If you don't find the one who makes you say, 'I could live without you… but God, I don't want to,' then save that part of yourself, Katie."

She always spoke like the world was a fairytale she hadn't grown tired of yet.

And me?

I never told her that I was only ever brave because I knew she was there, watching. Cheering. Catching me if I fell.

And now she was gone.

Gone, and I was here—trying to solve the kinds of murders I couldn't stop before.

Trying to make sense of death so hers wouldn't be the only ghost following me around.

I didn't become a Forensic Analyst because I loved the science.

I became one because I had to understand the monsters.

Because I'd already met one.

Fault Lines in the Pattern

Katherine

The conference room air felt stale, over-circulated—coffee gone bitter, dry marker ink, and tension thick enough that hadn't eased in three months. Glenna's photo glared from the projector, the image already etched into memory: scorched cloth fused to skin, hand mutilated. Her ring finger gone.

Brandon's voice dragged over the ME notes we'd all heard too many times. "Heat origin localized. Accelerant likely, but lab results were inconclusive. Ring finger removed postmortem. Tool markings…" He hesitated, like the pause might make them sound new. "Consistent with previous victims."

Kali leaned back, clinical detachment wrapped tight around every word. "And that's it. The finger. Everything else? Noise."

Cheryl crossed her arms, eyes hard on the photo. "He's never burned a body before. This isn't him. All the others were honored."

"It's a deviation," I said. "Killers adapt. They test boundaries."

"Or it's a copycat," Kali's tone cut. "Someone who's read every article, memorized every word you've ever given the press. Glenna was getting married. That made her a target, yes—but also an easy prop for someone trying to stir your obsession back into the light."

The word lodged like glass. Obsession.

I kept my voice steady. "The cut was surgical. He took his time. This wasn't impulse. It was deliberate. Posed."

"Posed differently," Cheryl countered. "Dumped, half-burned, in a service alley. That's not art. That's panic."

Brandon flipped through case files, paper edges frayed from weeks of handling, like the answer might shake loose after the hundredth read.

Kali pressed harder. "Maybe you want it to be him. Maybe you can't stand that he vanished. That someone else might've taken his place while he went dark."

Her words needled, because silence had always been the worst part.

Brandon slid a photo across the table—Glenna's hand. The missing finger. "Tool use is consistent. But yeah… beyond that? We're still in the dark."

Still. Always still.

The others filed out, leaving me with the projector hum and Glenna's face flickering against the wall. Three months, and it still felt unfinished. Not just about answers anymore. About winning. If I failed here, if I misread this fault line, it wouldn't just be another case gone cold. It would be the start of something worse.

Outside, rain hit like needles, sharp and grounding. I curled my fists against the burn in my chest. He wouldn't stop. Not yet. And I couldn't afford to break—not when the silence was already breaking me.

A Man in the Terminal

The Lonely Heart Murderer

The arrivals gate was the most honest place in the city.

No one wore masks here. Not really. They smiled too wide, paced too fast, clutched flowers or signs. Waiting made people raw. It peeled back the skin.

He stood behind the glass just long enough to feel it—the yearning. The tension.

He remembered the first and last time she walked through this terminal.

Alone, unaware she was being seen.

Shoulder bag slung over one arm, hair pulled back, her walk more natural here than anywhere else.

She bought gum she wouldn't chew. Paused too long in indecision in front of the coffee counter. Her face tilted up as she scanned the crowd—not for anyone, just out of habit. She always scanned. Always searching.

But she didn't see him then. She never did.

Today wasn't about her.

But she lived behind everything now. Even this.

He drifted with the crowd, unremarkable. Clean lines. Tailored coat. His reflection bled against the glass: controlled, forgettable. No one remembered the man who didn't demand space.

Except the one he was watching.

Khaki coat. No carry-on. Shoes too clean. Wedding ring, but no phone calls. His eyes darted in clipped patterns, not random—trained. Law enforcement? Private security? Or just paranoid?

He matched his pace for a while. Not close. Just enough.

The man bought a sandwich and threw it out after one bite. He checked his phone. Looked behind him. Twice. Then slipped into the unisex restroom near Gate 17.

That was the signal.

He waited—ten seconds. Stepped forward.

And froze.

The door pushed open, but not with khaki coat. Another man slipped out, head lowered, sunglasses on indoors. He moved quick, casual, too casual. The real kind of casual that came with training. PI, maybe. Security. Hired eyes.

Khaki coat emerged only after, wiping his hands, oblivious. Wrong man. He'd been following the wrong man.

He turned back just in time to see the restroom door rocking closed again. The lid of the trash can ajar. Gloves on top—black leather, deliberate, not discarded. A plant.

Something tugged at him, low and sharp.

He backed out.

Walked quickly, eyes sharp.

Both men. Gone.

Then, just beyond the edge of a janitor's cart, half-caught beneath a scuffed heel—something white.

A photo.

He stooped. Plucked it off the floor.

Katherine. At the vigil. Candlelight haloing her face.

His pulse didn't spike. His breath didn't hitch. But the lights of the airport seemed to dim around him.

He turned the photo over. Nothing written.

She'd been watched. Documented.

Someone else had eyes on her.

This wasn't rage. It wasn't possession.

It was proof that someone else had noticed. Proof that someone else was trying to pull the strings—someone had hired this man to follow Katherine.

It wasn't just him anymore. There was more to this game. He tucked the photo inside his coat, pressed his fingers briefly to his chest.

She didn't know. No idea how many eyes were on her.

No idea how beautiful her end would be.

The Scream That Split Everything

Katherine

***

It was supposed to be our escape—just the two of us, no expectations.

The summer of 2000, we were twenty, invincible, high on freedom and togetherness. Elisabeth had her sights set on becoming a paralegal. I was working on my psych degree, still pretending like I knew what I was doing with my life.

But none of that mattered then.

We just wanted time—time to be sisters again, to laugh, to breathe outside the chaos. Myrtle Beach. Windows down, music too loud, the sun glinting off the hood of my beat-up car. I drove while she slept, her arm draped over her stomach, lips parted just enough to let out that soft rhythmic breath I'd known since we shared a crib.

I missed our exit. No big deal—we needed gas anyway. I figured I'd loop back.

I spotted a wide shoulder and eased over to turn around. Then, the car jolted. I didn't curse. Just sighed and parked.

She didn't stir.

I'd changed tires in the dark, in the rain, on gravel so cold it cut through my jeans. This would be easy.

I got out, popped the trunk, jacked the car up. Routine. Mundane. Safe.

Then I heard her door creak behind me.

"What's going on?" her voice groggy, half-asleep.

"Just a flat," I said, "It's fine. Go back to sleep."

She didn't. Instead, she screamed. "Katie! *Run!*"

My heart kicked. I froze. Turned. Her face—white. Lips parted. Eyes locked on something behind me.

What? Snake? Someone messing with us?

No—No, not that.

She was too still. Too quiet.

And me? I didn't move. Didn't run.

Not until it was already too late.

That was the moment everything cracked open. The last moment I had a normal life.

Hands. Too fast. Too strong.

One moment, I was crouched beside the tire, the next— arms locked around me, breath ripped from my lungs.

A sting at my neck. Sharp. Burning. Then darkness.

Heavy. Endless.

When I came to, the world had shrunk to four stained walls, a metal toilet, and a thin mattress shoved up against beige paint peeling like old scabs. No windows. No light but a faint bulb overhead. No sound but my own breathing—and the silence where Elisabeth should've been.

I called her name until my throat was raw.

Nothing. Just echoes. Just emptiness.

Maybe she got away. Maybe she was with Mom and Dad. Maybe they were already looking for me.

Please, please let her be safe.

Time blurred. Hours, days—maybe months.

I counted the minutes by the pain in my stomach, the rot in the air, the chain that dug into my ankle. The shackle just long enough to reach the toilet.

I scratched at it until the metal bit skin. I left blood on the floor more often than I realized.

I thought about her constantly. Was she alive? Was he hurting her? *Could I trade places? Offer myself if he'd just let her go?*

He'd storm in, reeking of sweat and fury, sometimes with blood smeared across his hands like war paint.

"Look what you make me do," he snarled through his voice changer. "Do you think your sister likes the games I play with her?"

I'd lunge, scream, beg—rage a storm even bound.

The duct tape muffled my words but not the hate.

He always left, slamming the steel door so hard the walls shook.

I never saw his face. Just that mask—plastic, expressionless.

That voice, robotic and inhuman.

Once, he knelt beside me, fingers cold and clinical on the gash around my ankle.

He always cared for it—like it mattered to him, like he didn't want me broken. Just everything else.

Then the alarm—distant, urgent. He froze. Panic. Behind the mask, I could see it.

He jabbed me with something. My limbs went liquid. Not out—just slowed. Tilted. Slurred.

He didn't lock the shackle. Didn't seal the door.

He ran.

I waited.

One breath. Two.

I crawled through that door like an animal, heart thrashing, half-blind from the drug, my mouth still taped shut.

I pressed against the walls, listening, feeling my way through blind corners.

The hallway twisted forever.

Then—

Light.

I was outside.

Alone.

The Wrong One Survived

Katherine

I used to think the scream was the worst part.

But surviving was louder.

Even after therapy, guided regressions, hypnotherapy—I still don't remember how I got away. Not really. That part of my mind is a locked box with the key rusted out. What I do remember is waking up in a hospital room in Charleston. Fluorescent lights too bright, my throat dry, my body aching like it had been dragged through hell and then left to rot.

Mom's hand was wrapped around mine, shaking, like she was afraid I'd disappear again. Dad was on the other side, dark circles under his eyes. He looked ten years older. They'd both been crying—pink rims around their eyes, faces bruised from sorrow.

The first thing out of my mouth was a whisper, broken and absolute: "Elisabeth is dead."

I didn't speak again for months.

After that, everything blurred. People talked around me like I wasn't there. Muffled voices, static. Detectives, doctors, even my parents—I heard them all in fragments.

We'd been missing for three months. That's what they said.

They said I'd been found walking barefoot along the edge of the interstate. My feet shredded. A state trooper saw me, thought I was drunk—until he noticed the duct tape still clinging to my wrists, the chain burns around my ankle. He approached slow, hands out like I was something wild. When he touched me, I screamed—fought like the shackles were still there. I don't remember the car. Just his voice calling it in—Jane Doe, female, injured, signs of captivity—before everything went black.

Later, after being released from the hospital, I found myself curled in Elisabeth's bed, surrounded by her perfume-soaked pillows and the stuffed bears she never gave away. I held one against my chest like it might breathe life back into me. I begged it for forgiveness.

Because I couldn't save her. I'd tried—I would have traded places with her in a second.

But he wouldn't let her go.

A few weeks later, a letter arrived. No return address. Just a sheet of paper with jagged, uneven handwriting:

"I hope you remember this every time you close your eyes.

You could have saved Elisabeth. But you chose your own freedom instead."

And I do. Every single night.

That moment plays again—his hands on me, my wrists bound.

Being drug down a hallway.

But I heard her. God, I *heard* her.

She was crying. Close enough that I knew she could see me. There had to be glass between us. I remember her voice breaking.

"Katie! Oh Katie! I'm so sorry. I tried to run, I really tried… but he was too strong."

She begged him. Pleaded.

"Leave her here with me. Please."

But he just laughed. That awful voice modulated, cutting through the dark like a blade.

He told us he'd always dreamed of taking a woman, breaking her down piece by piece, until she was his—alone.

And now, he had two.

Twins. A matched set.

"We'll have so much more fun this way," he whispered to me, breath hot against my ear. "You do exactly what I want when you cry. When you beg. This is even better than I imagined."

I wasn't a person to him. I was a toy.

The thought of what he might've done to Elisabeth still makes bile crawl up my throat.

Sixteen years.

Sixteen years without her.

Sixteen years of waking up to the sound of her scream, only to realize it's in my head.

My therapist says I did everything I could. Says I should be proud I even made it out alive.

But the guilt?

It doesn't go away. It waits for the quiet. For the dark. For the moment when I'm too tired to fight it off.

They say twins share a bond deeper than anything else. When one hurts, the other feels it. When one's in danger, the other knows.

Sometimes at night, I swear I still feel her. Just outside the edge of my consciousness.

Breathing. Waiting.

Then I slam the door on the feeling. Tell myself it's just grief. Just trauma. That we never found her body, and that's why my brain keeps trying to bring her back.

But I know the truth.

I'll never get to say goodbye.

And that truth haunts me more than anything else.

Hairline fracture

Katherine

The rain hadn't let up when I made it back to my apartment. The sound of it hammering against the windows had been a constant hum in my head, but I didn't mind. I needed the noise.

The tidal wave of memories in my head was too loud.

I didn't sleep. Not really. The same memories kept turning like a broken record.

When the morning came, I was back at work, the weight of it already settling over me as I walked through the precinct's door. The hallway smelled like printer toner and burnt coffee. Someone had spilled sugar packets near the copy machine. My boot crushed one as I passed, the soft crack sharp in the silence.

A rookie detective laughed about wedding hashtags and getting ghosted as I walked by. Cheryl shot him a look that could cauterize a wound, but I kept walking.

Before I knew it, I was standing in front of the glass wall outside the evidence board room. My reflection hovered over it—blurred, ghostlike. I lifted my hand before I thought better of it. Fist curled. Then—impact.

The glass gave with a sharp crack, splintering out in a spiderweb of fractures. Not broken. Just damaged. Like me. Blood welled from my knuckles, bright against the gray.

The bullpen stilled. A chair scraped back, someone's pen clattered to the floor. Then silence, everyone pretending not to stare.

Cheryl was suddenly at my side, steady as ever. She didn't scold. Just pressed her hand to my elbow and angled me down the hall, away from the board, the eyes.

"Sit," she said once we were clear. No softness, no sharpness either. Just firm.

I sat. The bench felt cold. Blood tracked down my wrist, dripping into my cuff. She tugged a tissue from her coat, pressed it against my hand. The sting made me grit my teeth.

"Better the glass than your own ribs," she muttered. Then she straightened, her job here done. "I'll send someone with gauze."

And just like that—she left.

Alone, I stared at the cracked glass through the open doorway, the web of fractures spreading across my own reflection.

A scream still rang in my ears. Mine.

And I realized—I wasn't trying to break the glass.

I was trying to break the silence.

I stood. Trembling but firm.

"Get me everything on Glenna's fiancé. All his contacts, every lead, even the smallest detail"

"If this isn't him back, let's find out who did this to her. And why."

Cheryl blinked, almost smiled. "There she is."

But I wasn't back.

I was just sharpening.

The Weight of Silence

Katherine

I used to think I was broken. Not visibly—just…cracked in the quiet places.

Too sharp for softness, too bruised to let anyone close without cutting them. Therapists called it "Trauma armor"—a way to feel safe. They said it was normal after what I'd survived. But normal still felt like a ghost story. People saw the badge, the precision, and assumed I had it all together. I didn't. I just knew how to fake it.

Sometimes, I wondered what it would feel like to let someone in—to sit across from someone and not scan the exits. To wake up beside warmth instead of nightmares. Not fairy tale stuff—just steady, kind. But the wondering scared me most.

Later, back at the apartment, I stepped into the shower, scalding water working the knots in my back. Water stinging my knuckles.

Wrapped in a towel, I moved on autopilot—brushed my teeth, changed into pjs. Before my body hit the mattress, my phone buzzed.

Brandon: *GET HERE NOW!*

I raced to the precinct, hair still damp. When I arrived, I didn't need to ask. I just looked at my desk.

A box sat there, my name written in bold ink. The weight of it hit me immediately—he was always one step ahead, knowing exactly where to aim.

The bomb squad had cleared it. I slipped on gloves and lifted the lid. Inside a letter.

I can feel your patience fraying, Katie…and I like it.

I pushed past the letter and found a small, ornate globe.

Was it a riddle? A gift of the world, maybe? Or something darker, more twisted?

I sank into my chair, the buzz of the room distant. I was too tired for this—and that's when he'd strike.

Resurrecting Katie

Katherine

Katie.

The name scraped at my throat, sharp like glass.

I hadn't heard it in years—hadn't thought of it. Now he was dragging her corpse back into the light—using it like it's his own personal pet name. It belonged to a girl who used to laugh in sunlit kitchens, who whispered secrets under bed-sheets with her twin, who believed in second chances and happy endings not soaked in blood.

That girl didn't exist anymore. She died in that room, the one with the rust-stained mattress.

I bit down hard enough to taste blood. This was how he worked—twisting memories like weapons, sharper than any knife.

My hands shook as I grabbed the nearest evidence bag and shoved the globe inside. Forensics can deal with it.

The others kept their distance, their eyes full of pity, fear—watching, just like he was, to see how I'd move next.

I didn't blame them. They didn't know how to stop a man who turned murder into performance art. Who turned me into a muse.

Are you not enjoying the personal shows I have provided for you?

I wanted to throw up.

He didn't just kill them—he arranged their bodies; it came back to me. I was the audience he craved, twisted love letter written in veins and broken bones.

I sank further into my chair, barely registering the leather biting into my back. My breath came in shallow bursts, my skin crawling with a revulsion I couldn't shake.

This time, I wasn't chasing a victim. I was the target.

But I wouldn't go without a fight.

Pull it together, Poe.

I stared at the globe; I wasn't seeing it anymore. I was back in time, back with Elisabeth.

***

We were sixteen.

I could still feel the sun through Dad's truck window, the leather seats burning the back of our legs. Elisabeth sat beside me, humming something off-key while she dug through the glove compartment for gum she'd already chewed. Her laugh exploded when I slapped her hand away and threatened to toss her purse out the window.

"You're such a troll," she said, shaking her curls like a shampoo commercial. "How are we even twins?"

"Superior genes," I muttered, shifting into third.

She kicked the dash. "You're gonna be the serious one forever, huh?"

"Someone's gotta be."

She smiled like she saw through me, like she always had.

"Someday, you're gonna let yourself fall in love, Katie," she said, voice dreamy, eyes glazed. "And it's gonna be this messy, stupid, inconvenient thing. And I hope I'm there to say, I told you so."

***

I snapped back to the present, fingers tight around the top of the evidence bag in my hand.

The globe.

I sat it on my desk. Felt personal. A message, wrapped in a riddle.

He knew I'd hate it.

You're very special to me.

I almost heard him say it, too close, too pleased with himself. And that's exactly why I'd take him down.

What the Quiet Conceals

Katherine

By mid-December, winter had settled in like the city was holding its breath—cold, suspended, waiting for something to break.

The silence wasn't relief; it was dread wearing a softer face. Worse than the sirens, worse than the press conferences or flickering morgue lights or late-night grainy CCTV loops. At least those things meant motion. At least they meant he was still playing.

Now? Nothing.

I didn't trust it. Couldn't. In his world, silence wasn't absence. It was incubation.

Still, the precinct moved like it always did—keyboards clacking, Cheryl barking over conference calls like nothing bled behind the walls. I went through the motions: logging reports, running through old interviews. But I was scanning faces, tones, undercurrents. Like if I blinked too long, I'd miss him slipping past again.

"You should take Newkirk," Cheryl voice interrupted. She dropped a folder on my desk without waiting for permission. "Body turned up in Jersey, not our guy, but jurisdiction's muddy and they want help."

I didn't look up. "We have a case."

"Not until he resurfaces," she countered. Her voice softened, but not enough to dull the edge. "You can't live in his shadow, Katherine. He's gone quiet. That happens."

I stiffened. "He's not gone. He's waiting."

Cheryl exhaled slowly. "Maybe. But until then, there are other women who need us. You can't stare at that map forever hoping it'll bleed answers."

But it might.

I didn't say that. I just nodded without agreeing, heat creeping up my neck.

When she left, I pulled the map out again. Still just that sliver of terrain, still taunting me. Still a message I couldn't -translate.

But I knew him.

He wouldn't vanish.

He needed an audience.

He needed *me*.

"You're gonna burn yourself out," Brandon said quietly as he slid into the chair across from me., offering a coffee. I took it without meeting his eyes.

"She could be out there," I muttered. "Right now. Alive. Waiting."

He didn't argue. Just let the silence stretch, then said, "You sure this is still about the case?"

My head snapped up. "What's that supposed to mean?"

Brandon didn't flinch. He never did with me.

"You've been chasing ghosts lately. I'm not saying you're wrong. I'm saying maybe he knows you'll run yourself ragged trying to read between every line."

"Because there *is* something between the lines," I snapped, louder than I meant to.

A few heads turned. I lowered my voice.

"He gave these to me. Not Cheryl. Not the task force. *Me.* That means something."

Brandon leaned back, calm as ever. "Okay. Then let's figure it out. Just... don't lose yourself in it. You don't owe him that."

But I did, didn't I?

Because if I missed something—if I let him disappear into the fog again—then it was on me. *Again.*

That night, I stayed late.

The map fragment on my desk, several stacks of maps, states, countries, I had widened the search, the rest of the precinct darkened and hollowed out around me.

I traced the bends in the road, the smudged crescent of trees. No new marks. No magic answer.

But something itched at the back of my mind.

A memory?

A shape?

I couldn't pin it.

I pressed my palms into my eyes. In the darkness behind my lids, I saw her. Elisabeth. Laughing in the snow. Pink mittens. Smudged wings in a crooked angel.

My chest twisted.

No.

I wasn't letting this go. Not again. Not because it was quiet. Not because someone else thought it wasn't enough.

"He's circling."

I whispered it aloud, just to remember the shape of the fear. Just to feel the truth of it.

And somewhere—I knew he was watching her.

Whoever she was.

God help her.

Auditioning Nicole

The Lonely Heart Murderer

I almost gave up. Not because I was tired—obsession doesn't tire—but because the city had gone quiet. Too ordinary. A bland landscape, like a fresh canvas with nothing left to stain it. I thought about moving, starting over. But then...

There she was.

It wasn't just coincidence. It never is.

A gust of wind lifted her hair as she stepped from the car—deep, glossy, mahogany against the pale December sky. The air bit at bare skin, sharp, but she didn't even flinch. She didn't even notice me. They never do.

But I noticed her. Everything about her.

Her body moved like poetry—fluid, soft. She wasn't perfect, no one ever is. But she could be. She *would* be.

He stepped out beside her, laughing like he mattered. I didn't care about him. He was just a placeholder, the accessory in the background of her life.

She lowered her sunglasses, winked. Not at me, but I saw it. That flash of green in her eyes, mossy agate. The kind of green you can't look away from, even when you know it's dangerous.

My heart skipped. My hands trembled. She was perfect.

She didn't know she was auditioning.

I followed, close enough to breathe her in, but far enough to stay hidden in the shadows. I didn't need to rush. She wasn't going anywhere.

They went cake tasting-ridiculous, quaint. A winter wedding. What a little fairy tale they were living. He smiled too much. She giggled like an innocent, too free to understand the fragility of her world.

It made me sick. Electric. I wanted to strip it all away—everything she thought she knew about safety, about love. The illusion would shatter. I would be there, waiting to pick up the pieces.

I stayed close enough to size her up. Five-seven, maybe a whisper more. Soft. Every inch of her carefully crafted. Just like the others—

They went to a brownstone in the Village, laughing like everything was fine, like nothing could touch them. Snow clung to the curb; cars iced at the edges. Their world was warmth and Christmas lights strung across storefronts. Mine was the shadow between them.

It made my stomach twist. So sweet. I couldn't stop shaking.

I gripped the wheel, the metal biting into my palms. My thoughts flickered, sharp as a knife. I wanted to paint her. To carve her. To possess her until there was nothing left of her except the *story* I'd written.

Nicole Bramble—I finally knew her name. Twenty-two. Every inch of her symmetry, or she would be.

Her routine became mine, too.

Every morning, she ran. Same path. Same time. Frost in her hair, breath ghosting the air like smoke. She bent halfway through, hands on her knees, her body trembling with each breath. Weakness. A crack in her perfect façade.

I watched her every step. Every. Single. Step.

She grabbed coffee. Black, two sugars. Every morning. Always. She didn't even taste it. She never did.

She showered, dressed and was gone by 8.

I knew her every move. Her world was control and structure. I could feel the cracks in her. I could smell the fragility. Routine? That's where they slip.

Lunch at 1 p.m. Sometimes Mark, fiancé, would meet her. Sometimes not. Either way, I watched.

I followed, lurking in the shadows, waiting for her to slip.

Nights were predictable, too. Nicole home by 6. Sometimes Mark came over. Sometimes not. She curled up with Netflix and a glass of red. The TV's light flickered over her face like it was dimming her soul.

I imagined her under real lights.

Last night. Something changed.

Another car.

Not Mark's.

Tall man, sharp pinstriped suit. He wasn't like the others. My pulse stuttered, but I didn't flinch. I ducked before his eyes could find me.

He knocked on her door like he belonged.

She didn't *slam* it in his face. She hugged him, kissed his cheek.

Like they'd known each other forever. She didn't have siblings.

Familiar. Comfortable.

I could feel my control slipping.

Nicole—my Nicole—shouldn't have done that.

I watched. Waited.

In the morning, he kissed her cheek. Lovingly.

Then she ran. Snow slick under her shoes, breath catching in the cold.

I squeezed the wheel until my knuckles burned.

She was supposed to be mine already.

But something worth drawing it out—enticed me.

The hunger's still there, but so is curiosity.

She has layers, I'll peel them back.

She's almost ready.

The Cost of Devastation

The Lonely Heart Murderer

I knew where she'd be. Every morning, like clockwork, she walked beneath the stone footbridge, the path slick with ice and shadowed in frost. Alone. Unaware. She thought she was safe, just another commuter wrapped in wool and routine.

But I saw it. I saw her.

The timing was perfect. My body coiled with anticipation, muscles tight and trembling with excitement. I crouched low in the frozen earth, hidden behind the boulder, breath sharp in the cold air. My hands burned from the chill, but I welcomed the pain—it kept me sharp. Her footsteps crunched steady in the snow, a rhythm that lulled me into the kind of stillness I could taste. The ponytail swaying, earbuds in place, her world completely removed from mine.

She was painting, unaware that her frame was already set, her role already written.

When she passed the rock, I moved. Fast. Silent.

My hands locked onto her skull like they were made for it. I slammed her head against the stone—an echoing crack that cut through the air like splitting ice. Not fatal—just enough to blur the world. Art needs time.

Her body sagged, blood smearing red across the pale stone, and I dragged her through the snow, her boots leaving broken trails behind us. Too visible. Too loud. I kicked snow back over the marks, smudging the red until it blurred gray, nothing more than winter's shadow. By the time anyone found this place, the storm would have painted it clean again.

She was my canvas now, not yet finished. We were gone before the crows even shifted in the branches.

Hours passed on the road. Her head lolled, blood matted in her hair, the rhythm of her breath shallow, fragile. I looked at her often—each breath, each rise and fall of her chest. She is beautiful. Broken. Honest. Her fear is the purest form of art I'd ever seen.

She woke with an hour left. Her green eyes locked with mine through the rearview mirror, panic flashing in her gaze.

It was intoxicating.

She thrashed, desperate to escape, but I'd already planned for that. Zip ties secured her wrists to the grab handle. The garrote—fine wire delicately wrapped around her throat—tightened with each jerk of her body.

Not enough to cut off air. Yet.

Just enough to teach her respect.

Her screams were nothing. Her pleas—meaningless. I was used to it. The winter forest devoured them whole.

I wanted to talk. I always did. The conversations were part of the art. The story.

So, I asked.

About him. The man who kissed her cheek. The one who wasn't her fiancé.

I needed to know. To test her. To see if she was pure—if her story aligned with the masterpiece, I was building.

She trembled, voice cracking as she swore it was nothing. *Chris,* she said. *My cousin. In town for the wedding.*

Mark was everything. She'd never betray him. He'd be devastated. Devastated.

The word gutted me. It burned, hollowing out my chest until rage flared in emptiness. She was mine, all of her. The centerpiece in my work, the stillness in the chaos.

I lashed out, my elbow driving into her jaw, silencing her with a jolt that snapped her head back.

No more talking.

The drive after that was heavy. Quiet.

When we arrived, the silence swallowed us whole. Snow lay thick across the roofline of my sanctuary, untouched, eternal. Time didn't exist here. Only art.

She slumped in the seat, bruised, beautiful, breath fogging the window—her last fragile trace of life.

The copper sting of blood clung to the cold air, mixing with the sterile tang of latex on my gloves. I leaned close, inhaling it.

It was time.

Time to set her frame. To make her mine. To make her eternal.

Paralyzed Elegy

The Lonely Heart Murderer

Car door open. Zip ties cut.

She ran.

I loved it when they ran.

Every footstep—every frantic movement—was music. A heartbeat in my symphony. Chaotic. Pleading. Brief. Fleeting.

Nicole bolted through the trees like a startled deer, breath ragged, shoes slipping on the icy underbrush. Ground cracked beneath her weight, brittle branches snapping, her breath clouding the dark like smoke. She had no idea how perfectly she played her part.

I let her go. I wanted to see it. The illusion of escape. That fleeing hope in her chest—her belief that she could get away. It made my pulse quicken.

She never saw me step into her path.

One second, her eyes locked forward, the next, she crashed into me.

The sharp, panicked gasp that left her lips was everything I craved.

Raw. Sweet.

I wrapped my arms around her like a lover—no rush. I let the moment breathe.

She didn't scream—couldn't.

I'd silenced her too well in the car. Too eager. Now she was starting to crack.

That pitiful whimper when I snapped her jaw back into place told me I'd pushed too far.

Her eyes rolled, body convulsing as she crumbled in my arms.

The satisfying pop gave way to a sickening crunch.

I hadn't meant to break her.

Not fully.

Now she'd never tell me about Mark. About their stupid little love story and what made him so special.

No dreamy anecdotes, no soft laughter between sobs.

Just choked breath and shattered bone.

Fine.

If she couldn't speak to me, she would still show me.

Her fear. Her devotion.

Her truth, in pieces.

I carried her—limp and heavy—as if she were nothing but a thing to be shaped, molded.

The room was already prepped—spotless and silent, a canvas waiting.

I laid her out on the table, her limbs trembling. It took little effort to strap her down. Ankles first. Then wrists.

I leaned in close, and her panic hit me like perfume—salt-stung skin, fear-slicked breath, a trace of jasmine that clung to her like memory.

Her eyes locked onto mine, wide and glistening. Fear etched in every inch of her face. Her breath came in shallow gasps, quick and desperate.

The way they followed my every movement, darting between the straps, the table, the pole—yes, I'd wheeled the IV in deliberately slow. Let her drink in every detail.

"Hydration is important," I whispered, voice soft enough to pass for kind. "This takes time. I need you alert."

I inserted the needle into her arm with practiced ease. She flinched.

The fluids flowed first, clear and cold.

Then Nimbex. That beautiful little drug.

It would still her body, make her mine completely.

But it wouldn't dull her mind.

No, she would feel *everything*.

She just wouldn't be able to run again.

Not even blink.

Her body stiffened slowly. I watched it take hold—muscles locking, breath shallow and fast.

When I unbuckled the restraints, she stayed just as I needed her.

Open. Helpless.

A perfect porcelain doll waiting to be made new.

I brushed her hair off her forehead.

"This is what love looks like," I murmured. "Still. Obedient. Eternal."

It was time.

Time to make something beautiful for Katie.

***

The chains bit into my palms as I tightened the final knot.

My breath came in clouds, sharp and fast, but I didn't feel the cold anymore.

My fingers burned from the work—hooking her just right, angling the lines so the early light would hit her the way I imagined.

It was grueling.

Nicole was... exquisite.

I stepped back, wiping the sweat from my forehead with a trembling hand, heart hammering with joy.

She wasn't just posed.

She was elevated.

Suspended like she was weightless—art made flesh, suffering made sacred.

The line of her throat, the way her arms stretched just so—it sang.

My best.

She was my best.

I almost laughed.

How the hell was I ever going to top this?

The ribbon flared under the work lights—black in the shadows, crimson when the beam caught it just right.

Midnight vein.

Because now the bar was raised, and I loved the climb.

That heat in my chest, that tremor running deep through my spine—that was her. *My Katie.*

The thought of her, jaw clenched, storm in her eyes as she studied my gift... our gift.

She'd been slipping, tired of our dance.

Ready to walk away from what we had.

I couldn't let her.

Not yet.

Not when I had so much left to show her. To give her.

I knelt, adjusted the chain near Nicole's ankle, just a hair's breadth tighter.

Details mattered.

Katie would notice the craftsmanship, the effort, the intention behind every loop, every bend of wire, every bruise like a brushstroke.

She would see *me* in it.

She would *feel* me.

This was more than a message. It was a moment.

One I carved out of flesh and steel and silence.

Morning would come soon. The square would burst alive—with the first stalls of the Christmas market creaking open. Strings of bulbs and pine garlands. Cinnamon and roasted chestnuts thick in the air. Families bundled in scarves, children dragging mittened hands.

Past the glittering lights, past the red ribbons and wreaths, to where she swayed above it all. Suspended. Eternal.

I turned in a slow circle, heart steady, eyes taking in every angle.

This would show her I was still *worth* the chase. That the story wasn't over.

"This," I whispered to the cold, "she will love."

I let the silence settle. Let the moment breathe.

I could almost see her already—Katie, jaw tight, lips pressed, that flicker of something just behind her eyes. That battle between revulsion and fascination.

The spark I'd miss if she ever caught me.

The war inside her I wasn't ready to surrender to just yet.

"This," I whispered again, smiling now, "this will make her see me differently."

I stepped back into the shadows, my pulse steady, my hands still shaking.

Let the curtain rise.

Stilled for Him

Katherine

The weeks bled together—sirens, press briefings, noise without answers. Panic without progress.

We tried everything short of screaming at the public to stay calm. But how do you tell people not to panic when a sadistic monster is turning brides-to-be into corpses?

Still. Silence. Again.

I hated the quiet more than the blood.

What was he doing to her—the one he had now? Was she dead already? Or was she still clinging to hope, wherever he had her?

And why me? Why had I become his obsession?

I didn't ask for this. I never—

The call came at 8 a.m. I didn't even finish my coffee. Grabbing my keys, a heavy weight settled in my chest.

The moment I turned the corner and saw the alley blocked off by a wall of squad cars, I knew.

I parked. Climbed out, and the air felt thick, as if it knew what waited for me. Snow clung to the gutters; tire ruts iced into pavement.

Flashing red-and-blues painting the bricks, voices murmuring in the background. I ducked under the crime scene tape, feeling the cold scrape across my cheeks.

And then—

The air shifted. Sweet perfume colliding with copper and rot. Too strong, too sudden. It clawed down my throat, made my stomach lurch.

I saw her.

The world didn't slow—it *slammed*. My body locked, every nerve screaming before thought could catch up.

My breath hitched sharp in my chest, then punched out.

I nearly staggered back.

No, this—this couldn't be real.

He hadn't just escalated.

He had obliterated every line I thought he wouldn't cross.

She hung there—suspended by hooks and rusted chains like a grotesque marionette. Fishing line coiled around her limbs, shimmering in the morning light.

Her dress—black and red, a gothic bridal corset—looked almost romantic. Purposeful.

But her face— Wide eyes locked in terror, mouth stretched mid-breath she'd never finish. The agony froze there, carved into her like ice.

It tore straight through me.

She'd been alive for all of it.

I didn't need the M.E. to confirm it. I *felt* it.

And the scalpel in her hand—she had cut herself open?

Had he made her, do it?

I couldn't breathe.

Dayna Cookson had been brutal.

But this? This was... *reverence*.

People were snapping photos, their phones raised like they were at an art exhibit.

I wanted to scream, shove them back. This wasn't art. This was a woman. A life.

I knew—that's exactly what he wanted. That's how he saw her.

She wasn't like the others.

They'd been posed, yes, but this one was dressed. Made up.

Her lips-stained red. Hair curled into soft spirals like she was about to walk down the aisle—not be butchered and hung in an alley.

Black satin gloves reached up to her elbows.

No. She wasn't trash to him.

She was something more. *Worshipped.*

He hadn't just stolen her life. He'd painted it. Preserved it.

Made her both: woman and art.

The thought shook me.

Was she the one? The one he had always been searching for. Or was she someone new?

Am I even looking at his work?

My mind warred with itself as we waited for the body to be processed. But I already knew.

When they let me approach, everything slowed. My pulse pounded in my ears.

I didn't want to touch her—I wanted to let her rest—but my gut told me to check.

I reached for her left hand. Peeled the glove back with shaking fingers.

And then I dropped to my knees.

Her ring finger. Gone.

I stared at the space where it used to be, bile rising in my throat.

It *was* him.

It had always been him.

But this time…

He hadn't discarded her.

He'd *honored* her.

Why her?

Aftermath

Katherine

She couldn't scrub her hands clean.

The water was cold, biting into her skin, but she left it running, letting the sting punish her.

Nicole's blood hadn't touched her—but it didn't matter. It was under her skin now.

She'd seen worse.

But this one—

Nicole had been real. A fiancé with big ears. A rescue cat named Maple.

She was warm. Nervous

And now she was *art*.

Her vision blurred, breath halted. She braced herself on the counter, fingers digging into the granite, but still she stayed.

Nicole had been alive just twenty hours before they found her.

The timeline didn't matter. The patterns didn't matter.

None of it helped.

The board, the maps the photos—they were just window dressing. All that data and still, she'd stood staring at a body posed like a twisted love letter.

Satin gloves. Pale lips.

And the finger.

Her stomach turned. She bent over the sink, coughed dry, but nothing came. Her body didn't want to grieve. It just existed.

The water stared back at her. Her breath fogged on the mirror.

"Katherine?"

Brandon's voice. Hesitant.

She didn't answer.

The door creaked open. Brandon stepped inside, closing it gently, like he was entering a church.

"I'm fine," she said, voice hoarse.

"You're not."

He stepped closer but didn't touch.

"You haven't slept." he said gently.

"I'll sleep when he's in cuffs."

"You've said that before." He implored.

She didn't answer. Didn't want to argue.

He leaned against the counter, arms folded.

"Cheryl says you've been living off caffeine and cold air."

Katherine turned the faucet off. The silence roared louder.

"She's worried," he added.

Katherine let her hands fall to her sides. They shook. She curled them into fists.

"Cheryl should worry about the press, or the mayor. or the family who's about to bury their daughter with a finger missing."

"Kat—"

She snapped her head up.

"You think I don't know that we missed it? That if we'd just—if *I'd* just put the pattern together sooner, she'd be alive right now?"

His mouth opened, but nothing came out.

Because there was nothing.

No comfort. No fix.

Nicole was dead. The killer was still free. Probably watching. Probably laughing.

"I'm supposed to be good at this," she whispered. "I was supposed to stop him."

"You're not a psychic, Kat."

"No. I'm worse." Her voice dropped.

"I'm a mirror. That's what he said last time. That I'm his mirror. I see the world the way he does. But maybe I don't. Maybe that's the problem. Maybe he sees it clearer."

Brandon flinched.

"You don't believe that."

"I don't know what I believe anymore."

The room went quiet again, long enough for the buzz in her ears to take shape. A low hum. Almost like—

She looked up, startled.

Brandon was still there.

But something inside her had shifted.

"I need air," she said abruptly. "I need to move."

"You need sleep."

"I said I need air."

She didn't wait for him to follow. She was already gone.

Quiet Knocks Loudest

Katherine

Later that night, waiting for Bella's text, the phone rang.

I jolted, almost dropping it. My pulse surged. For a second, my mouth couldn't form words.

"Hello?"

A pause. Then a deep, unfamiliar voice.

"Umm… Katherine?"

Telemarketer.

"How can I help you?" I asked, narrowing my eyes at the unfamiliar number. "Who's calling?"

Didn't have time for this.

"I'm Devin. Cheryl's friend—we were supposed to meet at The Saffire Grill a few weeks ago?"

Wait. *What?* I crossed my arms, defensive. My voice came out tighter than I meant. "How did you get my number? I told Cheryl I'd call when I had time."

Damn it, Cheryl.

"She told me it'd be okay to call." He added. "Thought maybe I could set something up with you directly."

His voice was gentle. Hopeful.

Too forward. But also… kind of gutsy.

I felt the smallest flicker in my chest—someone asking about me—not the case, not my trauma, just *me*.

I pressed a hand to my forehead, half expecting to find a fever.

"I appreciate the call," I said carefully, "but I've got a long day tomorrow. Can I call you when I come up for air?"

His exhale was quick. "Yeah, sure. That would be great. Whenever you get a chance. Talk soon"

He hung up.

I stared at the phone, stillness settling like a held breath. A stranger with my number, who wanted to date me.

I should be angry. But behind the instinctive walls, something stirred. Assertive. Confident.

Maybe I'd call him. Eventually.

Later, after a too-hot shower and the familiar ritual of checking locks twice over, I slid beneath the covers.

I waited for the usual parade of nightmares to march in behind my closed eyelids.

But that night?

There was only quiet.

And for the first time in months, I slept.

Downtown Canvas

Katherine

The Garment District smelled like last chances.

Fifth Avenue was a polished lie—windows full of mirrored promises—but between Eighth and Ninth the streets were honest about their bruises. Steam hissed from sidewalk grates; wet cardboard soured in the gutters. I liked it better here. Nothing pretended.

Brandon and I cut across 37th. Slush seeped into my boots, the cold biting through yesterday's caffeine. He flipped through invoices while we walked.

Ten nights ago, she'd been found—corseted in black satin, arterial red ribbon. Whoever dressed her hadn't ripped fabric from thrift bins; he'd sourced it. Quality. Purpose.

We'd pulled three supplier codes off fragments in her bodice lining—tiny heat-pressed numbers. One had dead-ended in Italy, one in New Jersey, and the third pointed straight to midtown Manhattan.

Brandon paused in front of a storefront. "He buys better than I do."

"Nicole was worth more than retail," I said.

Inside, bolts of fabric stood like silent choir rows—silks, brocades, velvets. The clerk, a woman with a silver hoop through her brow, eyed our badges like unpaid rent.

Brandon laid the invoice copy on the counter "Recognize it?"

She chewed her lip. "Black silk satin, fifteen-ounce weight. We only had five yards in stock that day. Gone in ten minutes. Cash buyer. Sunglasses. Gloves."

"Date?" I asked.

"Exactly one month ago."

I wrote it down. We asked about cameras; she laughed—no footage, no card, no name.

At the next shop, crimson silk ribbon, 200 yards, purchased in cash. The owner remembered the buyer's question—*Could the ribbon withstand direct rain for at least four hours?*

My stomach twisted.

At the third, a sixty-year-old tailor remembered custom-cut spiral steels. *Not many knew how to size those anymore.*

"He does," I whispered.

The sky bruised toward dusk, neon signs sputtering awake. We hit three more stores. Same story: single male buyer, cash.

"He's not just dressing them," Brandon.

"He's engineering them, Nicole wasn't a costume; she was a blueprint." I confirmed.

One shop left—Luce Blu Textiles—a narrow, showroom lit by weak candles and worse fluorescents. The clerk a woman in a cardigan, studied the ribbon SKU.

"He called it midnight vein," she said, pulling an invoice. "Said it needed to look black until a flash hit it, then flare red. He knew his pigment chemistry."

She slid the paperwork across. Alias, burner number, a Manhattan PO box. Paid in full.

"Anything else?" I asked.

She hesitated, then leaned in. "He smelled like violets and bleach. Odd combination, but unforgettable."

Violets. My pulse stuttered—memory of orchid petals in another woman's mouth.

Brandon caught my shoulder. "Kat?"

"I'm good," I lied. "We've got what we need."

Outside, the winter air slapped color back into my face. The map in my head redrew itself—suppliers like pushpins, routes like veins. The killer moved through these streets like a designer, turning silk and steel into his haven.

"We're close," Brandon said.

I studied the invoice fluttering in his hand, red dye fingerprints on my glove, black ink bleeding where snow landed.

"We're closer than he thinks," I answered.

A delivery truck rumbled by, sending steam curls around us. I watched it disappear down 38th, back gate flapping.

Somewhere in this city, new bolts were being cut—fabric just as rare, just as reverent. Measured for a body that hadn't stopped breathing yet. And we had his supply chain. A silk footprint. A thread to strangle him with.

I took a breath that tasted like metal and rain. Then we turned east, into the glow of Seventh Avenue, following the trail he thought was invisible.

The Ones I Couldn't Save

Katherine

Katherine stared at the crack in her ceiling like it owed her something—answers, maybe.

Or an apology. Her arm draped over her eyes, but the jagged line of plaster sliced through her vision. The radiator groaned louder, but she was too tired to turn it off.

Replaying every detail from downtown. None of it fit, yet all of it did. Her eyes burned, blinked too long, and sleep took her before she could resist.

The moment her lids fluttered too long, the room changed.

✦

The crack in the ceiling shifted, becoming a seam in a veil—white, laced, fluttering. The bed beneath her melted into something softer, cleaner. And the air thickened with lilies. Not the smell. Their presence.

She sat up, slowly, and found herself standing.

The world around her blurred. Muted.

And at the end of the hall—Nicole.

Barefoot, her veil still pinned. The dress pristine, soft. Not bloodstained, not yet.

Nicole didn't speak. She just looked.

Katherine's breath caught in her chest.

"I'm sorry," she croaked, voice jagged, "I tried. I swear—

Nicole tilted her head.

You didn't try hard enough.

The words didn't come from her lips, but they rang clear.

Katherine took a step forward. The lilies thickened, suffocating. The hall stretched—like she wasn't getting closer. Nicole, out of reach.

"You were texting your sister about cake flavors," Katherine whispered. "You'd picked lemon lavender. You didn't get to taste it."

Nicole's eyes shimmered.

Another step.

Katherine reached out her hand. "I see you now. I see you."

Nicole blinked. Then her mouth opened—and it wasn't her voice that came out.

You're not the mirror, the voice rasped. Low, male. Familiar.

Katherine's heart froze.

Nicole's face twisted, smeared like wet paint.

The mirror is cracked, the voice growled again, from somewhere beneath her skin. *You can't see me anymore.*

Katherine jerked back. The lilies rotted. Black and curling, the walls bleeding ink. Her boots stuck to the floor, the hall warped. Twisted.

✦

She woke up gasping.

Her throat was dry, her shirt damp with sweat. The room was cold. The ceiling crack still harmless. But her fingers dug into the sheets like they were torn from a grave.

Nicole was gone.

But not far.

Katherine sat up, cradling her forehead in her palms.

She didn't sleep again that night.

The Tipping Point

Katherine

The drive was a blur. One moment she was in the car, fists clenched, the next, the sterile light of the precinct slammed into her vision. Too bright. Too clean.

She didn't stop to think—just moved. Away. From the dreams. From the suffocating stillness of the girl's sculpted face. From the weight of not saving her.

She needed the noise. Anything. Phones ringing, papers rustling. Anything to anchor her.

"You're late." Cheryl's voice snagged her. Not sharp. Just worn out, tired.

Katherine didn't stop. Her bag dropped with a thud on a desk, but her feet kept moving. Straight to the evidence room.

She needed to see something. Anything. Just not stillness.

"You're not cleared," Cheryl called, footsteps chasing hers.

Katherine's laugh cracked dry in her throat. "Nicole dropped by last night. Veiled and glowing—like she hadn't been carved up and left for me to find.

Cheryl followed. "That's not trauma. That's your guilt playing dress-up with someone else's death."

Katherine spun. "Don't pull that therapist crap on me."

"You've been circling the drain, "Cheryl said, voice cutting.

Katherine looked away, weight in her throat was worse than shame.

I said quietly. "I can't sleep. I jump at nothing. Sometimes I catch a whiff of something sweet—soap, flowers long dead—and I freeze like he's behind me. I see fingers in my food. I can't eat. I can't breathe right."

Cheryl stepped in. "I expect you to be alive long enough to stop this guy."

Silence hit hard. Katherine blinked. "He's escalating. If we stop now, we're complicit. I'll carry the weight. I just can't carry silence too."

Cheryl exhaled—like it bruised something in her ribs. "Then stop pretending you can do it alone."

The words hit like gravel in a blender. She didn't nod—just shifted, a body too tired to fight.

"Come with me," Cheryl said softly. "Five minutes. Then decide what more you can carry."

Katherine's instinct lit up, ready to bite. But the argument fizzled. Died. She just... followed.

The hallway felt too long. Her boots echoed. Her pulse tried to choke her.

Closing the door. Cheryl leaned against the desk. "Last time you slept more than three hours?"

Katherine sat staring at her shoes. "Sleep's irrelevant."

Cheryl nodded like she'd already written the answers down. "You're burning out."

"I know."

"Well, I care." She said gently.

Katherine's head snapped up. "Why? I'm a walking red flag. I'm barely holding it together"

"You're the only one he's building this for," Cheryl interrupted. "You're the axis. If you break, we lose our only leverage."

Katherine's throat clenched. She wouldn't cry.

But her hands curled tight in her lap.

"I can't stop looking," she said. "Even when it hurts. I can't look away."

Cheryl crouched beside her, eyes steady. "Then don't. But let someone hold the flashlight."

Something in Katherine cracked. Breath leaked out slow, real.

"Five minutes," she whispered. "That's how we survive. Five minutes at a time."

Postmarked: Hell

Katherine

I was supposed to wait five minutes. I lasted four.

The weight of Nicole's silence dragged me here. I couldn't sit still, couldn't breathe without knowing. What had he done to her? How had he turned her into this grotesque thing?

The morgue doors hissed as they shut behind me. Formalin hit my throat before the sterile cold crept through my skin. It wasn't the chill that made me sick—it was the dread pooling in my stomach.

Bella glanced up from the exam table, her eyes flickering with a knowing sadness. No questions, no words. She didn't need to ask why I was here.

I stood on the other side of Nicole's body, arms folded tight to hold my cracking composure together. Her dress was already gone—packed up for evidence. I studied her, eyes tracking the lack of surface lacerations. No ragged wounds like the others. Her makeup had been wiped away, but under the foundation, a dark bruise bloomed across her jaw.

My stomach twisted. He hit her. Hard.

"Scrape under her nails," I ordered, my voice thin. "Check for defensive wounds."

Her hands hung limp now—slack and cold, too still.

I couldn't look away as Bella described the wound. He split her skull, from crown to throat. If he opened her while her heart was pumping, the alley should've been a slaughterhouse—spray, cast-off. But only clean vertical droplets had been logged.

He drained her first. Or did it somewhere else.

She's been alive for it. Every breath was forced through that gaping wound.

And the fishing line?

It wasn't an accident. He stitched her like a puppet.

Nicole Bramble. Twenty-two. Full of life. A wedding on the horizon. A fiancé. A future ended.

The clock ticked as Bella's voice buzzed in the background. My mind couldn't hold onto it. I had to know more.

***

We tore apart Nicole's life. Her apartment—perfect. Her texts—mundane. No wild admirers. No signs of obsession.

Nothing.

The door creaked open.

"Excuse me, I'm looking for Katherine Poe."

I snapped my head up. A courier.

Brandon stepped forward. I rose immediately, the unease crawling up my neck. "I'm Katherine Poe," I said.

The man handed me a clipboard. "Sign here."

I scribbled my name, already frowning. No return address. No sender.

"Where did this come from?" I asked.

He blinked, "part of my route," shrugged, disappeared like a shadow.

I almost tore the envelope open but stopped myself. Gloves. I slid them on, hands shaking.

Inside, a photograph. Nicole—alive, walking down the street. Her coffee in hand. More pictures followed.

Her undressing. Bound. Gagged. Hooked. Cut.

The paper reeked of fresh ink. Chemicals. My stomach churned.

And then the letter.

Katherine, my dear Katherine, I was so pleased to see the look on your face as you discovered my present for you. I knew this would be the one where you'd start to appreciate all that I've done for you. That flush as you stepped from your car, wrestling with your scarf…It was comical, truly. I will never tire of that expression. It holds me over. Until we're face to face. Soon, Katie. Very soon.

--Your Admirer.

I couldn't breathe.

He had seen me. Close enough to describe my scarf. Close enough to watch me—watch me and know how I felt.

My hands crumpled the letter before I forced it flat again. I scanned it, but the words blurred.

I went to the computer, searched every piece of footage from the scene. He had to be there. The ego was too large to stay hidden. He'd wanted to see me, wanted me to watch him stand triumphant over Nicole's death.

He was a ghost.

Ghosts didn't breathe down your neck.

And they didn't describe your scarf like they owned the moment.

I slammed my fist on the desk, a wave of cold dread crashing through me. He was closer than I wanted to believe.

But it wasn't enough. Not yet.

I couldn't shake the thought.

Let him remember the scarf. When I catch him, I'll be the one tightening it around his neck.

Chain of Custody

Katherine

The evidence vaults always smelled like cold metal and paper cuts—clean, dry, clinical. A place that didn't allow grief, only procedure.

Strip the human away. Reduce a life to catalog numbers, tamper-proof tape.

Katherine signed her name on the chain of custody form for the third time this month. Her signature was starting to look like someone else's—half the loop on the K, no flourish.

Efficient. Tired.

"You know there's a rumor you sleep here," Bella said without looking up.

Katherine didn't glance at her. She was busy cross-referencing fiber samples from Victim Sixteen.

"You know there's a rumor you have a secret romance with the ME from Queens," Katherine said dryly.

Bella snorted. "Please. He labels his organ jars with emojis. That man couldn't handle me."

Katherine cracked the faintest smile. Just enough to acknowledge it. Then back to the evidence.

The sealed tray held a single envelope—torn but pristine where it mattered. No DNA, no prints. But the paper felt...too smooth. Too intentional.

Handmade, maybe.

Bella glanced over her shoulder. "He's not just meticulous. He's romantic."

"Romance usually involves consent," Katherine muttered.

"Still. The ritual of it. The poetics. He wants you to feel seen."

Katherine's stomach churned. "I know."

They worked in silence for a while—gloves whispering against trays and folders. Each item tagged, logged, re-examined.

Tedium didn't lie.

"He's pivoting," Katherine said. "A shift in the staging. Less destruction, more curation."

Bella looked up sharply. "You think we're entering endgame?"

Katherine didn't answer.

Because yes.

She could feel it. The precision. The restraint. Something massive coiling just beneath the surface. A final act in preparation.

She signed off on the last item in the ledger.

"Want me to walk you out?" Bella asked.

Katherine shook her head. "I'm good."

She watched Bella disappear, her boots' echo swallowed by the hum of climate control.

Then Katherine reached into her own pocket.

A different envelope. Unlogged. No return address. Just her name—scrawled in a hand she didn't want to recognize.

She opened it slowly. One line.

Would you recognize your own ending if I handed it to you in lace?

Katherine didn't flinch. She folded the note, sealed it in a new evidence bag, and placed it in the box with the others.

The vault swallowed it whole.

The Room Without Corners

Katherine

She hadn't meant to end up here.

But silence—even in the vault—only went so far.

This room was quieter. No sharp corners—just soft curves and muted light. Designed by someone who understood trauma too well.

The chair wasn't uncomfortable. Just indifferent.

Katherine sat, arms folded, elbows clutched tight, bracing herself, angled away from the woman across from her.

"Did you sleep last night?" she asked, gentle.

Katherine's eyes flicked up, hard. "Define sleep."

Delaney didn't smile, just waited.

"It was the room again," Katherine said after a beat. Her voice felt distant, like it belonged to someone else. "The floors were too clean. I don't remember them being clean."

"What do you remember?" she questioned.

Silence.

"The humming," Katherine said finally. "Not a tune. Just... his breath. Vibrating in his throat. Like a wire being plucked."

She hadn't told anyone that before.

No pen moved. No notes. Just presence.

"And when you wake up?" she asked.

"I smell him," she said. "Not sweat. Not anything sharp. It's warmth. Woodsmoke, maybe. And something singed—like a warning that never fades."

"I think they're doubting me again,"

"Your team?" she asked.

"They don't say it. But Glenna rattled them. They think I spiraled."

"Did you?" she implored.

Katherine's jaw locked. "I never spiraled. I saw what they didn't. Symmetry. Posing. The missing ring finger. Now another woman's dead, and it's exactly what I warned them about."

"Have you told them how that feels?" she asked more gently.

"They're not the ones in therapy."

"That doesn't mean they're not carrying it." She added.

Katherine exhaled, sharp. "They're good people. But they haven't lived inside him."

"You have?" she inquired.

"They're catching up. But I'm done waiting for them before I act."

She nodded.

Katherine stood, her hands clenched at her sides.

"He's not playing with them," she said. "He's playing with me.

Vindication

Katherine

Later that evening, the bullpen was quieter than usual.

Too quiet for a room full of analysts and detectives who should've been arguing over timelines and cross-jurisdictional warrants.

Instead, only the occasional cough and the hum of flickering fluorescent lights filled the space.

Katherine stayed seated. Let them come to her.

She didn't flinch when the door to the glass office opened.

Cheryl stepped in first, followed by Kali—both avoiding eye contact, like grief had made the walls too reflective.

Katherine waited.

Cheryl cleared her throat. "We should've listened."

Kali folded her arms, tight across her chest. "Glenna was enough. She should've been enough."

Katherine didn't respond. She simply shifted a page in the file before her, not for effect, but to keep her hands from curling into fists.

Cheryl tried again. "We thought maybe you were too close to it. Seeing ghosts."

"I was," Katherine said, voice calm, like winter glass. "He's always the one."

Kali looked down. "Nicole—victim sixteen. Her ring finger missing the symmetry of the wounds. It's exactly how you described. Exactly what Glenna's should've told us."

"No," Katherine replied, voice cold. "It meant he was perfecting."

They stood in the rare silence that followed, none of them able to dress it up as professionalism.

"I'm not angry," Katherine said finally. "You weren't supposed to feel it. Not like I did."

"But now we do," Kali said softly. "It cost another woman her life."

Katherine closed the file. The sound was sharp in the hush, like a gavel.

"Then we don't let it cost another," she said. "We move when it feels wrong. We listen when the air shifts."

Cheryl nodded. "You have point on this. Whatever you need."

Katherine stood, eyes level, voice steady. "Then we start with the photos. He's not hiding anymore. He wants to be seen."

She brushed past them, silent, motioning forward.

Remorse wasn't a correction. It was a catalyst.

What They Owed Her

Katherine

The breakroom was empty.

No hum of vending machines. No clink of coffee pots. Just the hum of silence and the brittle sound of her own breathing.

She hadn't meant to sit, but her knees had finally caught up with her spine.

The file was still in her hand, closed now, the edge of the manila folder leaving a faint crease in her palm.

They'd apologized.

Not grandly. Not with groveling. Just… honestly.

And that almost hurt more.

Because Glenna was still dead.

Now Nicole.

Katherine stared at the far wall, where chipped paint had been lazily covered with a sticky note—someone's half-written shopping list. Almonds. Soap. Coffee.

She almost laughed. The world kept spinning, even when it cracked.

A small part of her—a cruel, quiet part—wanted to throw their remorse back at them. Remind them how it felt to scream underwater while everyone else smiled on the shore.

But she didn't. Because stopping wasn't an option.

Her fingers slid across the folder. Nicole. Glenna. Dayna. The others.

He wasn't done.

And now they all believed her.

That was the shift she'd been waiting for.

Not power. Not pity.

Permission.

She stood slowly, tucked the file beneath her arm, and walked out without turning off the light.

It was time to stop whispering to ghosts.

Time to answer the *invitation*.

Chosen and Eternal

The Lonely Heart Murderer

When I was younger, I used to lie awake at night imagining the moment—the first cut, the way her breath would hitch, the way her eyes would lock on mine and beg without words.

The movies never got it right. They always rush the moment, always treat it like some crude act of violence.

But not me.

I saw it for what it was.

A symphony.

She would be my first. *My Angel.*

I could already see her—soft, trembling, watching me like I held the moon in my hands.

And in that moment, I would.

She wouldn't scream. Not at first. She'd tremble instead, just a soft shake in her wrists, like a violin string tightening before it breaks. The fear would come in waves, slow and poetic. I'd whisper to her, guide her into understanding what this was—not cruelty, but a kind of transcendence.

Artists don't *kill*. We reveal.

The world would remember her because *I* had seen her. *I* had chosen her. No one else would've known how perfect she was—how her body could become something ethereal.

There would be no bloodlust, no chaos.

Just... *beauty*, stretched and suspended in quiet awe. A sculpture of devotion.

People would look away, too afraid to see what I had created.

But Katie—*my* Katie—she'd see it. She'd *feel* it.

The message was always for her.

She was the reason I started. The reason I refined my technique. She made me want to perfect every angle, every position, every moment frozen in time. Because one day, when we finally meet face to face, I want her to understand that I've always done this *for her*.

Every model a message.

Every scene a love letter.

Every breath taken in their final moments, a whisper of the devotion I've never been allowed to show her.

She'll see it soon.

She'll see *me*.

The First Stillness

The Lonely Heart Murderer

Before the frame.

Twelve-years-old. And the silence pressed in like a second ribcage.

Not the kind that came when a room emptied out—this was the silence that bloomed *after*. *After* screaming turned to air. *After* the belt snapped drywall and splinters rained like dust motes in the kitchen light. *After* the glass stopped its skittering crawl across the linoleum.

The silence after violence always had weight. It settled in his sternum and refused to leave.

Knees drawn tight to chest beneath the table, chin resting on denim. Cold vinyl floor against bare feet. Breath shallow, not from fear—just instinct. *Don't draw attention. Don't shift the air. Don't invite another round.*

Red dripped down the edge of the fridge. Slow. Sticky. Thick enough to hold a reflection before it broke and fell.

Not his.

Not hers.

Maybe the dog. Maybe that tabby from next door.

He didn't check. Didn't move. Just watched.

The house held its breath with him.

No doors latched properly here—nothing ever sealed all the way shut. People always left like weather—suddenly, without warning. He learned not to ask why.

Maybe his father was still inside. Maybe not. The walls never told.

No tears. Not that night. Not after.

Only the pattern.

The way blood dried in ridges, curling at the edges like burnt paper. Fossil shapes. Fractal spirals.

There was something in that—something ancient. Something trying to speak if you looked hard enough.

He memorized it.

One week later, the slingshot snapped.

He hadn't meant it. Not really. But when the crow hit the ground, the sound it made—wet and final—it stitched into him.

Wings spasming. Leg kicking once. Neck crooked, beak open in a frozen scream.

He crouched beside it. Not out of pity. Not curiosity. Just *need*.

The need to see.

Its feathers weren't black. Not really. In the sun, they bled green. Purple. Oil-slick shimmer.

Color that only revealed itself if you stared long enough.

Five feathers. One by one, plucked. Careful not to bend the shafts. Pressed flat between notebook pages, dated in block letters.

A record. A beginning.

It hadn't felt wrong.

It hadn't felt like anything.

Except still.

Still was good.

Still meant quiet.

Still meant no one moved unless he said so.

Years would pass before he'd learn the word for what he was. Before he'd hear it whispered in courtrooms and textbooks and true crime podcasts.

But under that table, blood cooling, eyes wide, lungs locked—

He already knew.

Silence was the frame.

And he was learning to paint.

Muse in the Window

The Lonely Heart Murderer

I walked slower than I should have.

I knew exactly where my feet were carrying me—her corner coffee shop. The one with the dull green trim and smudged windows where she always ordered that ridiculous oversized muffin and a black coffee she rarely finished.

And there she was.

Right where she always sat—tucked into the far corner, one foot curled under her, leaning just slightly over whatever report she was pretending to focus on.

My chest tightened, a breath caught somewhere between reverence and hunger.

God, she was radiant when she didn't know someone was watching. That slight crease between her brows as she read—so serious, so precise. And when she reached for her cup, she smiled at something in her mind.

That smile wasn't meant for the world, and I wanted to bottle it. *Steal* it.

I only let myself look for a second. Just one heartbeat. Any longer and I risked the air shifting—the way it always does when prey senses the eyes on them.

But Katie was never prey.

She was the muse.

I'd been still for so long. Four years. No art. No blood. No canvas. All because watching her was better. *More* fulfilling. She moved like thought incarnate—disciplined, beautiful, wild when she believed no one could see.

Her laugh with her family in West Virginia, that fleeting dance in the kitchen as she stirred hot chocolate for her family, the way she looked up at the first snowfall like it was made just for her.

Her hair was always twisted tight for work, but I'd seen it down. The way it fell in waves, curling at the ends like it knew how to tempt gravity. It bounced when she jogged, when she swayed to the music in her earbuds, when she forgot the world was watching—or didn't care.

She didn't know she was mine.

That I had memorized every tilt of her head, every look of frustration when she thought she'd lost my trail.

She came alive when she chased me. That was her most breathtaking version—hunter and hunted in one body.

I pushed too hard with the first clue. I know that now.

But she'll figure it out—she *must*. She was made for this. For me.

Still... watching only satisfied the ache for so long. And now, it was back. That rising current inside me, hot and violent and eager. It clawed through my chest, demanding release.

My fingers twitched.

My mind began forming lines and edges, the first strokes of a new piece.

I could already smell the antiseptic, the copper, the sweat.

Katie could wait.

It was time to create again.

The Unworthy Subject

The Lonely Heart Murderer

Later that evening work consumed me.

My urges dulled beneath the weight of endless hours and deadlines, muffled like a scream underwater. But I still knew. I still saw her.

She wasn't like the others—no delicate green eyes, no chocolate waves of hair that glinted red in the light.

She wasn't my muse.

Not because she fit the gallery.

Because she insulted it.

The one who dubbed me '*The Lonely Heart Murderer*.' Like I was some common creep with mommy issues and a scalpel.

No art. No elegance.

Just another headline for her byline. She reduced my work to a punchline—and got applause for it.

A bonus. A disruption. A mistake I had to correct.

I stepped out into the night, the air cool against my face, and there she was. A shape in the dark that didn't belong—until it did. Until I saw the potential in her angles, the piece she could become.

I turned to leave, a thrill already twisting its way through my spine—and that's when it hit.

It started in my ears. Blood, loud and fast, roaring like a tide. The air grew thick. My throat closed. Heat crept up my neck, flooded my face, scalded me from the inside out.

I staggered.

The world narrowed to a pinpoint, and I was drowning in nothing, flailing in a vacuum I couldn't see or fight.

Clammy hands. Trembling limbs.

I was collapsing in plain sight but the world around me stayed upright.

No earthquake. No warning.

Just the sick, stuttering gasp of panic clamping its jaws around me.

I ran.

I barely made it to my car. I gripped the steering wheel so tight my knuckles turned bone white. My chest heaved. My vision blurred.

The sobs ripped out of me like an animal clawing through its cage.

It didn't stop until I was wrung out and hollow, a shell sitting in the driver's seat with salt on his lips and no breath left.

Panic. *Again.*

I hadn't had one since I was thirteen—since those early kills, the small ones. The animals. The ones I didn't want to hurt but had to.

When I'd lie awake for days, guilt twisting in my stomach, bile rising like penance.

I never wanted to feel it again.

I thought I'd buried that part of myself. Controlled it. *Owned* it.

But this wasn't the same.

I wasn't planning to kill some helpless creature.

I was creating.

So why did it feel like my insides were tearing in half?

I got myself home. Barely. My limbs felt disconnected from the rest of me, like they were carrying the weight of the question I couldn't answer. I crawled into bed fully clothed, my thoughts crashing into each other like broken glass.

Then it came to me.

She wasn't part of the design.

But neither was defacement.

And I was still *The Artist*.

Even if the next piece had to be a warning.

My body would learn to accept that.

It had no choice.

It didn't back then. It wouldn't now.

The Byline Bleeds

The Artist

Her scarf was red—sharp, daring. She wanted to be seen.

He stayed two cars back. Close enough.

She walked fast, the practiced pace of someone chasing stories. Unaware, confident in her invisibility.

She stopped at the coffee shop on 9th, almond milk, two sugars. He watched her stir, always counter-clockwise. A small ritual, a perfect detail. He took a seat across the street. The reflection in the coffee shop glass—a woman oblivious, unaware of the story being written about her.

Natalie Crane. The journalist who gave him his name.

The Lonely Heart Murderer.

Vulgar. She framed it that way, made it her headline.

He would correct her.

Lady Justice—he called it. Blindfolded, but with wax. A set of scales. A pen, the one she used in court sketches, resting beneath her tongue. And the red scarf.

She made herself loud. He would make her silent.

She left the shop, unaware of him. Easy.

He followed. No chloroform this time—quiet. The moment would come, though.

She didn't fit the pattern—blonde hair, blue eyes, sharp tongue.

But her mockery needed to be silenced.

The city still buzzed with the last scene I'd left for her. The police were chasing shadows; Katherine was chasing me. But this one wasn't Her's.

The gallery would gain its most ironic addition.

He waited in the alley. She re-applied her lipstick in the mirrored window. Her ego in full view.

He watched.

The needle slipped in. She didn't feel it until her knees buckled.

He caught her before she hit the ground.

Shhh, sweetheart. Now you'll listen.

No sweetness this time. This was steel and stone.

Justice, as she claimed to champion.

He dressed her in white, like a statue, a ghost. Blind-folded, sealed eyes. The scale in her hand—cold, rusted. He placed the recording of her most vicious podcast on one side.

The other side—a goat heart. Not hers, but close enough.

He left her hanging, arms outstretched, lips still stained with her last broadcast lipstick.

Lady Justice.

LIAR.

The word felt good in my mouth, even if no one heard it. No satisfaction, though—just quiet. Always the quiet.

Liar

Katherine

The air was sharp, too clean—like bleach battling something darker beneath it. Sirens had quieted, leaving only murmured voices and generators' hum. Katherine ducked under the tape. *Two weeks since the last body, and now this.*

She didn't need the backstory.

Natalie Crane. Or what was left of her.

Suspended in the courthouse threshold. White dress. Blindfolded. A scale in her hand.

"The Lonely Heart Murderer strikes again!" The voice looped.

Katherine flinched. Natalie's frozen grin. The blood-red smear still on her lips.

One side of the scale held a heart. The other, a recorder with one of her latest podcasts talking about The Lonely Hear Murderer.

The word etched in stone: **LIAR**

Katherine studied the flaw in the R, the slip only she would catch.

It wasn't just murder. It was vengeance.

He'd staged her to send a message. To Katherine.

"I see everything. I choose what's true," it said. "Say the wrong thing, and I'll rewrite you."

Katherine stepped back, cold rage flooding her chest.

He thinks he rattled me.

It didn't. It sharpened her focus.

Four victims left.

And so was he.

Threadbare

Katherine

She hadn't been cold yet.

That's what stuck.

Natalie's skin hadn't fully grayed. She'd been staged fresh. Which meant he waited. Waited with her body—blindfolded her,

posed her, timing the playback.

Theatrics weren't new. This was proximity.

I'd barely made it to my apartment before I collapsed on the kitchen floor, boots still on, jacket half-off.

Natalie's face kept blinking behind my eyes. That smirk. That smear of red.

The heart. Goat heart.

She'd mocked him. I knew that. Said he was a "fragile brand," a man hiding behind symbols.

But I'd said it first. Offhand, like it didn't matter.

And now she was dead. No—displayed.

He wanted me to see her. To *remember* my words.

I braced my elbows on my knees and pressed my palms to my face.

I should've felt sick. I should've cried.

Instead, I counted.

Sixteen victims.

Natalie was an outlier. Not part of the bride pattern. Not green-eyed, not brunette. No veil, no vow.

She was an editor's note.

A red mark across my mouth.

He was watching me closer. Listening. Tightening the net, around me, not him.

This wasn't about showing the world who he was.

It was about showing me who I was. What I'd missed. What I'd said wrong.

But either way, it was my name carved into the bottom of her silence.

Case File: Me

Katherine

I couldn't sleep. It had been two nights since Natalie Crane's display.

The bed was too soft, the silence too loud. My thoughts spiraled, thick and feverish, crawling under my skin.

The name—*Katie*—echoed in my mind, a razor between syllables.

My mother used to say it with honey. Elisabeth used to sing it like a secret. But on that paper, scrawled in a patchwork of typefaces, it felt like a violation.

No one called me that now. No one *should*.

I reached for my phone, thumb hovering over the screen. I'd already searched the name five times. Nothing explained why this monster knew it—why he kept using it like it belonged to him.

I squeezed my eyes shut.

It could've been a leak. An old friend. But no—this wasn't a recycled nickname casually mentioned by someone at a bar.

It was *intentional*. A breadcrumb meant to keep me circling back.

You have disappointed me, Katie.

I pulled the letter from the drawer again. The edges had curled.

That tone—intimate, condescending—like we were playing house, like this was a damn *relationship*.

I swallowed hard. I needed to think, but not out loud. Not on paper.

I sat at my laptop, opened an encrypted folder, and started typing into a fresh document—off-network, no auto-sync, no cloud.

1. Leak Check — Inner Circle

Brandon: my partner. Trusted, but... he's been more distant lately. Would *never* call me Katie. He calls me Kat. But could he have mentioned it to someone else?

Cheryl: too chatty. Set me up with that guy, Devin. She could've used it without realizing.

Devin: barely knows me. But persistent. He called after I cancelled. *How did he get my number again?*

Action:

Pull Cheryl's call records if possible. Run background on Devin. Confirm phone number source.

2. Recent Access to My Private Info

I use "Katie" as a username for *nothing*. Where's it coming from?

Old notebooks? Boxes in storage? Someone would've had to physically go through my things.

I never speak the name. *Never.*

Action:

Check if anything's been touched in my storage unit. Review security cam logs for the building. Pull recent badge swipes at my office after hours.

I sat back, fingers trembling slightly.

This wasn't just about solving a case anymore.

This was *personal.*

He wasn't leaving clues for the department.

He was curating a gallery for me alone.

And I had a sick feeling the final piece he wanted to unveil wasn't another victim—it was *me.*

And I wasn't ready to be on display.

Not again.

The phone lit up on my nightstand, slicing through the dark like a blade. Unknown Number. *Again.*

My pulse ticked higher. A slow, familiar thrum started at the base of my throat—half dread, half curiosity.

I hovered, thumb over screen.

"Hello?"

Goodnight, Katie

Katherine

"Hey, Katherine. I hope this isn't too late. It's Devin."

I sat up, tension knotting between my shoulders.

The voice was warm. Friendly. Confident in that casual, practiced way people are when they assume they're welcome.

"Oh," I said. My voice caught on the word. "Devin. Hi."

Cheryl's friend. The almost-date I never showed up for. Right. *Him.*

"I know this is out of the blue," he said, chuckling softly like we were already in on the same joke, "but Cheryl mentioned you've had a lot going on lately. Said I might need to be persistent."

God help me, I smiled. Just a little. *Against my better judgment.*

My smile held, but something under my ribs flinched.

"She also said we'd be a perfect match," he added. "And Cheryl doesn't usually go out of her way to set people up."

"She doesn't," I said, throat dry. "She's usually terrible at it."

A laugh from him. Not loud, not over-the-top—just genuine enough to rattle something inside me. I shifted the phone to my other hand.

"I get it," he said, voice low. "Life gets messy. But... if you've got room for coffee sometime, or even just a phone call that doesn't sound like a cold case briefing, I'd really like that."

My stomach twisted.

He was saying all the right things. Calm. Steady. Not pushy—persistent, but not aggressive.

And that scared me more than if he *had* been pushy.

Because men like him—they were never suspects.

"I'll think about it," I said, soft but not cold. I wasn't sure if I meant it.

Maybe I did. Maybe I wanted to.

Hell, maybe I just wanted to feel *something* that didn't come wrapped in duct tape and trauma.

"I'll take that as a maybe," he replied with a grin in his voice. "Goodnight, Katherine. Or *Katie*, if I'm lucky enough to earn that someday."

My breath caught.

The warmth in my chest turned to ice water.

I didn't move, didn't speak, until the call disconnected.

He didn't know. *He couldn't* know.

Katie was a name buried in the dirt with my innocence.

Cheryl must have mentioned it by accident. Must have. Right?

Tomorrow, I'd start digging into Devin properly.

Because if he was harmless, I needed to be sure.

I wasn't about to be anyone's art piece.

No Exes, No Scandals, No Flaws

Katherine

Katherine stared at the screen long after Devin's name disappeared from the call log. She exhaled, tension settling low in her chest. Something didn't sit right.

Her thumb tapped Cheryl's contact without thinking. Cheryl answered on the third ring, chipper as ever.

"Hey! Everything okay?"

Katherine didn't bother with pleasantries. "Did you give Devin my number?"

There was a pause. "Well," Cheryl finally said, drawing the word out, "I might've encouraged him to call. You've been buried in that cave of yours for months, *Katie*, and he's a good guy. Steady. Normal."

Katherine flinched. "You... call me *Katie?*"

Cheryl laughed. "Yeah, sometimes. It slips out when I talk about you."

"Devin said it." Katherine said flatly.

"Devin picked it up from me. Sorry, didn't think it'd weird you out." Cheryl added.

Katherine didn't know what to say. It *did* weird her out.

But she also understood. Cheryl had been trying to play matchmaker since the day Katherine moved back. The nickname wasn't sacred. Not really.

"I just wasn't expecting it," Katherine said, forcing her voice steady. "It caught me off guard."

"I get it." Cheryl softened. "But he's solid. Honestly, kind of a unicorn. You should give him a real chance."

Katherine's jaw tensed. "Maybe, what's his last name?"

Cheryl questioned, "Why are you doing a background check?"

Katherine said matter-of-factly, "You know I am."

"Grayson," Cheryl said, "But I don't foresee you finding anything bad."

They exchanged a few more casual words before she hung up.

Her thoughts, however, refused to do the same.

Katherine ended the call with Cheryl and let the phone fall to the couch beside her. *Katie.*

Hearing it again from someone she barely knew scraped against something too soft inside her, like a memory she'd buried alive. But Cheryl had said it so casually, so dismissively—*I use it when I talk about you*—like that made it fine. Like it didn't matter.

Maybe she was spiraling, again, searching for meaning in places that didn't deserve it.

Her fingers tapped against her thigh as she stared out the window into the dark.

Cheryl said he was steady. Normal. Kind. The kind of man a woman like her should want.

She opened a browser window and typed:

Devin Grayson Manhattan.

Dozens of results exploded across the page. Grayson Foundation. Charity galas. Photos of him with mayors, CEOs, smiling with polished teeth and suits that cost more than her rent. *Of course there was.*

She narrowed her search.

Devin Grayson West Virginia.

She clicked through article after article—philanthropy, real estate holdings, old family money, invitations to speak at business schools. No arrests. No exes selling stories. No scandals. No flaws.

Her eyes burned. She saved every bit of it.

She pulled up public databases. Real estate records, business licenses. There was a property in Montauk. A suite in Tribeca. A black car registered to a corporate holding company.

Just... careful. Cautious. She'd earned that.

No Sound, No Mercy

Katherine

The precinct felt submerged. Every motion sluggish, every voice muffled.

Katherine kept blinking, trying to wake up, trying to shake off the shadows under her eyes. Sleep deprivation wasn't new. It was routine.

The conference room smelled like dry ambition. A new analyst spoke about victim positioning, using phrases like "psychosocial signature" as if they meant something, as if words could fill the hollow silence after a body was found.

Katherine stared at the projected photos—locations, not bodies. Trees. Carpet. Theater seats. A backdrop, not the performance. But she knew better. The Artist had staged every inch intentionally.

Her temples throbbed, and her spine ached. Her mind pulled her sideways, down corridors she hadn't walked in years. Gripping her pen, the room blurred at the edges.

Lunch came and went. She didn't eat. She told someone she had errands, but she sat in her car, palms clenched in her lap, bracing for a wave that never came.

By the time the sun dipped, her muscles buzzed with exhaustion from not moving. She returned to her office, shut the door, and didn't bother locking it.

She told herself just sit for a second. Write the report. But her body slumped. Her eyes fluttered.

✦

She was twenty again.

The hallway stretched longer than it ever had, the wallpaper seams yawning open like wounds, bleeding light through the cracks.

Her bare feet slapped against wood that didn't echo. No matter how fast she moved, the door at the end pulled farther away.

She could hear Elisabeth screaming. But the sound was wrong—too muffled, too much like her own voice underwater.

The doorknob wouldn't turn.

She pounded on it, fists thudding against the wood, sobbing now, because she *knew* what was behind it. Knew what was happening inside.

The smell of iron and bleach burned in her nostrils.

Then silence.

Then his voice.

Whispered against the back of her neck even though she was alone: *"You were supposed to watch her."*

✦

Her body jerked awake.

Elbows cracked against the desk edge. Her breath came in ragged pulls. The nightmare clung to her skin like sweat-soaked linen.

Her hand flew to her holster. Still there. Safe. Sort of.

The office was quiet, lit only by the flicker of her laptop. The satellite overlays, the map grids, the chess piece she hadn't deciphered.

Her eyes burned.

She hadn't slept through the night in years, except a few times. Not since *him*. But it was getting worse again.

The bodies piled up, the more vivid the dreams became. In every dream, her abductor had a voice, blaming her.

Elisabeth hasn't screamed once today. The phrase stuck to her ribs like thorns.

She rubbed her face with both hands and reached for her phone.

2:47 AM. No missed calls. No alerts.

Sleep was a luxury she couldn't afford.

But lately...

Maybe he was already inside her head again.

Contamination

The Artist

He crouched behind the burnt-out generator behind the rec center, breath syncing with the soft thump of bass echoing through the brick walls.

The gym closed at ten, and she always left by 10:04.

Predictable.

Routine made people weak.

That's what he liked about her.

Her name was Madeline. She worked at the pet hospital. Red water bottle. Cropped hoodie. Always tied her shoes before unlocking the car, like it was a superstition.

She hadn't seen him yet—not ever. Not when he followed her through the cereal aisle. Not when he stood behind her in line at the gas station.

He'd picked her for how perfectly she moved through the world without suspicion. The way she smiled at strangers and hummed to herself when she thought no one could hear. The way she reached down to pet stray cats outside her apartment complex.

She deserved to be seen in full bloom.

Preserved.

He'd chosen the spot carefully. No active security cameras. Broken floodlight above the gate. Trees like shadows melted down the edge of the alley.

The cloth in his sleeve was damp with ether and lavender oil—something soft for her.

He inhaled deeply, calmed his pulse, stepped forward—

And she turned.

She looked *directly* at him. Not past him. Not through him. At him.

He froze. Just for a breath.

That's all it took.

She screamed. Loud. From the gut. Like a throat full of broken glass.

He lunged—too late.

The cloth smacked her cheek instead of her mouth.

Her elbow cracked against his jaw.

It wasn't elegant.

It wasn't controlled.

It was *chaos*.

She slipped from his grip, hit the ground on her knees, and scrambled backward like a cornered animal. Her scream turned into a series of sobbing gasps as she fled.

The moment fractured.

He stood there, blinking, paralyzed in the shards of what was supposed to be.

She ran.

And the world rushed in.

The headlights.

The neighbors.

The shriek of a distant car alarm.

She was gone.

And with her—

Everything he'd built for the last three weeks.

He backed into the alley and vanished, slipping through a drainage corridor and into the sprawl of the city like ink down a drain.

By the time he got home, the taste of blood and lavender still coated his tongue.

He pulled the ledger from the shelf, flipped to her name, and crossed it out. Not once.

Repeatedly.

Pen carving through the paper until it shredded.

Her name meant nothing now.

The broken brushstroke of a failed masterpiece.

He wasn't angry.

He was *violated*.

There had been order.

There had been rules.

This wasn't improvisation. It was *contamination*.

Something foreign and unclean.

He sat for hours, still in his coat, staring at the cork-board where the next four victims had been tentatively outlined.

Madeline was gone.

His fingers twitched.

He needed to restore balance.

The Hum Beneath My Skin

The Artist

She almost slipped past me.

If I hadn't been standing beneath the cracked awning across from the florist's window, waiting for the rain to ease, I might've missed her completely.

But then—she stepped outside.

Paper-wrapped bouquet in hand, hair tumbling in thick waves the color of dark molasses, catching beads of water like they *belonged* there.

My breath hitched.

Not because she was beautiful, though she was—not in the obvious way, no, not the type that begs for a camera.

She had the kind of face that took time to understand. A little uneven. Real.

Her green eyes scanned the street like she was already somewhere else. Thinking ahead. Dreaming, maybe.

I felt it the moment I saw her—a hum under my skin, like tuning a stringed instrument.

This one had music in her.

She wore long sleeves despite the warmth. A pale blue cardigan with sleeves pulled down past her wrists.

Trying to disappear? Or hide something?

I watched the way she carried herself—shoulders drawn, but her chin up.

Defiant. And kind.

I could always tell the kind ones.

They didn't know how to protect their soft parts.

I followed her when she crossed the street. Not too close.

The trick is to breathe at their pace.

Blend.

***

I knew every crack in the sidewalk between her flower shop and the corner bookstore by now—her Thursday routine never changed.

But today, something was different.

She hesitated before going inside. Turned her face to the sky. Let the rain fall. Eyes closed, lips parted. Like she was tasting it. My fingers curled around the edge of my coat pocket. I had to ground myself, keep from crossing the street and reaching out to touch her right then.

That wouldn't do. Not yet.

Inside the shop, she leaned against the counter and talked to the old man. I moved closer, let the door of the bodega next door swing open behind me so I could hear her laugh when she handed him a bag of licorice. She remembered his favorite. Of course she did. I felt a flash of warmth that scorched more than soothed. She had tenderness for strangers. It meant she had no idea what the world really was.

She had no idea I was watching. Always watching.

She tucked the poetry book into her canvas tote—worn corners, fraying handle. There were initials stitched in one corner. Not hers. Someone else's? A gift? It mattered. Everything mattered. I needed to know who she loved and why. What made her cry. What she told no one. I had to unearth it all to make the art real. Intimate. Eternal.

She glanced toward the window, and I felt a lurch in my gut. I stepped back into shadow, heart pounding against my ribs like it wanted to be seen. Heard. Touched. But her gaze didn't land on me. Not yet.

Still. I would have to move faster now.

Lena.

I had overheard her name when her coworker called it out to her across the flower shop the day before. Lena with the dark waves and meadow-glass eyes.

She wasn't part of the original design.

But I would adjust the canvas.

She was going to be magnificent.

Stars on the Ceiling

The Artist

She wasn't supposed to matter.

But something about her did.

Lena.

I'd been watching her for days now.

Following the delicate rhythm of her life like a song half-remembered. Mornings at the flower shop. Afternoons at the library or the corner café.

And Thursdays—Thursdays were different.

That's when she left late.

After the shelter closed.

After the stories were shared, the coffee gone cold, the chairs put back into place.

She always waited until the last woman left before turning off the lights.

As if she needed to be the one to close the door on their pain.

Tonight, I was waiting.

Not in her path. Not in her way.

Just near enough that when the alley swallowed her in shadow, *I became part of it.*

She didn't scream.

There was a flicker of fear—yes—but no struggle. Just her breath catching.

Her hand raised slightly, palms out.

A gesture I knew too well.

Don't hurt me.

I didn't.

Not yet.

The van door shut with a quiet finality.

I drove in silence, the city unraveling behind us.

***

She woke slowly, lashes fluttering like moth wings.

The light in the studio was soft, golden, warm.

She didn't speak at first. Just looked around.

Noticing.

I waited.

"I've been here before, "she said finally. Her voice hoarse. "Not this place. But…this moment."

I sat across from her, brush in hand. Not painting. Not yet. Just holding it.

"You wore long sleeves," I said. "Even when it was hot."

Her gaze snapped to mine.

"I thought it was modesty. Shyness. But wasn't."

I reached forward and gently took her wrist, letting her see I wasn't going to force anything.

Rolled the sleeve back slowly.

Yellowing bruises bloomed like pressed flowers across her skin.

Higher up, older scars.

Neat. Straight.

She didn't flinch.

She just stared down at her own arm like it belonged to someone else.

"Doesn't matter now," she murmured.

"It does," I said.

Silence stretched between us.

"When I saw seven," I told her, "My father broke my mother's nose for dropping a plate."

She blinked.

"I cleaned the blood. My hands were so small back then. Couldn't carry much."

She looked at me—not with pity. With *understanding*.

"She never left him." I said.

"I did," she replied.

I nodded. "I know."

I stood and began the work.

Not hurried. Not cruel.

She didn't cry. Didn't beg.

She just watched me with those green eyes.

Like she saw every layer of me. Down to the rot and the splinters.

"I was never going to be a bride," she whispered, "But you chose me anyway."

"I know."

"You don't have to make me pretty." She said more gently, nodding off to sleep.

I made sure she was comfortable before the end.

"You already are." I whispered.

***

She wore her pale blue cardigan.

I left it on her.

Pulled her sleeves down over her wrists the way she always did.

Her body was arranged on a soft bed of dried florals—baby's breath, statice, strawflower.

Things that held their color long after death.

She lay curled on her side, like sleep had taken her gently.

I painted vines along her collarbone, trailing down her arms, blooming over bruises like armor.

Her lips were left bare.

No theatrical rose clays this time.

Just the pink of reality.

Above her, I lit the ceiling.

Not fairy lights this time.

Stars.

Tiny glass fragments I'd glued in constellations.

They caught the LED lights and scattered it like glitter across her skin.

The letter I left was folded carefully beside her hand.

Katie,

She knew pain before I did. She wasn't afraid of me. She saw the stars. You will too.

Even Flowers Bruise

Katherine

The call came through dispatch at 2:13 a.m.

"Possible 10-54. Female, unknown location. Envelope addressed to Investigator Poe left at the scene."

No name. No address. Just a letter.

The enveloped had been tucked behind the handle of the precinct's front doors.

Inside: coordinates. Latitude and longitude scrawled in ink.

It wasn't a mistake. It was a summons.

My gut turned. The coffee I'd forced down minutes earlier soured in my stomach. I was already driving.

***

The building was a warehouse—abandoned, half-swallowed by vines. No alarms. No power. Just quiet and rot and the hum of distant traffic.

The team swept the entrance first. I didn't wait.

Inside, it smelled like lavender. Not fresh. Dried. Dozens of sprigs scattered across the floor, arranged like breadcrumbs. Not a drop of blood in sight.

My boots echoed on the concrete as I followed the path.

She was in the center of the space—beneath a low ring of light. Not overhead. From the floor. Reflected upward through shards of mirrored glass arranged in constellations.

She was laying on her side, arms tucked beneath her cheek, wrapped in a pale blue cardigan with the sleeves pulled all the way to her hands. Like she'd fallen to sleep trying not to be noticed.

Her lips were bare. Her hair braided. No makeup. No veil. No bridal lace or ribbon.

Just her.

Wildflowers circled her body. Not fresh-cut arrangements-dried stems, faded purples and yellows, woven into a loose crown around her shoulders.

Paint trailed across her skin. Vines. Inked with care. They bloomed over bruises.

Old bruises.

Fingertip-sized. Some healing. Some not.

I crouched low. Closer. Her wrists—red, raw in patches, like she'd spent years pulling her sleeves over them.

This wasn't a kill site. It was a stage.

But not for a bride.

The note was folded beside her hand.

Katie,

She knew pain before I did. She wasn't afraid of me. She saw the stars. You will too.

My throat closed. I stood too fast. The light fractured across my boots.

I turned to the forensic lead. "I want every shelter within ten miles combed. Volunteer logs. Intake rosters. She is a victim of domestic violence, but she seems to have escaped it—*only to find worse*. Find out who she is, and I want to know her last forty-eight hours."

He nodded.

No ring on her hand.

No finger removed.

Nothing cut.

Nothing missing from the body.

So why her?

Why like this?

I closed my eyes and saw it—the way he positioned her. The tenderness in the line of her body. The cardigan. The ceiling.

Stars made of glass.

He wanted me to see what she saw. And he knew I would.

This wasn't escalation. It was evolution.

He hadn't taken her to make a point.

He'd taken her because he recognized something in her.

And maybe—

Maybe I would see him.

***

Back at the precinct.

A tech scrambled toward her with a file bag.

Katherine ripped it open. "Lena Renee Marquez, 27" Her eyes skimmed. No record of engagement. No fiancé. No wedding registry. No venue booked. No dress on order.

"Run her socials," she told her team. "Every post. Every message. I want to know if there's anyone she was hiding. But this—" her voice dipped, shaky for the first time, "this doesn't match."

She wasn't afraid of me..." Katherine could barely finish reading. Her hands trembled. *You will too.* That line clung like frost. Not *we*. Not *they*. Just *you*.

It was a message for her and her alone.

Katherine's stomach twisted. Her mind spun.

Was this a mistake? A warning? Or was Lena never meant to fit the pattern?

Was she an outlier?

Or a shift?

She turned to her partner. "I want every florist order Lena's shop filled in the last three months. Wedding bouquets, deliveries, anything connected to a bride. Track them all."

If Lena wasn't a bride... maybe she was the connection to one.

Or maybe she was just the beginning of something new.

Something worse.

Something meant for her.

Like a Match

Katherine

The evening had been… off.

She didn't remember ever fully agreeing to dinner—just a vague *maybe* tossed out in a moment of emotional fatigue.

Coffee, yes.

Dinner, maybe.

But somehow, *maybe* had turned into *this*.

Cheryl vetted him, she would try.

Devin had picked the restaurant. A boutique spot tucked into the corner of a side street, all reclaimed wood, moody pendant lights, and amber candle jars that made every table glow like a secret.

It should've felt intimate. Instead, it felt… designed. Like someone had staged it for effect.

For her.

And then there was him.

Six-foot-two, broad-shouldered, built like a man who knew how to fill out a suit but chose to wear it like an afterthought.

His dark brown hair—almost black—was tousled in that irritatingly perfect way, like he'd run a hand through it once and the wind had done the rest. A sharp jawline. Clean-shaven. Olive-toned skin.

Eyes like iced whiskey—gold-flecked, amber in some lights, near-honey in others. Warm. Sharp. Hypnotic.

Too perfect.

He smiled when he saw her, and something in her ribs pulled tight.

Not because of the smile. Because of how it landed.

Every woman in the vicinity looked. Not at her. At him.

The bartender straightened. Two women at the corner table whispered. One even adjusted her lipstick.

He was *that* man.

The kind you didn't meet at random.

The kind who didn't have to try.

She followed him inside. Her breath felt shallow, like her body had started preparing to react before she even understood why.

***

He was already telling a story across the table—something about a pretentious client who'd mistaken a Rothko for a red garage door. He chuckled at his own punchline, fingers wrapped elegantly around a crystal tumbler, pinky barely grazing the base.

She tried to smile. Tried harder to listen.

But her eyes kept getting stuck—on the way the candlelight caught the sharp line of his cheekbone, the deliberate grace in the way he moved his glass, the subtle precision in how he sat.

He was composed.

Every detail curated.

"You can't fake intention," he said, voice smooth as a violin's last note. "You can copy a style. But real work bleeds."

A flicker pulsed low in her gut.

Not attraction—she knew what that was.

This was something else.

Like her subconscious had registered something before her logic could explain it.

She didn't trust herself around men like this—not because they were dangerous, but because she always convinced herself they weren't.

He leaned forward, forearms resting just right on the table, sleeves rolled halfway, revealing sinewed forearms and the glint of a worn leather watch strap.

"What's going on in that head of yours, Katherine?"

She blinked. "What do you mean?"

"That face." His smile was soft, attentive. "You look like you're watching a house burn and trying to figure out if you're the one holding the match."

She forced a breath. Reached for her drink. Raspberry something. Tart.

Then, before she could stop herself, it came out.

"You ever feel like someone's lying right to your face… and you're the last person in the room to figure it out?"

It was too honest.

Too fast.

It fell between them like a truth neither of them asked for.

Devin's laugh was low and smooth. "Only every time I file taxes," he said.

She gave him a smile that never reached her eyes.

Later, she wouldn't remember the check. Or the walk back to the car. Just the moment his hand brushed hers across the table. Just the warmth of his skin.

And how it left her feeling like her blood had gone cold.

Relief in a Sketch

Katherine

It had been three days since the dinner. Since Devin's words lodged somewhere she couldn't shake.

But this case hadn't paused for her gut.

Madeline Brookshire sat stiff in the interview chair, hands bandaged, voice low but steady. Her wrist trembled every time she lifted the paper cup, but her eyes never left mine.

"He came out of nowhere," she said. "I don't know how long he was watching me, but it felt...planned. Like he was waiting for the exact second I turned my head."

She shifted in her seat, then winced. Her cheek was mottled with the shadow of a bruise, half-covered by makeup that couldn't quite hide it.

"I'd parked like I always do. Tied my shoes, reached for my keys—and he was just...there. I didn't hear him walk up. But I felt it. The air changed. I looked up, and he was staring at me. Not like a mugger. Not even like someone mad. Just calm. Like he already knew how it would end."

Her fingers twitched on the cup. "He tried to put something over my mouth. Cloth, I think. It smelled like lavender. But I hit him—I don't even remember how. My elbow got him in the jaw. I fell, and I just...ran. Screamed like hell."

She breathed out hard, shaking her head. "I don't think he expected me to fight."

I didn't move. Didn't breathe.

"He didn't say anything," she added. "No threats. No creepy speech. Just this one thing—after I hit him. Like a whisper. I couldn't make it all out, but it was something like, 'not perfect anymore.'"

A cold sliver crawled up the back of my spine.

"Are you sure that's what he said?" I asked, keeping my tone even.

She nodded hard. "Exact words. I've heard them a hundred times since. I didn't dream that part."

"What did his voice sound like?" I asked.

"Low. Controlled. Not angry. Just…disappointed."

I leaned back

I hadn't admitted it to myself, not fully. Some part of me had been suspecting Devin. Watching for the crack behind the smile. The mask slipping. It was stupid—he was too polished, too controlled. Too perfect.

But that was the problem. He was *perfect*.

I leaned back just a little as the sketch artist entered. "Let's take it slow," I said to her. "One detail at a time."

She nodded. "He was tall. Six-one, maybe six-two. Built—not like a bodybuilder, but solid. I think he had on a hoodie, but I saw his neck. Light stubble. Sandy-blond hair. Cut short, like someone who cares about keeping it clean."

I didn't blink. Didn't speak.

"Eyes were icy. Light-colored. Blue or gray. Kinda dead-looking, if I'm honest."

"What about his face?" the sketch artist asked gently.

"Angular. Sharp jawline. Pale skin. I think… I think he had a scar here." She traced her finger along her cheek. "Left side. Small but real. Oh—and his nose had a bump, like it'd been broken once."

The sketch began to take shape—each pencil stroke layering onto the page like a curtain closing.

And with each detail, that cold sliver inside me started to melt.

It wasn't him.

It wasn't Devin.

No dark waves, no warm brown eyes. No sun-kissed skin, no elegant features softened with charm. This man she saw was rough. Blue-eyed. Scarred. Not someone who could pass for a gallery curator, let alone charm a room.

Not someone like him.

Not someone like *Devin*.

I stood slowly as the sketch artist turned the pad toward me.

She nodded, eyes fierce. "That's him. I'd bet everything."

But it wasn't.

It wasn't even close.

Relief hit me like a weight sliding off my chest. Not all the way to the floor—but far enough to let me breathe again.

It wasn't him.

I tucked the sketch into the file, thanked her for her courage, and stepped out of the room.

The hallway was quiet. I leaned against the wall, let the cold tile press into my back.

It was a mistake to suspect Devin. I had let the case bleed into places it didn't belong. My paranoia had started seeing ghosts.

I'd been wrong.

The killer was still out there.

But not *him*.

The next model in his gallery frame? That was still coming.

And now... I had a new face to find.

Even if it wasn't the right one.

Permission to Try

Katherine

She stared at his name for the fifth time that hour.

Devin.

The contact hadn't changed. Still the one Cheryl insisted on introducing her to. Still the one she'd grilled quietly over dinner the first night, testing his expressions like puzzle pieces.

Still the one she'd secretly held up against the profile in her head—the possibility, the *what if*, the nightmare scenario.

And now?

Now he wasn't that.

Not after the sketch. Not after the girl who got away described a man too tall, too soft in the jaw, too *something else*.

Devin didn't match.

And somehow, that felt... disappointing.

Not because she wanted him to be the killer—but because it meant the pull she felt toward him didn't come with an obvious warning label. No excuse to walk away. No built-in danger to justify her own resistance.

One who looked at her like she wasn't damaged goods.

Her thumb hovered over the call button.

"You're being ridiculous," she muttered.

This wasn't a tactical op. It was just a second date. A maybe. A dinner.

But she still sat there, breath shallow, hoodie strings wound so tightly around her finger the nail had gone pale.

It wasn't fear—not really.

It was that other thing. That unnamable ache that lived just beneath her ribs, the part that remembered what it felt like to want something soft and normal before the world hollowed her out.

Her phone vibrated in her palm.

Devin – *Just checking in. No pressure. But I'd really like to see you again. Dinner's on me this time.*

She smiled.

Actual smile. Teeth and all.

God help her.

Her thumb hit **Call** before she could second guess it.

Ring one. Her pulse kicked.

Ring two. She considered hanging up.

Ring three—

"Hello?"

Same voice. Same calm warmth.

The kind that slipped under defenses and rewired the way she held tension in her shoulders.

"It's me," she said. Then winced. "Katherine. I mean. Sorry. That was—"

She rolled her eyes at herself. He couldn't see it, but it helped.

"Hey, Katie," he said, gentle. "Glad you called."

It landed different this time.

Katie.

Not condescending. Not invasive. Just… familiar.

"I was thinking," she said. "I've got some space in the schedule. Would you want to grab dinner this week?"

A pause. Just long enough to scare her.

"I'd really like that," he said.

Relief hit harder than expected. She exhaled, finally, and leaned back into the couch.

"Somewhere quiet," she added. "Not weird quiet. Just… easy."

"I know a place," he said. "You'll like it."

And for a minute—just a breath of one—it felt like she might.

They worked out the details. She jotted down the name of the place even though she knew she'd memorize it.

When they hung up, she sat there staring at the screen.

The apartment was still.

The case files were stacked just feet away.

But none of it pressed in the same way.

She didn't owe anyone an apology for wanting this. For saying yes.

It didn't mean she wasn't still hunting monsters.

It didn't mean she'd forgotten what was waiting out there.

For once, she'd give herself permission to try.

Even if it broke her later.

Too Close to Real

Katherine

She hadn't worn the black dress since the last time she let herself believe someone might be good.

It still smelled faintly of cedar and something older—an echo of a life that hadn't imploded yet.

The restaurant was too warm. Too intimate. Too exposed. Her back was to the wall. Not the door. She'd let him have the view of the exit. Rookie move. She'd been too tired to argue when the hostess pointed. Too tired to be on guard and charming at the same time.

Devin laughed across from her, eyes crinkling, voice low. Grounded. Assured.

The kind of voice that made women lean closer.

She didn't lean. She hadn't touched her wine.

He noticed. Of course he did.

He noticed everything.

Katherine kept her fork moving, drawing lines through a smear of sauce she hadn't tasted.

Her head ached from not sleeping. Three hours, maybe, the night before. Not even deep sleep—just that fractured kind where you surface every ten minutes gasping, ribs aching from clenching.

She didn't know what he was talking about anymore. Something about lilies. Or no, someone named Lily. A coworker? A neighbor?

Her heart thudded once. Then twice. *Stay in it.*

She nodded at what felt like the right beat. Smiled, almost. Her cheeks resisted the pull.

"I'm rambling," he said, sheepish. "You look like you're somewhere else."

Because she was.

Because she always was.

She forced herself to lift the wine glass, the stem cold where her fingers trembled slightly against it.

Focus. Drink. Respond.

"No, I'm listening," she said.

The lie came easy. Reflex.

"I just—long week."

Devin leaned forward. "Want to talk about it?"

She could feel the room pulse around her like a lung—inhale, exhale, every face a blur.

Her chest tightened.

"No," she said too fast. "No, I... I'd rather just be here. With you."

His smile was soft. Kind.

It made her want to flinch.

How long had it been since someone didn't want something from her?

She hated how safe he made her feel.

Because safe wasn't real.

Safe was a trick your brain played on you right before it all went black.

He reached across the table. Not far. Not insistent. Just enough. His fingers brushed hers, and she let them. God, she let them.

"I am having a good time," he said.

She couldn't breathe for a second. Her throat clenched around air like it was glass.

Don't ruin it. Don't dissect it. Don't pull it apart like you always do.

"Me too," she whispered.

And hated that she meant it.

Because somewhere deep, beneath the warmth of his touch, beneath the ache of the wine she hadn't tasted and the headache she'd pretended didn't exist—

She knew it wasn't going to last.

A Pattern That Doesn't Fit

Katherine

The hum overhead had become a low, buzzing ache behind her eyes.

Katherine sat at the edge of her chair in the glass-walled conference room, sleeves pushed up, palms pressed flat to the table like she could hold the whole thing together by force. The board in front of her was a chaos of photographs and red string, but Lena's face sat dead center.

Bare lips.

Closed eyes.

Too much peace.

God, she hated that he'd given her peace.

Lena wasn't a bride. No veil. No registry. Just a pale cardigan and that look in her eyes that she'd finally stopped bracing for something. It hadn't fit the pattern. None of it did.

So why her?

The forensic tech's voice droned somewhere to her right, words bleeding into the air like static. Something about restraint marks. Tox screens. Nothing conclusive. Nothing useful.

"She didn't fight," she said, too suddenly.

Lozano glanced up. "You think he caught her off-guard?"

Her throat tightened. "No. I think she didn't want to."

The room stilled. Even the hum seemed to pause.

Katherine leaned forward, tapped the photo of Lena's forearm with the back of her knuckle. Paint swirling into bruises. Old ones. Familiar shapes.

"She'd fought before," she murmured. "Hands-up, teeth-bared kind of fight. You can tell. But not this time. Nothing fresh."

"She wasn't even a bride," one of the junior analysts said cautiously. "Could it have been a mistake?"

Her gazed snapped to the girl like a lash. "He doesn't make mistakes."

The analyst blinked, sank back in her chair.

This wasn't random.

This wasn't wrong.

"He pivoted," Katherine said, more to herself than anyone else. "Or he's shifting the frame. A new pattern, or a new message."

She pushed away from the table, the chair scraping harsh against tile. Her pulse thundered in her ears.

"Get me the full client roster from her shop—last six months. Weddings, anniversaries, standing orders, whatever they've got. Cross-check it with the bridal web. Names, dates, overlaps."

Kali already had her pen moving.

"She volunteered at a shelter," she added, words sharper now, faster. "Rosters. Staff logs. If he didn't choose her for the pattern, he chose her for who she touched."

"There won't be digital records for that," someone said quietly.

"Then knock on doors. Pull street cams. Bank footage. Talk to her coworkers. Talk to her ghosts, I don't care. I want to know who leaned on that damn counter and told her things they shouldn't have."

No pushback. Not this time. Just scribbles. Screens lighting up. Boots hitting tile.

Katherine didn't sit back down. Her hand slid along the table's edge as she turned, eyes snagging on the board again.

Lena's faced stared back—frozen, glowing under that fake ceiling sky. She hadn't slept. Not really. Not since that night.

He's changing the story.

The thought came like a whisper she didn't mean to say out loud. "He's changing the story," she echoed, barely audible.

"Trying to get my attention in a new way."

She swallowed hard. Her voice dropped. "And he has it."

The board stared back, useless. A silent wall of paper gods and red-thread omens.

Everyone else had left. But she stayed, frozen under the buzz of dying fluorescents, waiting for the thread to pull tight again. For anything to click back into place.

She didn't want to go home. Didn't want the quiet. Didn't want to sit in the dark and wonder what else she was missing.

She just wanted the pattern to make sense again.

But it didn't.

And that scared her more than the blood, the bodies, or the bastard who left them behind.

Linger

Katherine

The knock came at 6:04 p.m.—soft, rhythmic.

Her fingers tightened around the mug. Still warm. Still full. The tea hadn't cooled, but her blood had.

No one buzzed. No message. No warning.

Her gut clenched.

Not press. Not a neighbor. Not him.

Then came the voice—low, steady, almost teasing.

"Soup delivery."

Devin.

What?

Her stomach twisted.

She moved to the door and cracked it, the chain still latched, eye peering through the narrow slice like it might be someone else. It wasn't. Paper bag in hand. That lopsided smile. Like he knew she was about to slam it.

"I didn't text you," she said, voice flat.

"You didn't have to."

Her muscles tensed at that. Teeth locked behind a too-sharp inhale. *He always says shit like that. Like he has the map of me memorized.* But the smell hit next—rosemary and garlic, slow-cooked chicken—and something traitorous in her stomach unfurled.

She stared at the bag, not him. "You keep feeding me like this and I'm going to start thinking you're trying to bribe your way into my life."

"Is it working?"

Katherine didn't answer. Just undid the chain with a small clack and opened the door wide enough to take the bag. Not an inch more.

He didn't try to cross the threshold. Didn't ask to.

The handoff was quick. Warm paper brushed her fingers, and something stupid fluttered low in her chest.

"Thanks," she muttered.

"You're welcome."

She was already closing the door when her mouth betrayed her.

"Devin."

He stopped, halfway down the hall, and turned just enough for the light to catch his face.

"You didn't have to bring it."

"I know."

No grin. No charm. Just truth, plain and inconvenient.

She shut the door. Clicked the lock. Bolted it.

Pressed her forehead to the wood and exhaled like it hurt.

The apartment pressed in around her, thick with the kind of quiet that let thoughts echo. She set the bag on the counter, unopened, untouched.

Too kind.

Too careful.

Too much.

Her hands hovered near the soup for a second longer, then retreated.

She didn't want warmth. She wanted control.

And he kept showing up with the wrong kind of comfort.

A Killer's Curriculum

Katherine

Text.

The lab report was useless.

Clean surfaces. No DNA. No prints. No fibers.

Not even a stray dog hair to chase.

It should have made her feel defeated.

Instead, it made her pulse spike.

Because he didn't miss.

He didn't forget.

If it looked clean, it was because he'd made it that way.

Katherine leaned back in the conference room chair, alone, fingers tapping the closed manila folder like it might twitch.

This wasn't evidence.

It was theater.

Every step he made was calculated—not to evade them, but to engage her.

She stared at the corner of the table where a few paper clips sat twisted into shapes.

Her work. Or maybe just a nervous habit.

But today, they looked like a map.

A spiral.

A noose.

She exhaled through her nose, slow. Controlled.

Not calm.

No one else saw it—not yet.

The shape forming beneath the chaos.

The way his choices were evolving.

The way the latest victim didn't quite fit.

It wasn't sloppiness.

It was something else.

A message.

Maybe not to them, but to *her*.

Her gaze drifted to the window, where dusk stained the skyline in layered pinks and greys.

West. Always west.

Her stomach tightened.

She thought of the road leading out of town, the one that curved hard and vanished into coal country.

The smell of sulfur.

Damp roots.

Her sister's laughter echoing through trees long since dead.

A buzz from her phone broke the silence.

Glanced.

A group thread. Brandon. Kali. Cheryl. None of it mattered right now.

She clicked the screen off. Sat still.

Tried not to feel the gravity pulling her inward.

Katherine stood.

Her jaw clenched tight, breath slow and shallow as she forced the panic down.

It was time to dig.

Into the town.

The mine.

The past.

Into *her*.

Echo Point

Katherine

The city could've collapsed outside the window, and she wouldn't have blinked.

Katherine sat statue-still, arms wrapped around her ribs like a splint, anchoring herself to the chair instead of the spiral.

She hadn't moved in forty minutes.

Maybe longer.

Her coat was still slung over the back of the chair, one boot half untied. The radiator hissed faintly against the silence.

Twenty.

The number scraped against the back of her skull like a warning too close to ignore.

Not seventeen.

Not a stretch of chaos.

A clean, deliberate count.

People don't choose round numbers unless they're trying to finish something.

Tick.

Tick.

Her gaze drifted toward the whiteboard.

The faces didn't look back anymore.

They waited.

Every one of them.

Quiet. Expectant.

As if she already had the answers and just wouldn't say them aloud.

He wasn't taunting her.

Not now.

He was teaching.

And the lesson was almost over.

She blinked.

Once.

Twice.

Her neck cracked as she turned it.

Her body felt wrong inside itself—sore where it shouldn't be, hollow where pressure should've built.

She stood.

Pacing without thought.

Three steps forward, one back.

Then the opposite.

Her breath syncopated to the rhythm.

Some part of him was always here.

Not in the room. Not in the shadows.

But behind her thoughts.

She leaned over the edge of her desk; palms pressed flat to the surface and let her head hang between her shoulders.

Just one more thread.

One more shift in the pattern.

Then she'd find him.

And he'd already know what she was going to do.

A Loop Instead of a Line

Katherine

The hallway lights flickered, humming faintly overhead like dying stars.

Katherine pressed the heel of her hand to her right temple; breath caught somewhere between a sigh and a curse. She hadn't slept in over twenty-three hours. The coffee in her thermos was colder than her will to keep going. Her desk looked like a crime scene of its own—half-eaten protein bar, scattered case files, and a post it with a name she didn't remember writing.

Nothing was clicking.

Not yet.

Lena had thrown everything off. No wedding. No ring. No severed finger. But the tenderness in her display, the intimacy of the note, the fact that she didn't belong to the pattern at all—Katherine felt like she was watching the storm veer off course while still being dragged into the eye.

She leaned back. The leather creaked. Her spine popped. Her eyes found the board—photos, maps, lines drawn like the Artist had planned it all before the first victim ever died.

This hadn't ever been chaos.

It was always control.

He wasn't unraveling. He was pivoting.

A loop instead of a line.

She rubbed her eyes, and the sentence came back—the one that had stalked her through two sleepless nights.

She saw the stars. You will too.

Her breath caught.

She tried to dismiss it. Metaphor, maybe. A flourish of language. But her gut twisted. Instinct shoved back.

She *had* seen the stars.

Above Lena.

Maybe Lena was who he craved. Maybe it was over.

She stood slowly, legs stiff, breath shallow. Her pulse outpaced her breath—too fast for reason, too slow for panic.

She drifted past the evidence room and into the deeper corridor. Archives. Cold cases. Files that hadn't made sense—until now.

Maybe Lena wasn't the outlier.

Maybe she was the warning shot.

And Victim 17… whoever she was…

She wouldn't be a warning.

She'd be the *message*.

Unseen Origins

Katherine

She hadn't opened the cold case drawer in over five years.

But the Artist's rhythm was too familiar—too deliberate—to ignore.

The drawer jammed halfway before sliding open with a metallic groan. Dust kicked up in lazy spirals. She coughed once, then waved the particles away and flipped through the faded manila folders.

These were ghosts. Misfiled tragedies and overlooked truths.

Her fingers hovered over a file marked *CASE 12-A*. Blocky, unfamiliar handwriting. Cold. Clinical. Not hers.

A whisper in her chest said: *Look closer this time.*

Melanie Grant. Age twenty-five. Vanished three days before her wedding. Found in a community garden. Posed. Peaceful. Ring finger removed. No sign of sexual assault. COD: Exsanguination. Marked as *disorganized offender*. Low risk of repeat.

She had argued against that assessment. She remembered.

She also remembered being dismissed—too new to challenge protocol, too young to push against a system already thick with assumption.

But now…

Now she saw it.

The symmetry. The silence. The way the body had been arranged, not abandoned. The hint of ritual disguised as randomness.

This hadn't been an outlier.

It had been a *prototype*.

Her chest tightened as she laid the photographs out across the linoleum floor, she dropped to her knees, barefoot on the cold linoleum. The chill shot up her spine.

It felt like penance. Like confession.

She studied the angle of the limbs. The curvature of the fingers. The exact cut across the throat—clean, no jagged hesitation.

Just like the Artist.

Her pulse thudded at her neck.

He hadn't started with Victim One—Dayna Cook.

He'd just started signing his name.

She swept through the old files like a hurricane held together by trembling hands. Other women surfaced. Brides-to-be. Unsolved. Some missing their ring fingers. Some not. Some posed like statues. Others curled like dancers mid-turn.

And yet... none of them had been connected. Not until now.

Not until her.

She sat back on her heels, heart thudding in her chest like a gavel slamming down on a verdict no one wanted to believe.

This wasn't a killing spree.

It was a portfolio.

And she was the one who had been invited to witness it.

Number Seventeen

The Artist

I noticed her by accident.

A yellow umbrella. That's what caught my eye first—an obnoxiously bright slash against a gray Manhattan morning. She held it like she was in a perfume ad, lips painted red, laughing like the rain was in on her secret.

I almost turned away. Almost.

Until I saw what was wrapped around her finger.

It gleamed.

Not just because of the diamond, though it was decent enough—three-stone setting, cushion cut. No. It gleamed because she admired it constantly, like it was sacred. Like it *meant* something. That promise. That illusion.

I knew right then she was one of them.

A bride-to-be.

Hopeful.

Blind.

I followed her with practiced ease. Not too close. Not obvious.

She wore her hair long and wavy, dark as espresso beans, bouncing just past her shoulders. Green eyes that searched windows like they were portals to another world.

Her name came easily—Rebecca Vale. A local baker.

I watched her first from a distance. Four days. She had her patterns. 7:45 a.m. coffee run to the place on 22nd and Lexington, always ordered the same thing—matcha latte, almond milk.

She hated waiting. She picked at the sleeve of her coat if the line moved too slow.

Her fiancé, Darren, kissed her cheek at exactly 6:50 every morning before heading to the gym. I timed it. Two kisses on Fridays. One every other day.

By day six, I'd found her apartment. A sixth-floor walkup. Tiny windows. No elevator. Darren only stayed over twice a week—he lived uptown, apparently. Parents didn't approve of them living together yet.

Old money. Old values.

Perfect.

On day nine, I brushed past her at the bodega. She apologized like it was her fault. Smiled.

I wanted to grab her hand and tell her to run.

Tell her that she'd already been chosen.

She'd started preparing the flowers for her wedding. Peonies, roses, eucalyptus. Soft. Feminine. She arranged them like she was choosing them for a Queen.

I wondered what prayers she said over the petals—if she believed they'd protect her.

By day fourteen, I knew everything I needed to know.

She jogged Tuesday and Thursday evenings in the park near the Hudson. Always took the inner loop, earphones in, oblivious.

I passed her twice during those jogs.

The first time, I kept pace beside her for a moment. She glanced at me—fleeting eye contact—and then back to the path. No alarm.

The second time, I passed her again, just after sunset, and I smiled.

She didn't smile back.

That made me like her more.

Her bridal fittings were at Bellamy's on 5th.

Her gown: lace-backed, sweetheart neckline, fitted to the hip, ivory. She looked at herself in the mirror like she wasn't sure she deserved it. That sadness—that tiny fracture in her self-worth—it gleamed too.

She was ready.

But I wasn't.

Not yet.

I needed one more thing. I needed her to trust a stranger. Just once. To say yes without thinking.

So, I returned the umbrella.

I waited by the bakery shop. She was unloading a box when I approached—umbrella in hand, pretending I'd picked it up from the park.

"I think this is yours," I said.

She stared, blinked.

Then she smiled. "Oh my god, I lost this days ago. I thought someone swiped it!"

"No," I said, and smiled back. "Just kept it safe until I saw you again."

She took it from me. Her fingers brushed mine.

"Thank you," she said. "That was kind of you."

I nodded, turned to leave. Not too fast. Not too slow.

The umbrella was a test. She passed.

I would take her the night before her wedding.

She would be number seventeen.

And her petals would never wither.

She would bloom in silence, framed just for Katherine.

With This Breath, I Thee Take

The Artist

I rehearsed it a dozen times.

Not the mechanics—those were simple. Chloroform, gloves, blind corner, soft approach.

It was the moment before I touched her that needed to be perfect.

That's where the art began.

That's when I became more than a man.

That's when I was born again.

Rebecca had one hand on the wheel, the other gently holding her bouquet box steady in the passenger seat, as though her blooms were children who might get carsick.

She was singing. I couldn't hear it, but I could see her lips forming sound. That's how intimate we'd become—she gave me music without knowing I was listening.

She always took the scenic road back toward town— where the trees arched like cathedral spires. No streetlights. No cameras. No one for miles.

I watched her brake at the spot where the road dipped—habitual caution for deer.

She was a creature of habit.

It was almost sweet.

Like she believed caution would save her.

It was 6:43. Right on schedule.

I stepped from the tree line, silent and smooth, flare light flickering low in my palm—not bright enough to blind, just enough to confuse. Just enough to make her squint. The golden hour haloed her face as she leaned out her window, voice soft with concern.

"Are you okay?"

She asked *me* if I was okay.

I wanted to take her gently, like a dance. But the second her pupils dilated—the moment recognition flared—I had no choice.

She reached for the gear shift, but I was already there, wrapping around her like a shadow. The chloroform rag pressed against her lips and nose.

She thrashed. Good.

I let her struggle. Not to make her suffer—no. It was about the *spark*.

I wanted her body to tell me she had lived before I stopped it.

She fought harder than I expected, and that thrilled something primal in me.

Her elbow landed square in my sternum—momentary white-hot pain, then nothing.

I had her by the braid, pulled just enough to tilt her head back without snapping her neck.

Her heels scraped the floorboard, knees kicking upward.

My hand stayed steady.

I whispered against her hairline, *"Shh. I've got you."*

It wasn't a lie.

Her movements slowed. Limbs folding like a marionette at rest. Her chest rose once more, then again—shallow. *Shallow. Still.*

I caught her before she slumped forward into the steering wheel, dazed but struggling.

Her pulse fluttered against my gloved fingertips, delicate and fading.

I opened the door—crunch of gravel underfoot.

The back of my SUV was already prepared. Lined, sterile, scent-masked.

I laid her on the blanket, adjusted her head so it wouldn't bruise.

I strapped her down—not tightly—just enough to ensure she'd arrive intact.

I needed her *exactly* as she was. *Exactly.*

Before closing the hatch, I stood there, just watching her sleep.

Her engagement ring glinted against the dimming sky.

I almost smiled.
She was no longer on her way to be married.
She was already chosen.

Caged in Grace

The Artist

I didn't blindfold her.

She deserved to see it.

The moment she woke—I was ready. The studio was still, light from the paper lanterns casting soft gold across her skin. I had warmed the room before bringing her in. Rebecca wasn't meant for coldness. That was never her purpose.

She lay cradled on a suspended gurney I had built from birch and glass. The straps were minimal—discreet. White leather, soft as gloves. I'd brushed her hair while she slept. French-braided it. One long curve from temple to shoulder.

Her eyes opened fully. Green. Like moss after rain.

"I'm so glad you're here," I whispered.

She tried to speak, but the paralytic was doing its work. Just the flutter of her lips, the tension trembling in her jaw. I traced a fingertip down her throat.

"This won't be like the others. You're not for the grotesque. Not for shock." I paused, watching her pupils dilate. "You're for awe."

On the table beside me, my tools were lined in a velvet wrap—curved blades, a scalpel I'd bought in Milan, and the small, elegant cigar cutter. Not for her ring finger. Not this time. That wasn't her place in the sequence. She wasn't for continuity. She was an interlude.

A moment of beauty before the crescendo.

I started with the ink.

Soft red. Watercolor brush. I painted veins along her collarbones, tiny branches blooming outward like ivy. She watched.

She *always* watched. I could feel her attention like heat. Her trust. Even now. It made my hands steadier.

"You're going to become," I told her. "No one else gets this. Not like you."

The incision began beneath her breastbone—clean, deliberate. Her breathing stuttered, but she didn't flinch. I wasn't rushing. I followed the painted vines with the blade, slow, precise slices through skin already trembling. I whispered to her as I worked.

I slid the blade around her ribcage.

"You don't belong to the world."

The draining process took longer than expected. I adjusted the angle of the gurney slightly, allowing the blood to fill the base beneath her. A pool of crimson glass. I watched the light ripple through it—reflections warping against the ceiling.

Liquid pouring into the glass.

When her heart began to slow, I leaned close, brushing her cheek.

"You were always art. I'm just making it visible."

Her eyes didn't close when her pulse faded. I left them open.

I carried her body through the back corridors of the greenhouse, gloves silent on her silk gown. Petals brushing my legs. Every step was intentional—no hurry. This was the second act, and she deserved to be the centerpiece.

The ring finger. I hadn't wanted to take it—but the primal urge to own her overruled me.

I knelt beside the chaise, face cool in the humid air. I retrieved the cigar cutter—slim, surgical. The metal gleamed under the broken skylight. She wore her engagement ring, still intact. I slid the blade...

And *snap*—clean. The finger fell. I held it for a heartbeat, imagining the sorrow it would unleash when discovered. Then I placed it carefully in a velvet-lined box I carried—a trophy, a confession he would never see coming.

She watched me, in my mind. Still alive in the hush.

I moved her into position beneath the grand central skylight. Ivy framed her like drapery. I bent overhead supports into a cage—arched, gothic. Not to constrain, but to exalt.

Her body hung suspended in mid-air, lifted just enough by nearly invisible lines. Arms splayed in graceful repose. Head tipped back like a marionette in its final pose—forever on stage.

I adjusted the last tether. Her dress billowed. The folds pooled into a mauve slip beneath her—seed petals dyed that shade of evening sky I'd chosen. The same petals lay scattered around her—blush orchids mixed with dried dust from the greenhouse floor. Contrast.

A halo of fairy lights circled overhead—soft, almost celestial. Illumination overlaid with decay.

I wanted her to look like she was in mid-dream. Not dead. Not yet. Just asleep in floral suspension.

Her torso. I had carved a delicate, rib-length incision—

Slow. Rhythmic. Reverent.

I stepped back and looked.

She was perfect.

A mausoleum of petals and pale skin.

 It was complete.

Thread by Perfect Thread

The Artist

The way she stepped under the yellow tape, like it meant nothing. Like she already knew nothing could shield her from what waited inside.

Katherine always carried herself like she was built from tempered steel—but I could read the strain in her shoulders today, the subtle shift in her gait as she neared the greenhouse door.

She hadn't slept.

Good.

That made two of us.

I stayed hidden in the cover of the sycamores, far enough back not to draw attention, but close enough to see everything. I didn't blink as she came into view beneath the fractured skylight. Light spilled across her face, and I watched her squint, made her look like an oil painting moving across shattered glass.

And then it happened—just like I'd imagined.

She stopped.

Right in the threshold.

Her brow creased first—just slightly—as her eyes swept upward, catching the lines of fishing wire, the delicate angle of the body suspended. She didn't speak, but I didn't need her to. I felt the breath leave her chest from where I stood.

That tiny pause... *it was admiration.*

She tilted her head.

Yes, Katie. Look closely. I wanted her to see the symmetry, the thought in the gown's pleating, the way the shadows fell behind the figure like angel wings. I'd adjusted them three times to get it right.

She stepped forward—slow, measured, reverent.

God, she was stunning when she was decoding. That mind of hers, all sharp angles and relentless pursuit, working overtime behind those tired eyes. I could almost hear her thoughts. She was trying to outpace me again. Trying to stay ahead.

But for this moment, she was exactly where I wanted her.

Here, inside my creation.

She circled the body, her gloved hand hovering near the air-dried flowers I'd woven into the subject's braid. She crouched briefly to study the blood basin, and I saw the moment her breath caught again.

She was inside the moment with me.

She rose, slower this time, and walked outside. Light spilled across her face, and I watched her squint, her hand shading her eyes. She didn't cry.

The curve of her cheek in the lens was all he had—for now. Close enough to touch, but not yet.

Her face slid from shock into something hotter, tighter. The muscles along her jaw flexed—one, two—as if she were grinding the words she wanted to scream into powder. A faint pulse beat at the hollow of her throat, thrumming beneath skin gone a shade paler than moments before.

Her mouth flattened, the soft bow of her upper lip disappearing into a blade-thin line while a single vein rose at her temple, pulsing like a metronome of fury.

I caught the flare in her eyes—the way blue iced toward gray when rage eclipsed grief. Even from the tree line I felt it, that low percussion of her heartbeat driving against the silence I'd built.

Anger vibrated off her like a hidden choir: steady, relentless, almost musical. My favorite aria.

Anger meant she couldn't forget me.

She turned and spoke to someone out of my line of sight, her hand gesturing toward the greenhouse with restrained force. I imagined her voice—low, clipped, trying to hide how deeply she felt it. Always trying to separate herself from it.

But I could see it in the way she held her hands too still.

Katherine Poe was unraveling, thread by perfect thread.

I stayed only a moment longer, until I was sure she'd entered the greenhouse again, back into the silence of my offering. Then I stepped into the shadows, vanished the way I always did.

But not before whispering aloud, so soft the trees might have swallowed it: "You were always mine, even in the light."

The Silence That Watched Back

Katherine

The smell hit first—rust and lilies.

Too much sweetness always meant death.

Katherine ducked under the tape and forced her lungs to obey. One breath in. Then another. The tension in her jaw had settled like concrete days ago, and now it pulsed with the weight of every clenched second. She stepped forward.

Not a sound except boots on wet gravel, the hiss of wind against broken glass overhead.

And then she saw her.

Suspended in the air, like a marionette he'd never intended to dance—only hang. The woman's arms were bent at gentle angles, palms up, as if offering something invisible. White gardenias had been pinned behind her ear. Her wedding dress was black at the hem where it soaked through, and from a distance, it almost looked like water. *Almost.*

Katherine moved closer.

She didn't remember ordering the team to hold back. Didn't feel the gloves slide on. Her body was moving on instinct now—methodical, detached, the only way she knew how to keep from breaking wide open.

The victim was posed. No—*displayed.* That was his word. His language. Displayed, like she was meant to be studied.

Every detail was intentional.

Hair braided. Soft curls worked loose near the face.

Eyes open.

God.

They weren't screaming. They weren't glazed over.

They were... *waiting.*

She forced herself not to look away.

Katherine stepped around slowly, scanning the angle of the body, the lines of wire holding her in place. It wasn't just gruesome—it was theatrical. Thought out. There was symmetry here. He hadn't rushed this one.

Her throat tightened.

One hand—left—was missing a finger. She crouched. Counted to four. Then again. No mistake. The ring finger had been removed with precision.

It was him.

And yet… something was off. This staging wasn't like the others. No violence on the surface. No visible trauma beyond the incision site. It was too clean. Too… *reverent.*

He cared about this one.

Katherine rose to her feet, heart thudding against the hollow between her ribs. She turned toward the nearest uniform and barked orders she couldn't hear herself giving. She was already three steps ahead.

Get the scene scanned. Pull every bit of footage within a five-block radius. She needed angles. Faces. Patterns.

She backed out of the warehouse and into the open air, yanked the gloves off, and stuffed them into her coat pocket.

The breeze slapped her in the face.

She wanted to scream.

Instead, she looked up. *Instinct.*

The rooftops. Fire escapes. Shadows.

Nothing.

But she felt it—that crawl between her shoulder blades.

The weight of being observed.

He was here.

He had watched her see it.

And he'd loved every second.

Katherine swallowed the bile at the back of her throat and walked toward the perimeter.

"I need a list of all nearby rentals, vacant buildings, anything with a clear line of sight," she snapped.

And she was done reacting.

It was time to *outmaneuver* him.

The Shift

Katherine

It wasn't until she stepped around the back of the display—past the low beam where the chain had been rigged taut—that she saw the envelope.

Tucked just beneath the bouquet pressed into the victim's limp hands. White. Heavy paper. Her name scrawled across the front in looping calligraphy.

Not "Investigator Poe."

Just *Katherine.*

Her breath caught like a hitch in a damaged gear.

She stared for a second too long. A beat passed. Then another. Her latex fingers trembled as she peeled it open.

A single sheet folded inside. Smooth. No creases except the one made with deliberate care. She unfolded it, eyes tracing each line even as her pulse jackhammered through her throat.

Katherine,

You're improving. I saw the way your head tilted—just slightly—as you studied her. You paused longer on the hair than I expected. That pleased me.

You're beginning to understand the difference between a corpse and a canvas.

I was never meant to be hidden. My work deserves light, attention, an audience. But not for applause. No, never applause. That would be vulgar.

This isn't for them.

This is for you.

*I left her eyes open because I wanted you to see that she was still look-*ing. *That even in death, she wasn't afraid—just waiting. Waiting for you to see what I see.*

You'll feel it soon, I think. The shift.

— The Artist

Katherine's knees locked. Her fingers crumpled the edges of the paper before she forced herself to breathe again—slow, deliberate.

She read it twice.

Then a third time, just to be sure the rage building behind her ribs wasn't irrational. That it wasn't personal.

Except it *was*.

Of course it was.

The Artist. He had named himself. As if he were claiming ownership over her time, her thoughts... *her*.

She folded the letter and slipped it into the evidence bag without a word.

It wasn't fear she felt now.

It was something older, deeper.

The kind of fury that didn't burn—it cut. A blade honed over years of quiet injustice.

And now it had found its whetstone.

The kind that never let you sleep again.

Honeyed Lies

Katherine

Later that evening, Devin's apartment was warmer than I expected. Dim light. Clean lines. The scent of bergamot and something faintly smoky—maybe beeswax or sandalwood. Nothing out of place, which meant everything had been carefully arranged to feel that way.

I kept my coat on.

The air felt *too* still. Like the greenhouse before I stepped under the skylight and saw her swaying.

He offered tea like it was the most natural thing in the world. A half smile. Relaxed posture. No pressure. Just a question hanging in the air like steam.

"Chamomile with lavender?" he said.

I paused. "How'd you know?"

He gave a small shrug, like it wasn't a big deal. "I have a good memory. You mentioned it once."

Maybe I had. *Maybe I hadn't.* My brain catalogued threats, not casual preferences. Still, I nodded.

The mug warmed my hands faster than I expected. I didn't drink it right away. He gestured to the sofa, and I sat on the far end. Angled toward the door. I never gave people my full back unless I had to.

His apartment was small but intentional. Books alphabetized. Artwork with taste. A chessboard sat mid-game on a side table, as if someone had just stepped away to think. I didn't ask who he played against.

"You, okay?" he asked.

Loaded question. The answer changed minute by minute.

"Long day," I said.

He didn't push. Just sipped his own tea and let the silence work.

I stared into the cup. The tea was the right temperature now. It smelled like something from my childhood—*a rare pocket of comfort in the middle of a war zone.*

"You ever feel like you're chasing a ghost?" I asked.

Devin didn't blink. "Sure. What kind?"

"The kind that leaves silk behind. And broken fingers. And makes it all look like art."

His brow knit slightly, not performative. Just enough to say he was listening.

"You mean the killer."

I nodded.

"It's precise," I said. "Too clean. Which means he's either slipping or planning something worse."

"Or he's trying to talk to someone," Devin said quietly. "Someone who speaks his language."

I looked up. Sharp. Too sharp.

He held up his hands. "I read too much true crime. Sorry. I didn't mean to sound... flippant."

I relaxed an inch. Just an inch.

The jazz record playing in the corner crackled into a soft horn solo. Smooth. Intentional. Not background noise—a curated vibe.

I glanced at the chessboard. Picked up a rook. "You play?"

"Against myself. Helps me think."

I set the piece down. "You always win?"

He grinned. "Or I always lose. Depending on the move."

He made it easy to be here. That bothered me more than if he'd been trying too hard.

The tea was almost gone. My gloves sat beside me, folded in my lap. I hadn't realized I'd taken them off.

My phone buzzed. I silenced it.

Devin glanced toward the window. "Want me to call you a car?"

I stood. "I'll walk. I need the air."

He didn't argue. Just followed me to the door, hand on the frame but not in my way.

"Thanks for the tea," I said.

"Anytime."

The hallway was cooler. Quieter. I made it all the way to the elevator before I realized I'd left my gloves behind.

The Brushstroke

Katherine

"We need to see the whole picture. Not just the brush strokes—step back, and maybe we'll finally understand what he's painting."

The room was too quiet, but Katherine welcomed the hush. Noise got inside her head lately—static behind her eyes, jangling like a loose wire. She tugged the black pushpin from between her lips and pinned the last photo to the wall. Glenna's body, staged in a dumpster.

Not mercy. Performance.

Behind her, Brandon exhaled. It wasn't loud, but it still scraped the edge of her nerves.

"Where do you want Rebecca?" he asked.

She didn't turn. Just nodded toward the open space beneath Victim 16.

"Put her to the left of Nicole. The alignment feels off otherwise."

They were silent for a beat too long. Then: "You're treating them like puzzle pieces."

Her voice came out flat. "They are."

She stepped back, palms open, letting her gaze drag over the wall. Photos. Maps. Case files with color-coded clips. One long red string trailed from crime scene to crime scene like a vein bleeding across the cork.

But it wasn't enough. Something fundamental was missing.

"Every display is different," Katherine murmured, half to herself, half to the ghosts pinned before her. "But the intention is always the same—devotion. Ownership. Craft."

Brandon scratched the back of his neck. "You think he loved them?"

"No," she said quickly. Too quickly. "Not them. The message. The art. Maybe even me. But not them. They were... mediums."

She walked to the board and circled the word *queen* in thick red ink. Then drew a line to *ribbon, coal scrip, blue, hooks, birch wood,* and *black corset*. Every item, every texture, had been selected. Not found. Not chance. Deliberate.

"These weren't souvenirs," she said, pulse thrumming. "They were brush strokes. He's telling a story. Building toward something."

"Then what's the climax?" Brandon asked.

She paused. Turned to the center of the board. And stared at a blank space.

"That," she said. "He hasn't painted it yet."

The Reserved Seat

Katherine

They filed out one by one—Brandon last, tapping two knuckles on the doorframe like a question he didn't dare ask.

The overhead fluorescents dimmed to night mode, leaving only the board's pinned faces glowing under a strip of security lighting. She could've gone home. She told herself she would—ten minutes ago… twenty.

Now the precinct felt abandoned, an empty lung waiting to collapse. Her pulse filled the silence: *thud… thud… thud*—louder than any ticking clock.

She dragged a chair across the floor, placed it dead-center, and sat. No phone. No coffee. Just the wall and the hum in her skull.

Focus on one detail at a time.

Glenna's burnt body. Nicole's black corset. Rebecca's veil of sheer muslin. Hooks.

He wasn't random. Not escalation—crescendo.

The emptiness inside her chest pinged—an echo chamber. The room tilted, or maybe it was exhaustion sliding the floor sideways. She pressed palms to her temples: *stay still—breathe—count.*

One—door.

Two—exit.

Three—scissors on the evidence cart.

Safety ritual. Useless comfort.

Her eyes found the blank center square on the board again. That space wasn't absence; it was invitation. He'd left it for her like a reserved seat at a funeral.

You're the finale. Can't you see it?

A tremor started in her right hand. She clenched her fist. It crawled up her arm anyway, a current under skin. God, she was so tired. Eyelids sandpaper, head spinning with static. Sleep had become a rumor other people indulged in.

Her vision blurred—faces melting into one masked accusation. Glenna's lips became Nicole's, became Rebecca's, mouths sewn shut by the red string she'd pinned. In the hush she heard the faintest hum—like the generator from *that room* long ago. Couldn't be real. Too faint. Too far. But it crawled in her ear and nested there.

Stop it—stop it—STOP—

She shot to her feet so fast the chair clattered over. Startled silence. Heart hammering. Sweat at the nape of her neck turned ice.

Get out. Get air.

But her legs locked.

If she left now, the emptiness would follow. Better to stay in the glow of the wall, with its awful honesty.

She swallowed, throat raw. "What are you painting?" she whispered to the photos.

No answer. Just the layered stillness of nineteen women's silenced lives.

The tremor stilled. She righted the chair, sat again, and forced herself to study the blank center.

Three more brush strokes, she thought. *And he'll sign his name.*

She didn't know whether the shiver that rolled through her was terror—or anticipation.

She forced herself to trace each thread one more time.

Not with a marker. With her finger.

She didn't even realize she was doing it at first—walking that taut red yarn from Glenna to Nicole to Rebecca. Her fingertip trailed along the seam like she was blindfolded and being tested. As if the answers were in the texture of string, not the pattern. As if her skin might know what her mind couldn't hold anymore.

He's not rushing anymore.

That thought punched low.

She wasn't sure if she'd spoken it aloud until she noticed the hollow ring in the room afterward. Even her voice felt foreign now. Hoarse. Unused. Like it belonged to the Katherine who wasn't failing.

Her knees buckled a little as she lowered back into the chair. She sat on her hands. They were shaking again.

Sleep-deprived eyes began playing tricks.

Glenna's pinned photo twitched. Not real, she knew that, but it twitched. A trick of the light, the tilt of her head. But now Glenna's smile curled just slightly—wrongly.

Katherine's throat closed.

Then Nicole blinked. *She blinked.*

She tore her gaze away, too fast, and the room spun sideways. Her hands gripped the chair's edge. *Reality, Katherine. Find it.*

The hum came again—faint, rhythmic, under everything. Not a sound. A presence. A memory unzipping at the edge of thought.

That basement.

The generator.

Her sister's scream.

A hand over her mouth.

The hot breath against her ear.

"Shhh. You're going to ruin it."

Her body jerked like she'd been slapped.

She stood, pacing now, trying to outrun it—but the hum followed. Beneath her ribs. Behind her teeth. Threaded through the very air. Her eyes burned from the fluorescents—too bright now, too white.

She hit the light switch.

Dark.

Better.

Only the glow of the board remained. The shrine.

She walked to it again.

Someone had written something. No, that was her own handwriting. She couldn't remember writing it. Had she blacked out? Had she—

It's all right. Just breathe. One... Two...

Something clicked. Not in the room. In her mind.

She was Meant To

Katherine

She was meant to survive.

That's what they all kept saying, as if survival were some gift—some sacred duty she hadn't earned. But he hadn't meant for both to walk out of that place. Just one. Just Katherine.

He wouldn't have needed to kill Elisabeth to break her. Just keep her. Just let time rot through what was left. That would've been the real punishment—for both.

And if that's what happened… then Katherine hadn't saved her sister at all. She'd damned her.

Sometimes when she closed her eyes, Katherine swore she could hear a voice whispering from the dark.

Not memory. Not dream. But something deeper. Something that sounded like Elisabeth.

Sometimes, when Katherine let her mind go dark, she imagined what it would be like if Elisabeth was still alive. Not the hopeful rescue kind of imagining—this was the other kind. The kind she couldn't stop once it started.

There was a time when she imagined rescue.

Not anymore.

Now she imagined the sound of bones breaking—not from violence, but from disuse. From silence.

No clocks. No calendar. Just the flicker of overhead light. She marked time by absence.

Daylight meant he wasn't there.

Moonlight meant he might be.

And the in-between—that stretched, breathless dark—was the worst. That's when her skin crawled. That's when breath became rationed. That's when he came, like a shadow pretending to be a man.

There were no windows. Just four walls and a single mirrored panel. Not glass. Not truth. A reflection pretending to be escape. She'd pressed her ear to it once, back when she still believed something might answer back. Back when she still answered to Elisabeth.

But he never used her name.

He called her *Echo*.

Because she wasn't the original.

Just a haunting in the shape of Katherine.

The first time he braided her hair, she'd screamed. Not from pain. From memory.

The rhythm of the strands—three, three, loop—was too familiar.

Katherine's braid. First day of school. Church. Funeral.

She couldn't scream again after that. She wouldn't give him the satisfaction.

He'd whispered, *"You're her root. You're how I remember her before she tried to forget me."*

She didn't understand then.

Now she did.

Katherine had run.

He'd caged her echo instead.

He washed her hair with shampoo that smelled like lemon balm and cedarwood. Childhood in a bottle.

Imported, he'd said. "Not a replica. The original."

Because Elisabeth was the prototype.

Katherine was the masterpiece.

The music box played *Clair de Lune* every time he left. She counted the notes now—117 before it rewound.

That was her calendar. That was how she survived.

The dress he brought her was blue.

No tags. No seams. Just soft cotton and expectation.

"You'll wear this when she comes," he'd said, laying it over her knees like a prophecy. *"She'll know it. She'll know you."*

She stopped bleeding months ago. Her body had surrendered time, but her mind?

Sharper than ever.

She read the same six books in rotation. She carved secrets into the margins with a bent spoon. Not *help*. That was too obvious. Too desperate.

Instead, on page 87 of *The Little Prince*, she wrote:

"Love isn't always good. Sometimes it's camouflage."

There were two cameras in the ceiling. She didn't look at them anymore.

But when she cried, she did it under the vent, where the blind spot lived.

That was her resistance.

He talked about Katherine like she was a shrine. A final form.

But sometimes his voice trembled.

Not devotion. Not awe.

Obsession.

She knew the difference.

"She was meant for me," he said.

But saints didn't belong to anyone.

He just couldn't tell the difference between a sculpture and a possession.

She rocked herself slowly, blanket clutched tight at the shoulders, teeth pressed to her tongue.

And the voice—her own voice—spoke from someplace hollow and wild:

"Don't come here, Katie. Please don't come."

The Tilt

Katherine

The body always breaks first. But the mind hears it coming.

Dark syrup fills her chest, slicks behind her eyes, smothers her thoughts.

She blinks, tries to stay upright, counting steps. Three to the cooler. Six to the bathroom.

Black dots bloom at the edge of her vision. Blink. Mistake.

She stumbles into the break room. Cold water. Her hands shake, barely cupping it, but she drinks anyway—desperate.

The tremors spread across her shoulders like bees under her skin. She splashes her face—ice shock, breath seizes.

Blink. Wrong again.

The mirror doesn't reflect her.

It shows a body. Corset tight, black velvet dress soaked in blood, no head.

Just a dress. Just hooks and a backdrop of stage-light glow.

Nicole. Hung like a gallery piece.

Katherine's stomach churns. It's not real. She's not real.

She grabs the counter, knuckles blanching. Her face returns—eyes too wide, skin too pale.

Losing it.

She leans on the sink, forehead against steel.

Breathe.

In. Two. Out. Four.

The numbers slip. A sound—fabric shifting, leather brushing canvas.

Close.

She spins, hand to her sidearm.

No one. Just the hiss of the vent.

But knowing the monster's name doesn't make it leave.

The black edges crawl in again. Her legs give way. Cold tile stings her cheek.

For a moment, silence.

Then—

Dark. Concrete. A hum.

Breath. Not hers.

"Come on," he whispers. "Stop shaking."

She whimpers. Doesn't care if it's memory or madness.

"Katherine!"

Light explodes. Too white. Too much. Hands grip her.

Brandon.

His aftershave hits her first. The safety almost undoes her.

"Stay with me," he says, distant. "Your pulse is flying. When did you last sleep?"

Words don't come. Her tongue's sand. The ceiling pulses.

"Call medical," he said.

"Don't," she rasps. "I'm fine."

He laughs bitterly. "Bullshit."

He picks her up and carries her down the hall. The murder board swims into view. Faces blur, fuse.

One woman. A veil. Red lips. Finger missing.

She jerks her gaze away.

They need you.

He's watching.

You can't fall now.

Tears hover. She swallows them.

A water bottle is shoved in her hands. She can't hold it. He does it for her.

"When did you last sleep?" he questioned.

"Thirty-six hours." She whispered.

A lie.

He grabs his phone. *EMT.*

"You're going to urgent care." He said firmly.

"No," her voice cracks. "He wins if you bench me."

"He wins if you die." He doesn't press send.

She watches him. Doesn't blink.

"Four hours. Then hospital."

He dims the light, leaves the door cracked.

She curls up. The buzzing fades a little.

Sleep creeps in. Just before it pulls her under, one thought cuts through:

If I'm the finale, he's already watching me fall apart. The dark closes around her.

Split Katherine

Katherine

Brandon took her home.

She didn't remember the ride. Just the slam of the car door. The hum of tires over asphalt. The static roar behind her eyes louder than his voice, louder than the world.

Now the sun slants through the blinds—sharp angles, mean light. She sits on the edge of the couch, one sock on, the other foot bare, frozen mid-motion like she forgot what comes next.

Did she make coffee?

The silence says no.

Her apartment smells off. Metal, paper... fear, maybe. That cloying, stale scent of too many nights lived in survival mode. Her hoodie still clings to the shape of her spine, damp with sweat and sleep and failure.

Across the room, the briefcase waits. Open. Still.

She hasn't touched it in several weeks.

The chess piece.

The green stone.

The lock of hair, tied with a ribbon so blue it doesn't look real.

Her stomach turns.

She doesn't know why.

That shade—

It's almost identical to the contacts she wears. *Cyan Blue*, she's used since her twenties. The color she picked to erase the girl in the mirror.

For a split second, something icy twists behind her ribs.

But then she shakes her head. No. Coincidence.

It's just a ribbon.

Could've come from anywhere.

She shifts her gaze. Forces herself not to look at the rest.

Behind her, something moves. A whisper behind the doorframe. Her head jerks—nothing. Just shadow. But last night, at 3:12 a.m., she swore there was someone in the corner of her room. Watching.

When she turned the lamp on, only the crooked coat rack stood there. Same shape. Same silence. Different weight.

Sleep isn't sleep anymore. Its two-hour stints stitched together with adrenaline and ghosts. Every dream ends the same—with stitched mouths and open eyes.

She scratches her scalp until the sting feels real. Crosses the room.

Her reflection halts her.

Not her.

Not quite.

Eyes sunken. Skin wrong. Like she's been replaced by someone who forgot how to pretend to be her.

The mirror has a hairline crack. Right down the middle. Between her pupils.

A split Katherine.

She steps back. The room pulses.

It's fine. It's nothing.

The sound of fabric falling—just her jacket off the chair—still makes her flinch.

Her phone buzzes.

The screen glows: Devin.

It rings. Stops.

The silence that follows feels like judgment.

She sinks onto the couch. Folds in on herself. Knees up. Face buried in the crook of her arm.

She's unraveling. Not metaphorically. Not figuratively.

And no one sees it. Not really.

Then the phone buzzes again.

A text.

FROM: Brandon

Get some sleep. Let us take the wheel for a bit.

Chasing Her Own SHADOW

Katherine

The drive blurred. Katherine didn't remember grabbing her coat or locking her apartment door—just the click of her boots echoing down the sidewalk and the hollow pulse of her breath.

She had gotten the text ten minutes earlier.

She says she got away.

No name. No details. Just enough to slice the morning in half.

Inside the precinct, everything felt too bright. Too staged. The fluorescent lights buzzed like stage lights warming up. The rookie at the front desk offered a nod, but she didn't return it. Her focus tunneled. A phantom ringing in her ears as she turned toward Interview Room 3.

Brandon was waiting just outside. His face gave nothing away. "Didn't want anyone else," he said, holding the door open without meeting her eyes.

Inside, the woman was already performing.

Late thirties, maybe. Carefully disheveled. Her makeup stopped just short of looking applied, her hair tugged into the kind of messy bun people practiced in the mirror. She sat with one hand wrapped around a chipped paper cup, the other flat on the table like she wanted to look composed—but couldn't quite manage it.

Katherine closed the door behind her. No clipboard. No pen. Just presence.

The woman straightened immediately. "Agent Poe," she said, too quickly. "I—I'm glad it's you."

Katherine didn't respond to the name. Didn't offer reassurance. Just sat. Let the silence stretch.

The woman fidgeted. "I never thought I'd be here. Telling this. But I saw your press briefing last week, and I knew it was time."

Katherine's expression didn't move. "Tell me what happened."

A breath. A slight tremble. Practiced, not natural.

"I don't remember how I got there," she said. "He drugged me, I think. When I woke up, it was dark. Cold. I don't know how long I was there—he didn't hurt me, but he said awful things. About how I didn't belong. How I wasn't the one."

Katherine's head tilted slightly. "Did he ever ·use a name?"

"No," the woman said too fast. Then added, "But he kept muttering... things. About feathers. And a queen. He said she would understand. That it wasn't time for his masterpiece yet."

Feathers. Queen. Masterpiece.

All of them lifted straight from publicized case leaks. Katherine had given exactly two statements since the investigation reopened—one of them had mentioned the chess symbolism. The feathers had been referenced in a true crime podcast the week before.

Nothing she was saying was new.

"Go on," Katherine said.

"I escaped when he left the door unlocked. I don't know why." Her voice dropped to a whisper. "He said I wasn't her. That he'd wait."

Wait for what?

The words weren't said. Katherine didn't have to. The woman wasn't looking at her anymore—she was watching her own performance unfold in her head.

Katherine stood slowly. "Thank you," she said. "We'll follow up if we need more."

The woman blinked. "Wait—you believe me, right?"

Katherine didn't answer. She opened the door and left it wide behind her.

Outside, Brandon was already pacing. "She's been asking for media protection," he said. "Claims she'll be targeted again if we let her go."

"Of course she has," Katherine said flatly. "Get her a blanket, not a microphone."

She didn't believe her.

Because the truth didn't stutter.

Because real trauma didn't beg for applause.

Because nothing about that woman had survived anything except her own need to be seen.

And deep down, Katherine knew—the real victim wouldn't be talking.

She'd still be missing. Or dead.

Or waiting.

The First Gallery

The Artist

His father had been the one to teach him how to hold a brush steady, how to mix color, how to make something ugly look beautiful.

He'd watched him work in the barn more than once, the air heavy with turpentine and something sharper—copper-sweet. The women all sizes and ages, but the blood ran just as red.

His mother never asked questions. The blackened eye and split lip she carried home from the kitchen floor told him she already knew not to. The barn had been the first gallery.

He could still see the dust drifting in the light that slanted through the warped boards, smell the metallic sweetness before he understood what it was. His father had stood at an easel, brush moving over pale skin instead of canvas, strokes deliberate, patient. A woman's hair spilled over the side of the workbench like a ribbon. She never moved.

His mother had passed the open barn door without looking in, one hand pressed to a fresh bruise on her cheek.

Mistakes were not tolerated. Chaos was punished. His father demanded order—in the home, in the work. A crooked frame earned the back of a hand. A stray brushstroke meant a night locked in the dark. Perfection was survival.

That demand lived on still, years later, long after the barn, long after the first time his own brush had touched skin.

Which is why Madeline's failure wouldn't leave him. She'd screamed. She'd looked at him. Not like a canvas. Like a man. She had slipped the frame. Shattered it.

It wasn't a disruption—it was dissonance. The kind of chaos his father would have crushed instantly.

And the thought kept circling: she had seen him. Perhaps that meant she needed to be…silenced.

He sat in silence, hands trembling—not from fear, but from fracture. The ritual had been disturbed. He needed control. Tonight, he'd reclaim it.

The gallery waited. He moved reverently through the door, the scent of cedar and bleach clinging to the air—preservation, not decay. The stage was set; each figure bathed in gold. The photographs, precise and glossy, lay across the drafting table like a gallery without walls.

Glenna was first. Half-burnt, half-beautiful, captured just after the flames gave up. Smoke curled like regret, her hand reaching toward her chest, even in death. A perfect contrast: ruin and ritual.

Next, Nicole. Suspended in air, her corset tight across her ribs. Grime framed her, a sacrifice, worship. She hovered impossibly, her head like a wilted flower. The light had hit just right, turning bruises into brushstrokes.

Rebecca followed—his boldest piece. A cage of iron arched over her, vines weaving through. She looked like part of the world, as though the world had grown around her. He lingered, fingers brushing the edge of the print.

In the back room, the freezer hummed. Seventeen preserved fingers. Each with a ring. A promise unbroken. He traced one carefully, precise, not sentimental. Each finger a signature.

He labeled the next slot—Rebecca—Confirmed. Another remained blank.

The finale would come soon, but not yet.

First, he needed the world to watch Katherine unravel.

He closed the drawer. The freezer's hum was steady, symphonic. Madeline had been a fracture. But the masterpiece would hold.

Cross-Examination

Katherine

Some obsessions kill in an instant. Others take their time.

The interrogation room smelled like rust and old air, and Katherine couldn't shake the sense that this wasn't about the man across from her—it was about her.

The suspect sat still, blinking too slowly. He was younger than she expected. Clean-cut. Nervous hands. A finance intern who'd followed his coworker home. Watched her. Tried to befriend her by learning her routine.

"Harmless," his lawyer claimed. "Lonely, not dangerous."

Katherine knew better.

But today, it wasn't him she was reading. It was herself. Reflected.

The room closed in. Windowless. Lights too bright. The mirrored wall to her left wasn't glass—it was memory. A screen playing every bad thing she'd ever survived in a loop she couldn't mute.

She sat across from him, spine rigid, hands clasped too tightly on the table. The young man stammered through his answers. Her voice steady—too steady, like a script memorized years ago.

"Why her?" she asked. Flat. Surgical.

"I didn't mean—I just liked how she looked when she smiled."

His voice pitched, boyish and scared. Katherine knew what it meant to be adored, admired. Just before the door closed. Just before the darkness swallowed them whole.

She blinked hard. The room warped at the edges.

Not now.

"You memorized her schedule," she said. "Her favorite coffee order. The kind of shoes she wears. But you've never spoken to her?"

He shrugged like a child who knew he was caught.

"I just wanted to feel close to her. That's not a crime."

Katherine's hands ached. She unclenched her fingers and realized she'd left crescent-shaped dents in her palms.

She heard her own voice crack before she meant to speak.

"She didn't even know you existed. But you made her the center of your world. Do you know what that *does* to someone?"

The boy looked startled. Maybe even guilty. She didn't care.

"Do you understand what it's like to be hunted? To have your life sliced apart and painted as devotion," She paused, "To be someone else's art?

"Detective Poe," the other officer said gently from behind the glass. "We got enough."

She stood too fast. The chair skidded. The boy flinched.

But Katherine didn't stay long enough to apologize. She didn't look back.

In the hallway, she pressed her palms to her face and leaned into the wall until the floor stopped trying to tilt—static in her ears.

She was unraveling. And she didn't know how much longer she could keep the pieces from showing.

Cobalt Silk

The Artist

The gown arrived before dawn—twenty pounds of history, a shipping label dissolved in the drizzle. 1937 silk faille, bias cut, modest train, hand-sewn pearl buttons. Cedar and limestones cellars clung to it. Perfect.

I unrolled muslin, laid the gown flat. No stains, just yellowing beneath the arms—a fingerprint of time. She would wear this—brunette, green eyes, pale throat bruised by silk's embrace. I called her Brontë because the wind seemed to like her hair.

The Hue of Devotion

Cobalt is devotion—silence that tilts a room beneath sapphire light, demanding to be seen yet never understood.

Cobalt denies the eye's hunger, deepening where light should live, flaring where shadow should fall.

In the steel pot, 185°F water. Alum, vinegar, sea salt, and cobalt aluminate oxide. The water darkened, and I stirred. Steam carried whispers of cedar, abandoned hymnals. Twelve minutes—sky after rain. Twenty—horizon at dusk. Thirty-two—true cobalt, a tone that silenced thought. I killed the flame, let convection finish the metamorphosis.

While the fabric cooled, I sketched her—fountain edge curving sharper, fingers splayed as if translating rain into sign language. One hand protective, the other outstretched in longing. Death with a grammar of absence. Left ring finger excised post-mortem; sapphire halo ring balanced on the stump.

Rinse & Revelation

Silk weeps dye for longer than most imagine. Four rinses before the water cleared. Even wet, it commanded. She will command.

Brontë—green-eyed, bittersweet, choreographer sidewalks. I have studied her palette: emerald, jet, cream, opaline. She avoids sapphire, cobalt waiting.

She wears hurt like couture—never begging. That is why she qualifies.

Stitchwork

I unpicked the pearl buttons, replacing them with faceted glass dyed to the same pigment—little infinities reflecting nothing but themselves. Each buttonhole reinforced by hand. The gown's history now braided with mine.

Shoes—navy Spanish leather, size seven. I sliced the ankle straps almost through for future forensic confusion. Hairpiece: pressed brass leaves, tarnish intact, wired with dried forget-me-nots stained. Symbolism whispers.

Her wedding was close—too close, in a deconsecrated synagogue on Norfolk Street. She practices vows in her apartment kitchen—eyes closed.

I remind myself: devotion, not haste. Three more observations. Only then will the invitation be extended. The gallery demands precision.

The cobalt gown waits, breathless, for the skin it will devour. I stand before it. The silk absorbs the last glow.

Soon, I tell the dress.

Silence answers—a cathedral's silence. Approval.

I lock the studio and step into the hallway. My pocket notebook is open before the elevator arrives. One line: *Confirm florist delivery of orchids (deep plum) for fountain staging.* Ink dries in the shape of a promise.

She has no idea how beautifully she will drown.

Compartmentalized

Katherine

She stared at the map again, the edges soft from over-handling, the paper curling like it was trying to fold in on itself. Katherine pressed it flat against the table and exhaled slowly through her nose, bracing herself for another fruitless pass. Every inch of it felt familiar and foreign at the same time, like trying to recognize a face distorted in rippling water.

It didn't match anything. Not New York, not Connecticut, not anywhere upstate or along the coast. She'd pushed it across satellite overlays, historical city maps, even grainy scanned topographies from decades past. Nothing. It was hand-drawn, that much was certain. The style was confident but careful, deliberate. Which meant it had to mean something.

And that drove her insane.

She traced the jagged ridges with her fingertip. They reminded her of the mountains back home. Appalachia. But even when she'd pulled up every hiking trail and hand-sketched forest map from West Virginia to Kentucky, nothing aligned. It was like trying to read a language she once knew in a dream.

"You, okay?" Brandon had asked her last night before leaving the office. He'd given her that look again. The one that said she needed sleep. That her eyes were too red. Her hand too shaky with the coffee mug. She'd just nodded. Said she was fine.

She wasn't. But survival had muscle memory.

A week had passed since the last body. Weeks since Lena. And somehow, that disturbed her more. The silence.

The lull between storms. It felt wrong, like he was watching her wait.

She took the waiting and buried it under protocol. Files. Another pass through the evidence. The chess piece. The coal scrip. The emerald paperweight. She logged everything again, made Brandon and Jacoby cross-check it all with missing persons, with symbols from the other crime scenes. Nothing new.

Nothing but dust and frustration.

She leaned back in her chair, the case still open beside her like a patient refusing surgery and glanced at her phone.

A message from Devin.

Had a great time last night. Hope you got home okay. I found that wine we were talking about. Raincheck?

Her thumb hovered over the screen. He'd been kind. Gentle, even. Charming in a way that didn't feel performative. And she had vetted him. There had been nothing that set off her radar. No strange ties, no unexplainable gaps. Cheryl had vouched for him, and Cheryl wasn't careless with the people she trusted.

Still.

She texted back, short and polite. *Sounds good. Let me know when.*

She told herself she could compartmentalize. That she deserved to spend a few hours not buried under death and dread. That Devin's smile didn't feel like a trap. That when he called her Katie it didn't make her stomach twist just slightly too hard.

Katherine shut the briefcase and locked it again. Her fingers lingered on the latch.

A sound outside.

She moved to the window quickly, the motion instinctual. But it was just a car. A delivery. Her hand unclenched from the curtain. She blew out a breath.

The clock on the wall read 1:12 a.m.

She needed sleep.

But the map still sat in her mind like a heartbeat.

The Color of Lies

The Artist

She shimmered in deliberate deception.

I first saw her outside the bookstore in a green velvet coat, her lips deep crimson. She was perfect—brunette, green-eyed, a thrift-store wedding dress hemmed into a cocktail number. Curated.

I followed her for seventeen days—never desperate, always elegant. One day in emerald with a black parasol, her movement choreographed. The next, neon tights, vinyl trench, miming for passing children. Every day a new mask, a new role. Her green eyes always stayed the same.

I cataloged every moment—how she unlocked her door, stirred her coffee counterclockwise, checked for scuffs on her shoes. She was intentional. Every step, every breath, designed for attention.

She wasn't vain. She was unknowable. That's why she mattered. She had an ache beneath the surface, a sadness that wasn't performative but real. She wasn't looking to be seen, just understood.

By Day Nine, I had the vision. She would be wrapped in vintage tulle, one hand lifted toward the sky, frozen in the moment before drowning or rising. A perfect subject.

But Day Twelve changed everything. She wore a red ribbon in her hair—a break in her usual style. It felt wrong. Then, on Day Fifteen, I followed her into a costume shop, and when she emerged, she was blonde. Her eyes, once green, were now blue. No wig. No contacts. Just her, and she smiled—not her performance smile, but a real one.

That's when it hit me. She wasn't my art. She was a collector, a chameleon. Someone who wore grief like jewelry but didn't feel lit.

I left before she saw me. I had almost honored her, but she lied—not in words, but in intention. She assembled herself to be found, but she wasn't what I was looking for.

Art is honest. It bleeds. It decays. She wasn't one of mine.

The gown remains, cobalt and breathless—not as tribute, but as indictment. Denied by a fraud. And still, it waits.

Unguarded

Katherine

3:17 a.m.
She didn't remember going to bed.

Katherine stood in the hallway, blinking at the shadows. She wasn't sure if she'd just woken or never slept at all. The cold floor bit at her bare feet, the air thick with burnt coffee and bleach.

The past few nights blurred together. Her dreams were wrong—faces without names, a woman with no ring finger. Sometimes the Artist's voice slipped into her mind, whispering only for her to hear.

Her therapist called it hypervigilance. Her captain, burnout. Katherine called it survival.

She sat at the kitchen table, turning the black queen over in her hand. *She was the last piece, but whose side?*

The light above flickered. It hadn't done that yesterday. Or had it?

Her thoughts were a tangled mess; everything filtered through the case. A man bumped her on the street, and her hand went to her gun. The barista asked for her name, and she trembled.

She glanced at the fridge. A photo of her and Elisabeth when they were kids. It felt wrong, like someone had painted over her memory. He was making her question everything, even herself.

Her phone buzzed, pulling her from the spiral. A message from Devin:

"Hey you. Got the reservations. You seriously need air—let me be the bad influence tonight."

His steadiness scared her. She hated that part of her still wanted to say yes.

Reservations

Katherine

Location: A quiet Italian restaurant tucked on a corner two blocks off the main drag—low lighting, brick walls, linen napkins, and a small quartet playing something soft and string-heavy in the background.

Katherine ran her thumb along the stem of her wine glass, not drinking. Just moving. Just doing something with her hands.

She smiled. Real, this time.

He caught it. "Was that a laugh?"

Katherine lifted a shoulder. *Maybe.*

Devin leaned in a little, resting his forearms on the table, palms open. He always did that—kept himself unguarded. No crossed arms. No quick glances to the door.

Still… she liked the way he looked at her. Like he saw things she hadn't shown him yet.

She let herself breathe. Slowly. Measured. Her stomach hadn't clenched once during dinner. She'd noticed it in the third course. *She hadn't checked the exits. Hadn't swept the room for watchers. Not once.*

That scared her more than anything.

She picked up her fork, stabbed a ravioli, and tried to ground herself in the taste of ricotta and black pepper and whatever this moment was trying to be.

"So…" Devin said gently, "You're not reaching for your phone every two minutes. Am I growing on you, Poe?"

That made her smirk. "You've always been a little fungus-like."

"Ouch. Beautiful and brutal. You should come with a warning label."

"I do," she murmured. "Most people ignore it."

There was a silence after that. Not the bad kind. Just the kind where two people let the quiet stretch and didn't need to fill it. She traced the rim of her plate with her pinky.

"I like this," Devin said. "Us. The—uh—ease of it."

It wasn't easy. Not for her. But maybe that was the point.

Katherine tucked a strand of hair behind her ear and met his eyes. "I'm not always like this."

"Good," he said. "Neither am I."

Later behind the wheel. Goodnight said. Headed home.

She didn't remember locking the door behind her. Maybe she had. Maybe she hadn't. But somehow, it was already locked when she got inside.

Burn Steady

Katherine

The candles made it look beautiful. That was the part that felt wrong.

St. Patrick's stood like a shadow against the night—tall, lit from within, spine straight against the noise of a city that didn't believe in stillness. But tonight, it quieted. Tonight, it made space.

Rows of votives lined the steps, trembling flames tucked into jars and teacups and recycled baby food containers. Names written in Sharpie. Messages scrawled in chalk and lipstick and pen.

They weren't all there. Not every family had wanted a public display. Not every victim had even been named in the press. But enough were here to make the air feel full—parents, siblings, coworkers, strangers who felt less strange in the soft light of grief.

I adjusted the paper in my hand. I didn't want to speak.

I wasn't good at this part.

Public grief. Open wounds.

But Cheryl said it mattered. Said the department needed a voice that wasn't wrapped in sterile press briefings. And I—I needed something, too.

I stood just left of the podium, behind a priest I didn't know and a city council member I barely tolerated, trying not to look like I was cataloguing the exits.

Brandon stood behind me. Quiet. A solid presence. He didn't say anything, but I could feel him there. That mattered more than words.

The councilwoman finished her statement. Something about resilience. Unity. Safety.

I stepped forward, ignoring the way my pulse rattled like glass in my throat.

The mic wavered as I adjusted it. The silence leaned closer.

"I'm not here to speak as an investigator," I began. "I'm here because I've seen what he does. I've stood beside the bodies. I've touched the silk he dressed them in. I've looked into the eyes of women who should've been brides—and weren't given the chance."

A breath. The kind that cracks ribs on the way out.

"He doesn't just take lives. He erases futures. He poses these women like artifacts and dares us to look away."

I glanced toward the candles, their flicker steady in the windless air.

"But you didn't look away. You came. You lit candles. You said their names."

I could feel their families watching. A mother in the front row clutched a framed photo of her daughter. The angle caught the candlelight just right—burning over the glass, washing out the smile.

My voice caught. Just once. I swallowed it.

"I promise you this," I said, quieter now. "I won't stop. We won't stop. He's not a ghost. He's a man. And we are building the truth around him—*frame by frame, stitch by stitch.*"

The crowd didn't applaud. Thank God.

They bowed their heads.

I stepped back.

The priest led a short prayer. The councilwoman handed out small candles. A quartet played something wordless and sad.

And I slipped down the steps.

Brandon caught up halfway through the crowd. "You did good."

"I couldn't do it; I am not good with public grief." He whispered.

"I don't think I said anything new."

"You didn't need to. You said it clean."

We stopped near a display table where laminated photos flapped under stones—each one bordered in ribbons and fake flower petals. Some had notes tucked beneath them. Some just had names.

A girl around ten stood staring at one picture. I didn't recognize the victim's face, but the name chilled me: **Lydia Cho**.

She'd been found in the Rose Main Reading Room at the NYPL. Doctoral candidate. Twenty-six. Her wedding dress had been folded beside her, untouched.

"She was my babysitter," the girl said, not looking at me. "She used to make up stories about the books I picked."

I nodded. "She sounds like someone who paid attention."

The girl looked up. "Do you think she knew?"

"Knew what?"

"That someone was going to hurt her?"

I crouched slightly, knees aching from the cold.

"No," I said. "I think she knew she was loved. That's what she carried."

The girl nodded, satisfied.

Her mother called her name from the curb. She ran off.

I stood slowly.

A woman touched my sleeve. "You're Katherine Poe, aren't you?"

I turned. Late sixties. Silver in her hair. Grief in her skin.

"Yes," I said.

Her lips trembled. "My niece was Nicole. The one in the corset dress."

I braced myself. For anger. For gratitude. For anything.

"She would've liked you," she said, voice breaking. "She liked women who didn't flinch."

I didn't know what to say to that. I nodded.

She pressed something into my hand. *A folded paper crane.*

"She made these when she was anxious. I found a whole box in her closet."

"I'll keep it," I said.

The woman smiled. "Don't keep it. Let it remind you."

I tucked the crane into my coat pocket like evidence.

The wind picked up.

The candles flickered—but they didn't go out.

Frame By Frame

The Artist

The city's arteries pulsed loud enough to drown out thought—delivery trucks coughing exhaust, the metallic clang of a security grate rolling down behind me. Perfect camouflage. Noise was the one indulgence Manhattan offered in surplus.

I walked without haste; a single glove tucked in my coat pocket so my palm could feel the cold through wool. Let sensation catalog the moment: wind funneled off the river—tonight, the avenues tasted of iron. Anticipation always leaves a trace on the tongue.

Across Ninth, neon bled onto the wet asphalt and spilled over a wall of plate-glass. Harvey's Electronics. Televisions stacked in sloppy rows, sound muted, captions crawling like ants across the bottom edge. Normally I ignored storefronts—mass-produced chaos offered no inspiration—but something flickered blue-white, magnetic.

BREAKING NEWS ribboned across every screen.

The feed cut to candles lining cathedral steps—tiny lights trembling in the night, each flame mirrored into eternity by the dozen panels. St. Patrick's. The vigil.

And there—center frame—Katherine Poe.

She stood behind a podium too narrow for her shoulders, fingers flattened on a single sheet of paper she never glanced at. A sleepless bruise colored the hollow beneath her cheekbone. The camera operator zoomed in when she lifted her chin.

I promise you this. I won't stop.

No audio reached the sidewalk, but I'd memorized her mouth. I read the vow in the vowels.

On the screen, Katherine stepped away from the micro-phone, flanked by department brass. Her blazer was char-coal, almost black; candles reflected along the lapel like fall-ing embers. She didn't twitch or swallow—steel welded to bone.

The camera cut to the families—mothers with framed photographs, fathers holding programs—leaning forward to catch her words. They didn't look at the priest or the coun-cilwoman. They looked at Katherine. She had become the axis around which their losses orbited.

Good. I wanted them tasting hope. Hope heightens the eventual break.

A woman pressed an origami crane into her palm. Kath-erine closed her fingers around it, jaw flexing for one heart-beat before she masked the ripple. Not a collapse. A glimpse. Vulnerability exposed for exactly one-third of a second.

I inhaled, savoring it.

When the feed cut back to commercials, the magic was over. I exhaled, fog blooming on the glass. My reflection swam among the televisions, features distorted by back-to-back screens.

Unseen, I smiled.

A police cruiser idled at the corner, lights strobed but siren silent. Patrol, not pursuit. I crossed against the red, hood low, stride confident. Invisible men wear certainty.

Halfway up the block someone banged a trash can lid—restaurant porter, end-of-shift. The clang split the air, ech-oed down scaffolding.

Another screen in a deli window replayed a clip of the vigil. Closed captions scrolled:

FRAME BY FRAME, SHE SAID, STITCH BY STITCH.

My words, stolen and repurposed by a woman who'd never stepped inside my studio.

I felt a flicker of ownership—part pride, part fury. She was right, of course. But she spoke as if frames were inert, as if silk were passive. She had never pulled a needle through flesh or felt a body stiffen into geometry. She had never waited for rigor to curve a wrist into the perfect pleading angle.

Soon she would.

But not yet.

Patience, like cobalt, deepens in the dark.

And if grief demanded fire to set the final contrast, I would oblige.

I reached the subway entrance at 34th. Down the stairs, wind smelled of electricity and spilled beer. A busker's violin scratched out *Ave Maria* to indifferent commuters. I lingered on the platform edge, eyes closed, letting the rumble of an approaching train vibrate bones.

When I opened them, the tunneling headlights carved twin white paths in the dark—parallel frames racing toward convergence.

Katherine had promised the families she wouldn't stop. I believed her.

I would reward that devotion.

The cobalt gown was waiting. Perhaps it had always been meant for her.

Then—frame by frame—she would see the picture complete.

My train screamed into the station. Doors sighed. I boarded, coat settling around me like stage curtains falling before the final act.

Inside the glass of the opposite window, my reflection flickered, cut by passing tunnel lights.

I was already gone before I had fully arrived.

The Ones Who Stay

Katherine

The phone rang twice. She nearly hung up.

Then—click.

"Hello?" A woman's voice. Thin, wary. Like someone who had stopped expecting anything good from the sound of a phone.

Katherine almost forgot how to breathe. "Mrs. Dalton?"

A pause. "Yes?"

"This is—uh—this is Katherine Poe. I'm with CID. I... you reached out to me a few weeks ago. About your daughter. Camille."

The silence that followed wasn't empty. It had weight. Texture.

"You're the one who's chasing that jilted freak," the woman said flatly.

"Yes," Katherine replied, voice raw. "I am."

She didn't say she used to ignore it. Or that she should've stopped him long before now.

"Do you have something to tell me, Agent Poe? Or is this one of those calls that goes nowhere?"

Katherine felt the sharp edge of shame press against her throat. "I thought maybe we could talk. In person. If you're willing."

Another pause.

Then: "If I make coffee, you better damn well drink it."

The house smelled like wood polish and pine. Too clean. The kind of clean that comes from distraction, from trying to scrub away ghosts embedded in carpet fibers.

Photos lined the mantle—Camille in braces, in ballet slippers, in cap and gown. Her absence screamed louder than any words could.

"I'll get to it," Mrs. Dalton said, setting down two chipped mugs. "But I want to see if you flinch first."

Katherine took a sip of coffee she didn't want. Burnt. Strong. She welcomed the sting.

"She was twenty-three," the woman began. "Wanted to open a gallery. Didn't give a damn about money. She loved ugly things. Found beauty in everything but herself."

"I told her not to walk home at night. Told her the city's full of shadows. But she always said monsters didn't wear fangs, they wore kindness." Mrs. Dalton's mouth pulled tight. "I didn't get to see her face. They wouldn't let me. Said it would 'interfere with my healing.'"

Katherine's chest tightened. "I'm sorry."

"Don't be sorry. Be useful."

It was a slap disguised as a plea. Katherine swallowed it whole.

"He didn't stage her, you know," the woman went on. "Camille didn't get flowers or ribbons or… whatever the others got. She was left like trash. You only started caring when he made it *pretty*."

Katherine closed her eyes for a beat, but the words hit bone. "That's not true."

"Isn't it?"

Katherine stood. "I don't know what he saw in her. Why she didn't make it into his art."

"She was *too good for it*," the mother snapped. "He couldn't make her small enough."

Katherine nodded once, slowly, then walked to the photos. There was one of Camille holding a stray with mange. Her smile wasn't perfect. But it was honest.

That photo felt more human than the entire investigation board back at CID.

In the car, she stayed still for a beat, breath catching as she forced herself back into center. She told herself to breathe, not knowing it was only the beginning.

She got six more voicemails that week.

Three fiancés. One sister. One daughter.

A father who didn't cry—just said, "I still make dinner for two."

Katherine listened to them all.

Didn't delete one.

Sometimes it wasn't the staging, the trophies, the symbols that stayed with her. It was the people still living. The ones stitched together with hope and voicemail calls.

Copycats

Katherine

The first body wasn't his. She knew it before she even stepped out of the car.

Katherine had driven four hours through fog and sleet to reach the lakeside chapel where the bride had been found. The local police had already cordoned off the stone terrace out back. The victim was young. A brunette. Green eyes. Pretty in the way they always were. But she hadn't been staged. There were no symbolic flourishes, no craftsmanship. She hadn't been elevated—she had simply been discarded.

Still, she walked the perimeter. Ritual, not hope. She took pictures. Noticed the dirt under the girl's nails. The faint smear of lipstick across her cheek. She asked questions the small-town detectives couldn't answer and wrote the same line three times in her notebook:

Not him. But someone else is watching.

Two days later, another body. Another mimic.

Katherine followed the trail through Ohio, Pennsylvania, and upstate New York. Copycats, she suspected. Or someone trying to bait her.

She didn't sleep much. The team noticed. Brandon had started tiptoeing around her like she was a ticking bomb. She supposed she was.

She took to laying out the contents across her apartment floor every night: the black queen chess piece, the lock of hair tied with ribbon, the coal scrip, the emerald paperweight. The old paper map, torn and scorched along the edges. Still unreadable.

One night, the emerald caught the light just right. Green, but not the cheap kind—deep and real, like the flecks in her own eyes when she forgot to wear contacts. Her stomach tightened, a flicker of something too sharp to name.

She pushed the thought aside before it could find shape. She moved on.

Until one night, hunched over her kitchen counter, she traced the faint outline of a coastline she hadn't noticed before.

Chincoteague Island.

Virginia?

She sat up straight, blood surging like it used to when she was young and still believed instinct could save lives.

Chincoteague—wasn't just a name. It wasn't a metaphor. It was a location.

But why there?

She started researching ferry routes. Population records. Real estate holdings. Anything that could hint—why.

He was pulling her east.

And still, no sign of victim 18.

False Notes

Katherine

The drive out had been a gamble, but Katherine couldn't ignore. A sliver dug under her skin like a splinter. Three new bodies in two weeks—all dumped, none staged. Nothing about them fit the profile, but what gnawed at her was the whisper of performance. Like a counterfeit signature scrawled across a blank canvas, someone was imitating the Artist, and badly.

She ducked under the tape in the alley behind a downtown jazz club that reeked of stale beer and cigarettes. The thump of bass through the walls. It didn't belong. The whole atmosphere felt too loud, too desperate. Not him.

Still, she crouched near the victim, her gloved fingers brushing a piece of damp cloth from the woman's cheek. The angle was wrong. The eyes weren't even open. Sloppy. Soulless.

Katherine stood, heart heavy but her mind still sharp. There had been a letter—folded beneath her windshield wiper when she left the precinct last night.

"Not every echo is mine, Katie. But I'm searching. You'll know her when you see her. The true 18. She'll shine like bone in moonlight. Patience. Signed, The Artist.

Katherine folded the paper slowly, fingers tight. He was rewriting the script again. Making sure she knew—he still controlled the silence between the bodies.

Fracture Point

Katherine

The photos wouldn't stop screaming.

She flipped through them again on the precinct tablet, fingers stiff with tension. Brick alley. Cement slab. No ligature. No poetry. Just a body dumped like garbage behind a jazz club that hadn't seen real jazz since 2006.

It wasn't him. She knew it. But she couldn't stop chasing the echo.

"Looks like your guy," Brandon said, hands on hips, standing behind her in the conference room. "Bride-to-be, ring finger gone, white ribbon in her hair—your checklist."

Katherine didn't look up. Her eyes traced the image of the woman's face—closed eyes, slack jaw, no staging. No intention. A signature without the pen.

"Wouldn't make it past the first round in his gallery," she muttered.

Brandon sighed. "Kat..."

The use of her name burned. Everyone called her Poe. He only used 'Kat' when she was fraying.

"I'm going," she said, already pulling her keys from her pocket. "There's something off. I need to see it again."

You already saw it. Twice."

"Not alone."

He didn't argue. Just watched her like she might shatter before she reached the door.

Outside, the rain was that fine, needling kind that didn't fall so much as cling. She drove for hours without turning on the radio, her mind looping the photos, the letter, the victims.

The copycat was noise.

But the Artist was silence. Purposeful. Surgical. He left symbols like teeth marks on her mind. He was *still out there*, and she'd wasted two days chasing a fake. She hated herself for letting the false trail sink its claws in her.

And the worst part?

He knew.

He'd left her that letter because he knew she'd fall for the decoy. Because he could see her unraveling.

She took the next exit. Cheap motels. One blinking sign. She didn't even check the price.

She just needed to be alone.

Needed to *feel* again.

You ever feel like the killer's laughing while you chase his shadow?

The motel smelled like bleach and old grief. She didn't bother turning on the overhead light. Just the cracked lamp by the sink, its flicker like a pulse about to fail. The buzzing filled the room like static in her head.

She hadn't spoken to anyone in two days—not properly. Not unless you counted Brandon's text that just said, *Anything?* and her thumb hovered over *No* so long the screen dimmed.

She peeled off the blazer, arms shaking from too much caffeine and not enough food, and let it slump to the carpet like a second skin. Her chest felt hollow. Not empty. Excavated. As if something had clawed its way out and left a vacancy behind.

The case files were already spread across the bed, curling at the edges from the humidity. She didn't remember laying them out. She just remembered the letter—*You'll know her when you see her.*

But she didn't. She didn't know anything. She'd crouched over that last body and felt... nothing. A cheap imitation. A bad joke. Her instincts hadn't flinched.

He was mocking her. And she was starting to crack.

She dropped to her knees by the bed and opened the briefcase again. The queen piece shifted in its felt-lined slot.

She picked it up. Solid. Cold. Heavy for its size.

It was black.

Why black?

Did he think she was like him? A shadow piece. Twisted. Ruthless. Made for the endgame, but not the hero.

Her thumb traced the curve of the crown, the narrow point at the top.

Maybe that was the message. Not just that she was playing his game—but that she already belonged to it.

She swallowed hard and set the piece back, throat dry.

The coal scrip rattled beside it. The emerald caught a glint of the buzzing lamp. She didn't look at either.

"What the hell do you want from me?" she whispered.

No answer. Just the radiator groaning behind the wall, the lamp's flicker like static inside her head.

Katherine pressed her palms to her forehead and slid down until she was sitting on the thin motel carpet, surrounded by puzzle pieces she couldn't force to fit.

He was winning. Not because he was smarter, not even because he was faster—but because he made her feel something—rage, obsession, a sickness in her blood—and she didn't know how to bleed it out.

"I'm losing it."

And for the first time—she meant it.

Between the Lines

Katherine

She didn't remember the drive back from the motel. Just the weight of the key in her palm and the quiet of her apartment, too still to feel like safety.

The briefcase was open again. She hadn't meant to reopen it, not tonight. But her fingers had found the latch like muscle memory.

It looked different now.

Not in the contents. Those were the same. But in their arrangement. They didn't feel like evidence anymore.

They felt like offerings.

The chess queen. The emerald. The ribbon. The lock of hair. All hers.

Something that couldn't be soothed by logic or case files. Something that whispered in her sleep and stirred in her gut every time she traced the map with her fingertip.

He wasn't trying to frighten her.

He was trying to connect with her.

And somehow, that made it worse.

She sat cross-legged on the apartment floor, back pressed to the couch, lamp on, wine untouched.

Her fingers hovered above the queen.

It wasn't a threat anymore. It was a mirror.

You think I'm the last piece, she whispered, not knowing if she meant to say it out loud.

The notes had changed since the first victim. Less detached. More intimate. Not gloating, not even poetic. Personal. A man baring teeth without malice. A man who thought this was love.

She picked up the lock of hair, bound with pale blue silk.

She'd never tested it. Never ran DNA.

Not because she forgot. Because she didn't want to know.

Because some part of her—buried, silent—already did.

Her breath hitched in her throat. Her skin prickled in waves.

What kind of man leaves a trail not just of bodies, but of metaphors?

What kind of killer doesn't want to be found... but wants to be understood?

Her thoughts flicked to Devin.

Kind voice. Warm eyes. A way of seeing her without flinching.

Stop it.

She shut it hard enough to make the latch snap. Her pulse thundered in her ears.

No.

Devin wasn't like that. She'd felt safe with him. *Too* safe.

And wasn't that the trap?

She stood abruptly and paced the living room, trying to outwalk the thought. But it trailed behind her like a shadow that hadn't belonged to her in years.

She put the kettle on the stove, placed a tea bag in the mug.

Walking to the window to look out.

There was a knock at the door.

She froze.

Her phone buzzed immediately after.

Devin: *Didn't want to scare you. Just dropping this off. Figured you hadn't eaten. Doorstep.*

She opened the door slowly. A white paper bag sat beneath the flickering hallway light. Inside: A sandwich and a cookie. No note. Just a napkin-plain, white—tucked neatly inside.

It wasn't proof of anything. Just food. Just Devin. But her mind refused to let go of the shadow it had already drawn.

Mouth Too Loud

Katherine

He stank of stale beer and bar smoke, slouched in the chair like the world owed him applause for being clever. Slick blond hair faded leather jacket, a smirk that belonged in a bar fight—not a murder investigation.

He winked at me before I sat down. "You're prettier than I expected, Sweetheart."

I didn't answer. Let the silence stretch until even his drunken confidence started to itch. The mirrored wall behind me caught his reflection—cheap, cracked at the edges.

"Name?" I asked flatly.

"Garrison Laine. And like I told the beat cops—I didn't kill nobody. Just said a few things to stir the room up. It was a joke."

Brandon leaned against the far wall, arms crossed. Watching. Measuring.

I slid a folder onto the table. Let the weight of it speak. "Witnesses say you bragged you knew where the 'Lonely Heart guy' dumps his women. What he cuts off."

That's public," he grinned. "New articles, Reddit threads. Just repeated it for flair. Girls like a little danger."

"Do they like hearing you say you could do better? That their mistakes were too easy?" I flipped the folder open, photos face—down so only I knew which woman stared up at me. "Explain why you say they should've chained the door together."

His smirk faltered.

"You think this is funny?"

"Nah. Just drunk talk." But his voice had thinned, trembling at the edges. "Wasn't me."

Brandon pushed off the wall. "You're not under arrest. Yet. But impersonating a serial offender is enough to hold you while we check every damn word."

The smirk died.

***

I watched him through the glass. Pacing now, his swagger rotting under the lights. A trapped rat.

Brandon joined me, rubbing a tired hand down his jaw. "He's a clown. But he hit too many details too close to home for coincidence."

I nodded slowly. The line about the cigar cutter—he shouldn't have known that. It wasn't in the press.

"No way he guessed it, "I said.

"Unless someone fed it to him." Brandon's voice was steady, but my gut twisted. Either Garrison was the man we'd been chasing—or someone wanted us to waste time chasing him.

"Hold him. Seventy-two hours. Run his name through every dump site log, every rental van, every traffic cam in a hundred miles."

"And if he's clean?"

"Then he still bought himself a stay in hell for playing dress-up with the Devil."

Brandon huffed. "Remind me never to joke around you."

***

The case board hummed behind my eyes. Strings. Faces. Gaps I couldn't fill.

Rebecca's photo stared back—veil still sealed in its packaging when we found her. Like she never even got the chance to unwrap her own future.

"We've had him almost forty-eight hours," Brandon said. "No prints, no fibers, no travel history that lines up."

Cheryl set her mug down with deliberate calm. "He's not our guy."

"He knew about the cutter."

Brandon sighed. "He could've overheard it. Cops talk. Bars leak."

- 248 -

Cheryl's gaze cut sharp. "We're not in the business of locking people up because they're obnoxious and drunk. That's not justice. That's fear."

I snapped my head toward her. "You think I'm doing this out of fear?"

She didn't flinch. "I think you're trying to force clarity out of noise. We all are. But he's a distraction. He wanted to be part of something he didn't earn."

"What if he is part of it?" My voice cracked sharp. "What if he's not the Artist—but he knows him? A cousin, a roommate, someone too close for coincidence?"

Brandon stepped in, pressure valve. "We're not throwing him out. But unless you've got more than a gut, we can't keep him beyond tomorrow."

Rebecca's smile watched me from the board.

The Artist took his time with her. Ritual. Method. Message. Garrison Laine was too loud. Too eager. The Artist never craved attention—he commanded it.

And still, something itched.

"I'm not saying he's the one," I murmured. "But if he's not—I still want to be the one to shut the door behind him."

Moonlight and Sorrow

The Artist

Shadows slice the courtyard in stained-glass shards. From the balcony above, the world moves too fast, too loud. People hurry even when there's nowhere to be.

Tonight, I hunt.

The counterfeits annoyed me—three careless imitations dumped. Someone thought they understood my work. They didn't. They copied the structure without touching the soul. That's the difference between art and forgery.

The chaos has a silver lining. It thins the herd. Makes the genuine shimmer brighter.

I've found her.

Her name is Elise. Bartender on the Lower East Side. Mauve lipstick. Green eyes. A diamond ring that catches every scrap of light. The wrong kind of man gave her that ring. I see it in the way she twists it when she thinks no one's looking.

But I'm looking.

I shadow her home twice, a half-step behind, hidden in New York's midnight noise. She has a pair of sugar gliders—Bernie and Babs. Feeds them before herself. Reads aloud while she cooks. She has dreams. Regrets. She deserves more than this world handed her.

The site already chosen—an abandoned uptown atrium, glass ceiling shattered by storms. I've swept it clean, draped it just so. Eighteen will glow there. The light will catch in her hair like fire and sorrow.

Tomorrow, I'll introduce myself.

Blood and Satin

The Artist

She didn't wake when I lifted her from the van. Her head lolled against my chest, her fingers curled around nothing, breath slow and steady. The paralytic worked gently this time—no violence, no spasm. Just stillness.

The atrium greeted us like an open mouth; silver metallic fabric draped across broken walls. I'd swept the shattered glass into neat piles earlier. The wind whispered through the skeletal steel beams above. Moonlight fell in fractured geometry through the missing panes, creating a lattice of silver over the marble floor.

She belonged here.

The space had waited for her.

I laid her across the pedestal I'd built from mirrored panels and iron. It wasn't meant to be a coffin. It was meant to reflect her—to let her see herself as she became more than flesh. More than memory.

A shiver rippled beneath her skin. I knelt, held her hand.

You're safe, I whispered. You're seen.

Her lashes fluttered.

Awareness.

Good.

I began with the dress—white satin, floor-length, sleeveless. Chosen for how it would contrast with the blood. I slid it onto her slowly, threading her limbs through like a doll being readied for a display window.

Then the incision.

I marked it first—charcoal down the center of her sternum, branching in symmetrical lines like tree roots. A breath. Then the blade. Slow. Precise. No hesitation.

She couldn't scream, but her pupils widened.

Fear bloomed in them.

I breathed it in like incense.

The ring finger came last. It always did. The cigar cutter clicked once—clean, circular, ceremonial. I dropped the finger into the velvet-lined box with the others. Eighteen. Almost complete.

But Elise deserved more than numbers.

I moved her to the suspension frame—black-painted, shaped like a music stand, curving into a neck like a swan. Metal prongs hooked under her shoulder blades, lifting her just off the mirrored platform. Her arms spread outward, palms up, gold thread wiring them into a dancer's-pose.

Lilies traced in ink along her collarbone. Shallow cuts at the hips. Blood spilled slow, staining the gown like wine

Votive candles ringed her body, their flicker scattering dozens of Elises across the ceiling. Dozens of possible lives, hovering, vanishing.

I opened her eyes.

Even glassy, they caught the moonlight.

Even lifeless, they looked at me.

For a moment, I stood still. Watched her watching me. The art complete.

Then I took the envelope from my coat pocket, placed it at her feet.

Katie,

Do you see the difference now? The real from the imitation? This one—she was worthy. I knew you'd come. I felt your breath in the air before you ever arrived.

Only two left. If you find me, you can stop twenty. I want you to try. Truly.

Signed, The Artist.

Kaleidoscope

Katherine

The call came just after 4 a.m. I was already awake. Couldn't sleep.

Again. The apartment was too quiet, the air too still—like the world was waiting for something awful.

When the dispatcher said, "*abandoned atrium, Uptown*," something in me stilled. My stomach dropped like the bottom fell out of me, and I didn't even ask for details. I knew.

It was him.

It had to be.

The others—those half-assed imitations dumped in alleys and loading docks—had been noise. This... this felt deliberate.

The building looked like a collapsed greenhouse from a dream. Broken teeth of glass curled along the roofline, silver fabric choking the support beams, dust curling under the soles of my boots. I ducked under the tape and felt it before I saw it.

That... weight. That electric ache in the back of my skull.

Like I was being watched.

She hung just above the floor, centered perfectly in a ring of candlelight.

Mirrors caught the moonlight and threw it in every direction, bouncing reflections of her—of me—into the cracked ceiling like some kind of grotesque kaleidoscope. The gown shimmered. Blood darkened the hem like deliberate brushstrokes. Her arms were posed, hands turned out like she'd surrendered. Or danced.

I couldn't move for a second.

My lungs worked too hard. My knees buckled too easy.

She had green eyes. Wide. Empty. Still open.

It took me a moment to see the finger. The left ring—gone. But this one—wasn't just a message.

It was a declaration.

He'd staged her not for shock value. Not for press.

He'd staged her... for me.

I crouched down beside the pedestal. A white envelope lay at her feet like an afterthought, but I knew better. I could already feel the dread pooling in my chest.

My gloved fingers slipped the letter free. The paper smelled faintly like pine and ink.

Katie,

Do you see the difference now? The real from the imitation? This one—she was worthy. I knew you'd come. I felt your breath in the air before you ever arrived.

Only two left. If you find me, you can stop twenty. I want you to try. Truly.

Signed,
The Artist.

I stood so fast I felt dizzy.

He was here. Or had been.

My eyes scanned the broken glass overhead, the catwalks, the vines. Every instinct screamed he was watching me even now.

The Artist. Eighteen kills. And he was inviting me to the finale.

Two left.

Unless I could stop him.

I looked back at her—She had a name. She'd had a life. But now she was... this.

And I was running out of time.

Cold Angles

Katherine

The conference room reeked of scorched coffee, damp wool, and stale adrenaline.

Katherine sat at the table, her hand bracing her jaw, her eyes still haunted by the victim's face—*that open eye*, locked in her mind.

Brandon broke the silence, voice steady and no-nonsense. "ID came through. Elise Romano, twenty-seven, engaged to Anthony Marcellano, Jr. Nephew of 'Uncle Vito.'" The name hit like smoke. The Marcellano family controlled half the underground in Manhattan.

Cheryl leaned forward, sharper, the edge in her tone deliberate. "She's strung up like this, they'll want blood."

Kali added clinically, eyes flicking to her notes. "Time of death to discovery: twelve hours. Paralytic, medical grade. No sign of struggle."

Katherine's chest ached. Elise had been posed—exalted. *Gloria in Splendore* embroidered into the dress. "He didn't just stage a kill," she murmured. "He dressed her for transcendence."

Cheryl lifted a swatch of silver thread, light glancing off it. "No prints. No fluids. Nothing to work with."

The door opened without warning. A uniform stepped aside, and the room shifted. Heavy footsteps. The air thickened before Katherine even looked up.

The Marcellano men entered like a storm—dark coats, silence heavy enough to pin everyone to their seats.

Anthony's nephew stopped at the head of the table. His men fanned out, watching. Waiting.

"You have answers?" His voice carried menace under restraint.

Katherine didn't flinch, though her pulse hammered. "You'll have them when I'm ready

The room froze at the audacity of it. But the words cut clean, leaving no space for challenge.

They filed out, the silence they left behind colder than before.

Katherine exhaled, her mind already sharpening. Elise's green eyes wouldn't release her.

She would uncover the truth. His truth. The one Elise had died carrying.

Pattern Recognition

Katherine

The precinct had the dull buzz of too many monitors and not enough answers.

Katherine stood at the whiteboard, arms folded, the tip of a red marker resting against her bottom lip. Across from her, Elise's photo stared back. *Suspended. Sacred. Eighteen.* It had been twenty-three days since they found her. Long enough for bruises to yellow. Long enough for grief to lose its edge. But not long enough to shake the sense that she was being watched.

She could still smell the candle wax if she tried hard enough. Still feel the ghost of the letter in her pocket.

And sometimes—when the room was too quiet—she thought she smelled the ink again. Sharp. Pine-sweet. It wasn't there, not really. But it clung too long, like breath on the back of her neck. Like memory refusing to fade.

Okay, she murmured, dragging the marker down in a swift motion. *Let's try it again.*

Cheryl straightened in her chair. Brandon exhaled slowly from the window where he'd been pacing. Kali clicked her pen without using it.

"Elise wasn't just a reset," Katherine continued. "She was a reclamation. The posing, the candle ring, the Latin embroidered into the gown—it wasn't for the press. It wasn't for the city. It was for me."

"But why now?" Cheryl asked. "Why come back after a lull and go bigger? Cleaner?"

"Spotlight theft. Those fakes. He's correcting the record." Brandon answered, nodding toward the board where mock crime scene photos had been pinned. The fakes. The failures.

Katherine circled a section of Elise's photo. The thread-work in the gown shimmered even under the glare of the overhead fluorescents. "He wanted to transcend the noise. Elise was his masterpiece."

Her phone buzzed in her pocket. The captain's name lit the screen.

She answered, his voice already tight. "Heads-up—this case just got political. Elise's fiancé is 'Uncle Vito's nephew.'"

Katherine's pulse skipped. They were already aware.

"The uncle's making calls," the captain continued. "Wants a meeting. If we can't find who did this, he will. And trust me, you don't want him finding the guy first."

"Understood," she said, hanging up before anyone in the room could read her face.

Maybe she did want them to find him first, take him off the board for her, save the last two women.

Cheryl crossed her arms. "So, we just sit here with our thumbs up our asses until he feels like showing off again?"

"No," Katherine said. "He won't vanish this time. He's building momentum. And he wants me to see it."

The silence that followed was less awkward now. Familiar. Worn in like an old sweater.

"So where does he go next?" Kali finally asked.

Katherine didn't answer right away. Her gaze drifted across the wall of photos—the map of sites, the evolution of staging. Glenna, Nicole, Rebecca, Elise. One curve of the spiral feeding the next. Each more refined.

"It won't be public," she said finally. "Not next time. Elise was spectacle. Now he wants intimacy. Control. A setting that isolates."

Brandon tilted his head. "He's drawing her in. You."

Katherine nodded once. "He always has been."

She tapped the board twice. "Pull all missing persons from the past two weeks, radius sixty miles. Focus on engaged women under thirty-five. I want eyes on, gown tailors, and anyone who's recently purchased wrought iron."

She left the room before they could ask more.

At the end of the hall, she paused, forehead resting against cool drywall.

She typed a message to Devin:

Dinner tonight, 7? Her finger hovered. The silence pressed back. Then she hit send.

Where the Guard Slips

Katherine

The warmth of Devin's apartment was the first thing she noticed—not the temperature, but the feel of it. Real.

The low light from the lamp on the side table spilled amber across the wood floors, catching her breath in her throat for a moment.

She toed off her boots, curling her toes against the rug as he took her coat. He didn't say anything at first—just looked at her like she was something fragile and permanent all at once.

"Wine?" he asked.

"God, yes," she muttered, leaning into the kitchen doorway while he poured. She let herself relax into the doorway frame, watching the quiet rhythm of him. No theatrics. No masks. Just him. She realized she knew the layout of his apartment now. Where he kept the mugs. The drawer that stuck when you pulled too hard. How his record player needed a nudge to start.

A subtle intimacy built not in declarations but in repetition.

She took the glass from his hand, their fingers brushing longer than necessary. She didn't pull away.

The couch was low and soft, and she folded herself into the corner of it while he put on one of his favorite albums—old jazz, the kind with rough edges. Nothing curated. She liked that. It didn't feel like he was trying to impress her. He was just letting her in.

They sat for a while, not needing words. The silence didn't press. It soothed. Her head drifted to his shoulder slowly, like muscle memory finally catching up to where her thoughts had already gone.

"You always get this quiet when you're here," he said, voice low.

"That a bad thing?" she asked, without moving.

"No. I think it's the best version of you."

That caught her off guard. She shifted just enough to look at him.

"What version do you get?" she asked.

He didn't blink. "The one that lets herself rest."

Her throat went tight. She set the glass down.

He leaned in to kiss her, it wasn't sudden. It was slow, like a page turning. He stayed close enough to register what he wanted and let her choose. It was earned. She leaned in without resistance, her hands curling in his shirt, his palm finding the back of her neck.

It didn't feel like a rush. It felt like landing.

They moved together with a quiet urgency, not the kind born of desperation but of recognition. She trusted him. Enough to let him see the cracks. Enough to breathe against his mouth instead of bracing for impact.

She lay on his chest, his breath rising under her cheek, and let him press his mouth to her shoulder—warmth and rhythm syncing in a way that felt inevitable. But for a blink—just one—she wondered how many shadows a man like him could hide in. Then she buried it.

"You ever think about disappearing?" she asked into the hush.

"Every day. But only if I could take you with me."

She laughed softly, eyes closing. "You barely know me."

"I know enough. I know you stay when things get ugly. That you carry more weight than most men could lift. And that you don't let anyone hold you unless you mean it."

She didn't answer. She just listened to his heartbeat and let the warmth settle deep in her chest.

It scared her, how safe he felt.

But she didn't pull back. Not from his breath, not from the warmth pressed into her bones.

Tension Points

Katherine

A month had passed since the atrium. Too long.

The silence felt weaponized—he was either quiet or hunting.

Katherine stood in the textile district warehouse; fingers tracing the moon-reactive fabric beneath fluorescent light. It shimmered faintly—silver laced with frost. The exact blend found on Elise. Cheryl had confirmed it. A cold shiver ran down her spine and embedded itself, he touched it too.

Brandon circled old shipping logs beside her. "You'd think for a guy who treats murder like an art form, he'd leave a prettier paper trail."

"He doesn't leave trails," Katherine said. "Only brushstrokes."

Cheryl's voice crackled through Katherine's phone. "Ran the name—no Dorian Nash. Fictional or borrowed."

Katherine pinched the bridge of her nose. "Keep looking."

"Dorian means gift," Cheryl added.

Her phone buzzed again—this time, not from Cheryl.

Devin:
Still alive?
If you're buried under case files, blink twice.

She smiled faintly and typed with one hand.

Katherine:
Very much buried. Probably decomposing.
Rain check on that dinner.

Devin:
If I get the next dance. You still owe me one.

Katherine:
Do I?
Devin:
It's in the fine print. Page four, section two. Love interest gets one spontaneous moment of levity per homicide lull.

Katherine didn't realize she was smiling until Brandon gave her a look.

"What?" she asked.

"You get weirdly happy when you're texting."

"Shut up."

"Tell your boyfriend hi."

"He's not—"

Brandon held up a hand. "Spare me the denial. I've seen your *non-boyfriend* grin."

Katherine shoved her phone into her pocket, ears warm. "Back to murder."

He tapped the paper again. "This seamstress says he requested the fabric specifically for moonlight photography. Said it needed to reflect in a way 'that transcended dimension.' His words."

"Ritualistic again," she said. "But this time, he's building a theme. Like a composer nearing his final movement."

"Means we're running out of time."

Katherine nodded slowly. "We've always been."

Her phone rang—Devin's name lit the screen. She let it vibrate once. Twice.

"Take it," Brandon said. "We'll finish cataloging. Go play normal for a second."

She hesitated, then stepped outside into the cold light of late afternoon and answered.

"Hey," she said.

"You sound tired," he replied softly.

"Am tired."

"Then just listen," he said, and there was something in his voice that warmed her all the way through. "When you're done chasing shadows and translating corpses, come home. I made pasta. Not great pasta, but edible. And I'll save you the crusty part of the bread because you pretend to hate it but always steal it anyway."

She leaned against the brick wall, eyes fluttering closed.

"That sounds unfairly thoughtful."

He made it sound easy, like normal life was waiting right outside the crime scene tape. A dinner table. A crust of bread. But ease was a stranger to her now, and strangers always came with sharp edges.

"Come let me be unfair," he said.

She nodded into the quiet.

"Okay," she whispered, knowing full well the word meant surrender—to the warmth, to the quiet, to him.

A Place for Her

Katherine

Katherine stood in Devin's office, caught off guard by the quiet. The building buzzed with city life, but inside, everything moved slower, softer. She hadn't expected it to feel like this, as if he had planned it for days.

Devin's office was a blend of clean lines and personal touches—walnut bookshelves filled with both law books and true crime novels, a photo of his niece on his desk. He handed her coffee, adding cream without asking.

They sat in comfortable silence, the kind that didn't demand anything.

"So, this is where the magic happens?"

"If you count tax law and estate litigation, sure," he said with a grin.

Katherine laughed. "You'd clearly never seen an evidence locker."

Devin moved closer, not crowding her. "I wanted you to see this part of my life. It's mine. I wanted you to know there's space for you in it."

Her heart tightened. "I'm not good at this. The letting-someone-in-part."

"I know," he said, his voice steady. "I'm not in a rush. I just like being in the orbit."

Katherine turned to him. "I'm still sorting through a lot. No timeline."

Devin leaned in, brushed a strand of hair behind her ear. "I'm not keeping the dark out. I'm holding the light."

It was the kind of thing a man in her nightmares would say—soft, steady, convincing. For a breath, she hated that she wanted to believe him

She kissed him slowly, deeply—letting the quiet between them be enough. When they pulled apart, breathless, he whispered, "Stay awhile."

And for the first time in weeks, the thought of staying didn't feel like a compromise. It felt like the beginning of something real.

Splinters

Katherine

The precinct was quieter after 10. The kind of quiet that left room for everything you didn't want to think about.

Katherine stood in front of the old evidence shelves, her badge clipped to her waistband, sweater sleeves pushed up, hair twisted into a loose knot. The fluorescent light overhead buzzed faintly, casting uneven shadows against cardboard lids worn soft at the edges.

These weren't the current boxes. These were the ones from West Virginia. New York. Pre-briefcase. Pre-Devin.

She didn't know what she was looking for.

Only that she hadn't looked hard enough before.

Her fingers hovered, then landed on the label: **Zara Benítez**.

Victim Thirteen.

She slid the box free with a grunt. It was heavier than she remembered. She brought it to the evidence table, flipped the lid. Documentation. Photos. Inventory sheets. A small Ziplock bag containing lace fragments. Another with a bent silver fastener— jewelry? Or costume hardware?

Zara had been found in her own Midtown penthouse; the floor arranged like a bridal showroom. Dozens of veil replicas— identical, sheer, hand-hemmed. He'd replaced her entire wardrobe. Undetected. Untraceable. Cameras had caught nothing.

But something had always bothered her.

She flipped through the veil fragments again, then paused.

There—beneath the corner of a fabric sample, something else: a translucent envelope she didn't remember logging.

Inside, a small object. Taped. Categorized, but unremarkable at first glance.

She peeled it open.

A tiny, opalescent bead. Not a pearl. Not glass. Something older. Handmade.

Katherine blinked hard, scanning the evidence tag.

Recovered near window track — secondary bedroom closet. Not part of original gown or veil samples.

It wasn't decorative.

It looked like a seamstress's pinhead. But why would it be opalescent? She pulled out her phone and checked her notes from **Joelle Cunningham**—Victim Fourteen.

Displayed under the blue whale at the Natural History Museum. Her gown shimmered green under the exit signs.

Joelle had no surviving family, no dress history they could verify.

But one line in the autopsy notes caught Katherine now in a way it hadn't before:

"Faint silvery residue detected on upper back near zipper line— non-metallic, iridescent, moon-reactive under blacklight."

She sat down hard.

It couldn't be coincidence.

The killer hadn't just posed them.

He'd dressed them.

With intention. With symbolism.

And if this pin belonged to him—or his process—it had made it from Zara's penthouse **to** Joelle's cathedral. From private to public. From veil to whale. Seam work and staging bleeding together.

Katherine rubbed the edge of the bead between gloved fingers. Her pulse was rising again, slow but sharp.

No names.

No witnesses.

But the thread was tightening.

And she was beginning to feel the splinters catch beneath her skin.

A Future She Almost Had

Katherine

The blanket had slipped halfway down her legs, but she was too warm to care. Devin's fingers traced idle circles on her bare shoulder, his breath even against her neck.

Outside, the city sighed—late buses, distant sirens, the occasional echo of a dog barking three floors below. But up here, everything had gone still.

Katherine stared at the ceiling, skin flushed, pulse slower now but still threaded with disbelief. She hadn't meant to stay the night. Not really. Nothing happened but cuddling and kissing. But somewhere between the bottle of red wine and the second time she laughed hard enough to forget her own name, it just... happened. Naturally. Like gravity.

"You're quiet," he said, voice low, words resting on her collarbone.

"I'm not used to this," she murmured.

He kissed the edge of her jaw. "To what?"

"Being calm," she admitted. "Being here. With someone."

Devin pulled her closer. His chest was warm against her back, and she hated how safe it felt. No—she didn't hate it. She feared it. There was a difference.

"What if I mess it up?" she asked before she could stop herself.

"You won't," he said simply. "And if you do, I'll be here when you realize you didn't."

She almost laughed. "You sound like you've rehearsed that."

"I have," he said. "For you."

She turned then, eyes meeting his in the dim light. A quiet war inside her she didn't want to name.

"I talked to my mom today," she said.

His brows lifted. "Yeah?"

"They want to drive up in a couple weeks. I told them or we come down there... maybe they could meet you."

Devin blinked once. "Really?"

She nodded, feeling foolish and giddy all at once. "It's not a big thing. Just dinner. Or brunch. Something low-key. I thought maybe we could drive down, just for a night or two."

His face broke into a slow, unguarded smile. "Katherine Poe, are you introducing me to your parents?"

She rolled her eyes but couldn't stop smiling. "Don't make it weird."

"I'm honored," he said, then kissed her like the promise meant something.

And for a second—just a second—she let herself believe in it. In this. The warmth of his hands. The rhythm of their bodies. The fragile peace blooming in her chest.

She didn't think about the case. Or the briefcase. Or the fact that her instinct had started whispering again, beneath the surface.

Not tonight.

Tonight was for the version of her life where she wasn't being hunted. Where he wasn't a shadow.

Tonight was for possibility.

She fell asleep with his hand in hers, the ghost of a smile still playing at her mouth. And outside, the moon shifted over the city like it had always been watching.

A Quiet Between

Katherine

The rain had stopped hours ago, but the city still held its breath. Pavement shimmered with the memory of water, steam curling from manholes like ghosts reluctant to rise. Katherine walked home instead of taking the train—coat open, hair in a knot that had half-unraveled by the second block. Her boots kept rhythm with her thoughts. Slow. Echoing. Uneven.

It had been nearly two months since Elise.

Since the suspended dancer, the cathedral stillness, the cruel elegance of that staging.

But Elise hadn't left her. Not really. The image of her body—midair, transcendent—was stitched behind Katherine's eyes like a second retina. She could still feel the latex pinching her wrists, the mechanical hum of the display turning behind her. None of it faded. It just grew quieter. Slicker. Like oil beneath the skin.

She could still feel Devin's hand in hers.

Not in a haunting way.

Not yet.

Her phone buzzed in her pocket. She didn't check it right away. She already knew.

Devin.

Earlier, he'd called to describe the shape of a cloud drifting outside his office window—said it looked like a sleeping dragon, all winged and smoky. She'd laughed. Let the sound fall into that hollowed-out place inside her where things still sometimes lived.

Now, the message was probably something small. A soft check-in. Maybe a photo of the soup he over-salted with a caption like "Needs you to fix it." He didn't know about the new lead Cheryl found. Or how Katherine had spent the afternoon combing through surveillance footage that blurred after minute four like a memory refusing to stay honest.

He didn't know that the whispering had started again.

Not the killer's. Not exactly.

Her own.

The kind that stirred in the hours before sleep. The kind that made her wonder how long she could keep touching two worlds—one warm, one wretched—without one of them slipping.

She keyed into her building. Took the stairs. Fifth floor. No hesitation. She used to think about what might be waiting behind her door—something unfinished, something sharp—but not tonight. Tonight, there was only stillness.

No television. No music. Just the fridge hum and the long breath of the radiator.

Her phone buzzed again.

Devin:

Still thinking about last night. Hope today wasn't too brutal. Call if you want. Or come over. I'll make tea. Or grilled cheese. Or both. You don't even have to talk.

A soft breath left her—half a laugh, half something else she didn't want to name.

She didn't reply. Not yet.

She turned on the faucet and let the cold water run as she rinsed her hands.

She pressed her palms into the towel, grounding herself in the texture, the normalcy.

Just movement. Just breath. Just enough to stay whole.

Then:

Katherine:

Thanks. I'm okay. Just need quiet tonight. You're sweet.

The dots bounced.

Stopped.

No reply.

She stood at the sink a while longer, phone screen dimming against her palm. He'd wait, and he'd mean it. She loved that about him.

But something in her had begun to shift.

Not a break. Not yet.

Just a splinter.

She curled up on the couch. Blanket up to her knees.

Her phone buzzed once more.

Devin:

Sleep well, Poe. Dream light things.

She whispered into the dark, "I can't."

Faultline

Katherine

The cursor blinked beside an unfinished sentence, daring her to finish it. Katherine didn't move.

The case report should have been done hours ago. The forensics summary, the surveillance log, even just the bullet-point notes she'd promised Cheryl.

She closed the laptop instead.

It wasn't fatigue. She'd had worse nights—longer stretches without sleep, darker cases. But this one was different.

No new victim in nearly three months. The lull should've felt like a gift. A breath. A reprieve. But instead, it felt like a trap with velvet teeth. Quiet enough to make her forget the danger. Still enough to make her start believing in the life she almost had.

She reached for her phone.

Devin's name sat at the top of her messages. No new text tonight. Just the thread from the night before—him asking about her favorite childhood food. She'd told him about her dad's potato soup. He'd promised to try making it. Even asked if her mom would give him the recipe. She hadn't replied yet. Couldn't.

A month ago, she would have smiled. Typed something back immediately. Teased him for being bold. Now her fingers hovered and stilled.

Because she knew what was happening.

She was letting herself soften. And soft things broke.

Their time together had taken shape—quiet evenings, inside jokes, his ridiculous impressions of forensic techs that made her snort water through her nose. They'd built something quiet, steady, uncomplicated. And for a little while, it had felt real. Solid enough to rest in.

But now?

She was checking her phone instead of reviewing blood spatter timelines. Skipping lab reviews to meet him for lunch. Hearing his voice in her head instead of the killer's.

And that scared her more than anything.

Because she couldn't afford to forget. Not even for a second. The moment she started imagining herself in this life—this warm, breath-slowing, monster less bubble—was the moment she stopped being sharp enough to hunt the thing that waited on the other side of the silence.

She crossed to the window. New York throbbed below. Not noisy, but alive in that way cities never stopped being. A honk. A siren. Someone yelling in Spanish two blocks away. It grounded her more than Devin's arms ever could.

She hadn't put her all into this. Not really.

The briefcase still sat unopened on her desk. She told herself she was waiting for something—clarity, a lead, the right frame of mind. But maybe she wasn't opening it because some part of her didn't want to. Because once she did, the clock would restart. The chase would pick up again. The next girl would have a name.

Maybe she'd rather just… stay here a little longer. In this stillness.

Her reflection in the window looked back at her—faded, tired, caught between two versions of herself. One wanted to go to bed and wake up next to Devin, laughing about burnt toast and chasing nothing more dangerous than a coffee date. The other remembered blood patterns and missing ring fingers. Remembered what it meant to be haunted.

She let her forehead rest against the glass.

I can't have both.

And she was right.

It wouldn't be sudden. It never was. But she could already feel herself starting to pull away. Answering texts a little slower. Canceling a lunch. She told herself she was protecting him. That this was what distance looked like. What survival required.

Like taking an eraser to a life, she'd started sketching in pencil, not ink.

Her phone buzzed. A new message.
Devin:
Soup came out edible. But missing one thing.
You.
Her eyes closed, she didn't reply.

The Softest Sabotage

Katherine

The precinct was quieter at night. Or maybe she was just louder inside.

Katherine stood at the murder board alone, arms crossed, breath shallow. The overhead fluorescents buzzed with the kind of fluorescent fatigue that settled into the bones. Paper edges curled slightly from the humidity of breath and time. She didn't remember pinning Elise's photo that high. Or maybe someone else had.

She stared at Elise's image like it might blink. Like if she looked long enough, the answers would unfurl in reverse—moon-thread unwinding, vines, body lifting back into warmth.

But the photos stayed still. Silent. Devastating.

A scribbled margin note caught her eye—her own handwriting, looping and rushed. Something about trace elements in the glove lining. She didn't remember writing it. When had she last taken real notes? Thorough ones? When had she last stared down evidence instead of... floating above it?

The realization came quiet.

She wasn't all the way in anymore.

Not like before.

Not like when her only compass was rage and the thrill of deduction. Now her thoughts wandered. Fractured. Skimmed the surface of memory, then slipped away into things that weren't part of the job.

Like the way Devin's voice dropped when he said her name.

The way his apartment always smelled faintly of bergamot and old wood.

The way he tucked a hand behind her neck when she didn't even realize she needed steadying.

She had let herself build a soft place.

And now it was getting in the way.

Her pulse skittered. She didn't move.

This wasn't distraction.

This was a fracture.

A war between the version of herself that hunted monsters and the one who had begun to believe she could build something with a man who might never know what she'd really survived.

She turned to her desk, opened the laptop again. Should've followed up on the seamstress lead instead of texting Devin photos of snow-covered rooftops and asking if he'd ever seen the Hudson freeze.

The guilt curdled slow.

She tried to click into the trace lab reports but her eyes wouldn't hold. Her hand moved instead to her phone, flicking to messages, rereading old ones. She was so far from the hunt she couldn't even pretend she hadn't drifted.

And still—

She missed him.

She missed him right now.

Her throat ached with it.

She opened a new file. Tried to draft an internal memo. The screen stayed blank.

Then, quietly, she closed the laptop.

Locked her drawer.

Shut off the desk lamp.

Walked out.

Her phone vibrated in her coat.

Devin:

Still up? Was thinking about you. No pressure. Just… miss you.

She stared at the screen.

Didn't answer.

Not because she didn't want to.

Because she *did*.

And that was the problem.

Katherine slid her phone into her pocket and started walking. Not toward the train. Not toward Devin.

Home. Alone.

The wind turned. She didn't pull up her collar.

Didn't slow down.

The cold helped.

She needed to remember what it felt like to chase shadows again.

Because the only thing worse than letting her guard down—

Was doing it while a killer was still watching.

Alone With the Noise

Katherine

She stared at the shower tile until her fingertips wrinkled. The heat had long since bled from the water, but she didn't move. Arms curled tight around her knees, head bowed beneath the stream like confession. Her breath fogged in short bursts against the glass. She hadn't meant to sit down. Just meant to rinse off the day. To scrub the scent of formaldehyde and grief from her skin. But the weight hadn't lifted.

Not with the water.

Not with the steam.

Not with the silence.

By the time she stood, her body was trembling. Not from fear. From something deeper. She dried off without thinking, avoiding the mirror entirely. She couldn't look herself in the eye tonight—not after what she'd seen in that atrium. Not after what had been staged so clearly for her.

Nineteen were gone.

No.

Eighteen.

Just eighteen.

Which meant there was still one left.

She dressed in a fog, throwing on an old tee shirt, no bra, no socks, just layers against the cold she couldn't shake. The apartment lights stayed off. Too much brightness felt obscene. Instead, she walked to the window and stared out over the city—fog curling between the buildings like smoke from a slow-burning fire.

Her phone buzzed on the counter.

She didn't move.

The name lit the screen.

Devin.

She didn't answer.

She already knew before this she was pulling away.

Not because she didn't want to. But because it felt wrong now. All of it. He'd been kind. Present. His warmth had felt safe for a moment—a breath of air when she was drowning. But that moment was over. She couldn't hold both things. Couldn't chase death and still expect to be held in life.

She picked up the phone and typed a message slowly, her thumb hovering before pressing send:

I'm sorry. I'm not in a place for anything real right now. Please don't wait for me.

The message marked *read* Nothing came back.

She turned her phone face down and leaned her forehead against the cool glass. Somewhere out there, another girl was laughing. Texting. Living her last free day and not even knowing it.

Katherine's jaw tightened.

She didn't know who the next one was. Not yet. But she would. She had to.

Because there was still one left.

Just one.

And the one she was given a chance to save.

And she was running out of time.

"You're already watching her, aren't you?"

What He Couldn't See

She didn't know yet.

But she was already mine.

I watched her for eleven days—not like a man waiting for a bus, but like a composer shaping the final crescendo of a requiem. Every subtle beat mattered. The way exhaustion flickered in her eyes. The way exhaustion flickered in her eyes. The practiced exhale that masked everything she tried to bury. She moved with fatigue carved deep beneath her skin, a quiet armor forged by a world that had long stopped offering softness.

Juliette wasn't meant to be adored.

Not like Elise.

Not like Katherine.

She was meant to be remembered.

A nurse, twenty-six, a bride-to-be wearing tiredness like a second uniform, draped over faded scrubs that never quite hid the lines beneath her eyes. Needed, but never chosen. Her beauty was effortless but unpolished—chocolate hair tangled from long shift, seafoam eyes that rarely lifted to meet the world. Most men didn't see it. She carried herself like a ghost who'd stopped asking to be noticed. But I did. I had to.

Her fiancé—Brian—appeared like clockwork, twice a week, but never truly present. A shadow beside her, kissing cheeks but not mouths, bringing food but never sharing a table. She loved him because he was safe. Steady. Predictable. A shield against loneliness, dull but reliable. And that was love enough—for her.

She didn't see me.

How could she, when even the man she'd agreed to marry couldn't remember her face?

She thought herself invisible. That's why her blinds stayed cracked just enough to let the city watch but never enter. Why her keys swung lazily, not clenched tight. Why her notebook was tucked into her coat, filled with poems and fragments, traced again in fading ink on her wrist by morning.

"I think I'd be beautiful if someone looked at me long enough."

I did.

Not for sparkling or shining. But for surviving. For enduring the invisible wounds. For showing up every damn day in a world that tried to erase her light. For loving when love felt like a broken promise. That was hers. That was mine.

***

She'd just finished a double.

I could tell by the way she moved—slower than usual, but still upright, still fighting the weight in her bones. Nurses were like that. Resilient until collapse. Quiet steel.

Juliette slipped out through the staff corridor, the one tucked behind the maintenance bay. Most didn't know it existed. But I did. I knew the ten-foot gap in security feed between the generator housing and the waste dock. I knew the vent rattle that masked footfalls. I knew the rotation of the cameras. Every blind spot. Every pause in motion. Every silence.

She adjusted her tote on her left shoulder—always left. Keys curled between her knuckles. A bottle of electrolyte water pressed to her chest. The bandage on her finger was fresh. Her body bore that exhaustion only healers carried.

And she had no idea her own would come next.

Her hair was damp at the nape; the scent of hospital soap clung to her like breath on glass. A single curl had slipped loose and brushed the corner of her mouth.

She didn't hear the footsteps.

Or the whisper of gloves.

Or the sound of the safety cap sliding free from the syringe.

She only flinched when I touched her.

Just once.

Instinctive.

A hand at her back, steady. And then—paralysis.

Her breath caught. Her shoulders locked. Her muscles went rigid. Her weight fell against my chest like confession.

Not a scream.

Not a fight.

Just…surrender.

I eased her down before she could crumple. One arm beneath her knees. One behind her shoulders. Her head lolled against my collar.

I've got you, I whispered.

And she believed me.

Not because I earned it.

Because she needed to.

Her eyes fluttered once. Just once. And then the last of her resistance drifted out with the breath she didn't even know she was holding.

That was the part I savored.

Not the stillness.

Not the certainty.

The trust.

It was the most honest thing I would ever take from her.

Galaxies Don't Scream

The Artist

The planetarium was my sanctum.

Not for its shape, but for what it held—silence.

No music this time. No whispered lullabies. No borrowed melodies to chase ghosts through the dark. Juliette didn't need a song to carry her. She needed stillness. Reverence.

She was already extraordinary.

I had prepared this space for her alone. The dome's shattered glass let in starlight that bent wrong at the edges. My projectors were ready. They pulsed faintly in the dark like machines waiting to breathe. And at the center, beneath the mechanical oculus I had reconstructed from fractured telescope mounts, stood the altar.

I laid her on silk.

Not bridal white. Not funeral black. But indigo—deep and endless. The color between sleep and death. I dressed her in midnight. Not a gown. A canvas. Sleeveless. Flowing. Bare-backed. Not to expose her—but to honor her spine, the strongest part of her. It curved gently now across the satin, her limbs resting with the ease she never had in life.

Her skin held the faint scent of antiseptic and lavender. Her nails painted black, her ring shifted to her thumb—a vow she never got to speak.

I did not pose her like the others.

No suspension.

No turning stage.

Instead, she remained grounded. Rooted. Reclined like a painting from another century. One arm folded beneath her ribs. One hand curled against her chest. Her legs bent slightly to one side, like a woman who had once fallen asleep reading and had never stirred again.

Her lips still curved faintly, like the ghost of the laugh she tried to hide in her sleeve two nights before.

Her eyes—I left closed.

Not in shame. But in peace.

Above her, constellations bloomed. The projector spun a slow arc of stars across the dome, and I tuned it carefully, so when the light touched her face, it kissed only her jawline, not her eyelids. *Cassiopeia reached down like a hand. Ursa Minor curled beneath her knee.*

She did not become the sky. She completed it.

At her feet, I placed the letter. Folded. Clean. No blood. Only ink, steady and intentional.

Katie—You always thought the quiet was safety. But silence is where the loudest truths live. Only one left. Come see her. Come hear her.

—Yours.

I lit only three candles. No circle. No theatrics. Just a triangle at her head and feet, to hold her in place. To bless the shape of her rest. The shadows they cast did not distort her. They honored her edges. They made her more real.

And in her palm—I left no artifact.

Only her own photograph. Folded. Worn.

A candid one, captured on her stoop two nights before. Barefaced. Laughing into the crook of her arm. The kind of image no one else would frame.

The room held steady. No sounds but the hum of circuitry and the soft flicker of flame. I knelt beside her and pressed my forehead briefly to the floor, not in prayer, but in gratitude. This wasn't about power.

This was about *remembrance*.

I placed the letter at the foot of her silk-draped bench. Folded. Clean. It bore no blood, no stains. Just ink. Steady. Intentional.

I stood once more and took a final breath before exiting through the broken side door. The stars still moved when I looked back. But Juliette did not.

And for once, that felt right.

Silence Where Her Name Should Have Been

Katherine

The building was already open when she arrived.

No forced entry. No sirens. Just a pin dropped through an untraceable text hours before dawn, sent to her personal phone.

You'll want to see her this way. Alone.

Katherine didn't wait for backup. Again.

She knew the story she'd have to tell later—contamination risk, timeliness, protocol.

But the truth lived deeper. Beneath the bones.

She had to see the girl before the world did. Before the noise came crashing back in.

The planetarium hunched against the skyline, its fractured glass dome rising against the pale gray of morning. For a moment, Katherine hesitated outside. The quiet unnerved her. Fog curled at her boots, reluctant to rise.

Inside, concrete echoed beneath her steps.

No smell of blood. No decay. Only dust. The faintest trace of lavender.

And then—Juliette.

Not suspended. Not staged.

Resting.

She lay across an indigo silk bench, back arched gently, hands drawn close to her chest, as if asleep with a secret pressed behind her ribs. No blood. No violence.

Overhead, stars wheeled in reverent slow arcs—projected, not real. The dome breathed light across her stillness, and for a moment Katherine forgot crime.

This wasn't a scene.

This was a monument.

Beside her, a small wooden plaque rested on a low easel:
Juliette Maynard
She stood tall when no one noticed.
Now she never has to lower her head again.

No taunt. No cruel poetry. This wasn't about Katherine. It was about Juliette.

At her feet—three candles.

In her palm—a photo. Faded. Creased. Juliette laughing bare-faced on her front stoop, the kind of joy no one saves until it's gone.

Katherine's throat tightened. He hadn't displayed her.

He'd honored her.

She knelt, close but untouching. Not because of evidence—because it felt wrong to interrupt something sacred.

For the first time in months, she didn't feel like she'd walked into a crime scene.

She felt like she'd walked into a eulogy.

The stars spun. Juliette did not.

***

The others arrived twenty-three minutes later.

Katherine stood at the base of the dome—shoulders squared, voice low. Brandon didn't speak right away. Neither did Cheryl. They saw her stance. They saw Juliette. They understood.

This wasn't performance.

This was memorial

Cheryl called for forensics. Brandon lifted his camera with slower-than-usual hands. Even Kali, half-gloved, lowered her voice.

Katherine briefed them: no weapon, no rig. Projector on separate power. Bench light—pine maybe. Silk leveled on uneven floor. No blood. No incisions. Just lips faintly creased. Hands curled as though they'd meant to hold something.

Cassiopeia blinked once overhead and went dark.

The evidence sweep.

Dusting the photo.

Prints from candleholders.

Fibers from silk.

Nothing traceable. Nothing that screamed him—until Cheryl spotted it.

Taped beneath the bench.

Vellum. Clean. Waiting.

Katherine's gloves suddenly felt wrong. Too worn, too stained. She peeled them off slowly, one finger at a time, as though something inside her might unravel with them.

"New pair," she murmured.

Fresh latex snapped. Flesh to vellum. She unfolded the letter like skin pulled taut.

Edges straight. No quiver in the script.

He never trembled.

But she did.

Katie—

I didn't take her for you. I gave her back.

Not to him. Not to the world that stopped seeing her.

To the stars. To herself.

One left.

She's already dreaming. You'll have to wake her.

Come quietly. Come soon.

You don't save her by running.

--Yours

P.S. Linus is going to miss her. Someone help him. But Brian won't. He doesn't deserve to know.

Katherine didn't read it aloud. The words sank heavy behind her ribs. One left. She'd known it. Felt it since Elise. Since the briefcase. Since her first blood-glass dream.

But this was different. Not a taunt. Not a threat

This was a final breath. The end of something sacred. Or the beginning of something she wouldn't survive.

Cheryl's voice broke the silence: "He's escalating."

Brandon's shutter clicked. Juliette's profile softened under projected stars, the ring glimmering wrong on her thumb.

"She looks peaceful," he whispered.

Katherine swallowed. "He made her that way."

The silence held longer than it should have.

Then she handed the letter to evidence and tilted her face toward the dome.

Not a sky. Just like on glass.

And still—it felt like something was watching.

The Quietest Ones

Katherine

Juliette hadn't been reported missing.

There was no file. No flag in the system. No alert quietly circulating beneath the surface.

But they had a name.

It had been carved into a wooden plaque beside her body, beneath a velvet dusk sky inside a planetarium turned mausoleum. Juliette Maynard.

Katherine wrote it on the board herself, in red marker, letters slightly slanted, just like the ones left on the bench. She circled it three times.

Brandon brought in coffee without asking. No one said much. They all felt it—the way this one had been different. The reverence. The warning. The grief hidden in plain sight.

Kali was the first to find her license. She lived alone on the second floor of a well-kept brownstone just off Columbus Avenue—quiet, clean, and tucked behind a tree-lined sidewalk. Not extravagant. But cared for. Like her. The kind of place people noticed only in passing, never pausing long enough to wonder who lived there.

"I heard barking," Cheryl said, frowning as she stepped into the hallway, gun drawn just in case.

Katherine moved first. She pushed open the door gently, the scent of dried herbs and medical-grade soap still clinging to the air.

The dog met them in the living room.

He didn't bark.

Didn't growl.

Just sat by the window—tall, statuesque. A harlequin Great Dane with eyes like storm clouds and a greying chin. Beside him, a food bowl with wilted spinach tucked into the kibble, like someone had tried to coax a picky eater into better habits.

"That's Linus," Katherine said softly.

No one asked how she knew. They didn't need to.

He'd waited by the door. Waited for her. Probably hadn't moved in days except to drink. There were no signs of struggle. No forced entry here either.

Juliette had simply disappeared.

"Who the hell is Brian?" Brandon asked, kneeling by a side table where a half-finished letter sat folded beside a set of keys.

It wasn't addressed to anyone. But the penmanship was the same. Clean. Sharp.

A note had been left at the scene, too—next to Juliette's name. It had said:

Linus is going to miss her. Someone help him. But Brian won't. He doesn't deserve to know.

No one had mentioned Brian before that.

Katherine stared at the apartment walls. No pictures. No engagement photos. No wedding plans tacked to the fridge. Just neatly stacked medical journals and a pinned bus schedule.

They found Brian two days later.

He didn't return their calls. Didn't answer the door.

But his fiancée had been dead for over a week—and he hadn't noticed.

When Cheryl finally cornered him outside his gym, he shrugged. Claimed they'd had a fight. Claimed she was dramatic. Said she liked to leave sometimes, and he liked when she did.

"Did you even look for her?" Katherine asked, not bothering to hide the contempt.

Brian shrugged then disregarded her. "I figured she'd come back; they always do."

He had another woman by then. One he didn't hide.

The man had already moved on—if he'd ever been truly present at all.

Juliette hadn't mattered to him.

But she had mattered to someone.

Someone who watched her leave that night from the hospital. Someone who moved without leaving bruises. Someone who laid her down in starlight and called it sacred.

Tipline

Katherine

The line lit up before Cheryl even finished the press briefing.

"Here we go," Brandon. Muttered, snapping on a fresh pair of gloves as if the crazy could travel through the receiver.

The tipline wasn't a desk anymore—it was an entire table, two interns, and a rolling whiteboard where *credible* leads went to die a slow, bureaucratic death.

In the first hour, they'd logged:

A woman who swore the killer was communicating with her through her cat's eye blinks.

A man certain the staging locations aligned with the ancient ley lines of Atlantis.

Three separate callers who "just had a feeling" it was their ex-husband, one of whom provided a seventeen-minute description of his "energy aura."

Someone claiming the artist was *definitely* Banksy.

By the second hour, the more elaborate ones began rolling in.

"He's hiding in plain sight," said one breathless voice. "At the wax museum. Look for the one that *breathes.*"

Another insisted the killer was a time traveler, "collecting women who resemble his dead wife in different centuries."

One man simply whispered, *I've seen the silk,* and hung up.

Most were harmless. Some were mean. All of them clogged the works.

Katherine skimmed the written summaries, her eyes half-glazed from caffeine and futility—until she hit a single line in neat block letters:

CALLER REFUSES TO GIVE NAME. CLAIMS FAMILY MEMBER WORKS SECURITY FOR 'THE MARCELLANOS" AND OVERHEARD CONVERSATION ABOUT A WOMAN 'WHO WON'T BE AROUND MUCH LONGER.'

She paused, reading it twice.

The Marcellanos. Not her case. Not this case. But Elise had been engaged to one of their nephews when she died.

"Where's this one?" she asked, already reaching for it.

Cheryl tapped a separate stack. "Pulled it aside. Could be nothing. Could be one of the usual mob rumor calls. You know how it is whenever we open a tipline."

Katherine slid the note into the back of the pile—still in the mix, but not high priority. If it connected to anything, it wouldn't be the Artist. Still, she'd keep it in her periphery.

She handed the rest back to Cheryl and moved toward the board, where Juliette's name still sat in red, circled three times.

Red Thread

Katherine

"We're missing something," she said, dragging a red string across the board. *He's not hiding anymore—he's inviting us in.*

She hadn't slept. Couldn't. The espresso in her blood was stale, her throat raw from shouting down dead ends. The squad room reeked of old takeout and sour tension. Behind her, the printer stuttered like it knew its reports didn't matter.

But the wall mattered.

The wall was growing.

Photos, notes, maps. Dates, times, faces—God, the faces. Victims 1 through 19 stared back in silent judgment, some blurred by years of dust and negligence, others so fresh the bruises hadn't left her memory.

A red thread had been tacked to each one. Her doing. One detail, one thread of control. The Artist's gallery wasn't just in alleys and abandoned churches. It was here. Staring them down.

Her handwriting took over every empty space available, except the blank space left for the finale.

Brandon was sorting through the box of letters again. His gloves crinkled against paper. "Same signature," he muttered. "Same ink, same pretentious tone."

The tipline had brought in hundreds of calls, most of them insane, but one stuck in her mind—Elise's face still lived in her memory, and the Marcellano name still carried weight.

It doesn't fit—but it won't let go.

She pushed it aside. *For now.*

She turned toward the whiteboard.

None of it made sense in pieces.

But taken together…

"You think we're looking at escalation?" Brandon asked, tapping a knuckle against the photo of Victim 12, who'd been submerged in a fountain.

"No," she said. "Not escalation. *Evolution.*"

They were being shown a progression, not a descent. The killer wasn't unraveling—*he was refining.*

She reached for a marker and began drawing lines. Staging location to victim. City to year. West Virginia. New York. Then the briefcase. She taped a copy of the map next to the board.

"These aren't trophies," she whispered. "They're bread-crumbs.

The Shape of Her

Katherine

The door clicked shut behind her, sealing in a hush that didn't feel like home.

The air was dense, as if it had been holding its breath in her absence. The hum of the refrigerator was the only sound, low and steady, like something pretending to be calm. A faint trace of rain clung to the room—not fresh, but leftover, stale in the carpet fibers.

She set her bag on the counter without looking at it. Her jacket slid from her shoulders and landed across the arm of the couch, forgotten. She didn't sit. Not yet.

Every Breath You Take, by The Police. still played in her head, each note sinking into the quiet like a drop of ink into the water.

She hadn't slept. Not really. Not since the last letter

Only one remains.

Chincoteague Island, Virginia. She'd confirmed it several days ago. But tonight wasn't about the *where*. It was about *why*.

Her gaze traced the jagged ridge of land, the curve like a crooked grin, the deep blue inland lake.

Her chest tightened. Not recognition exactly. But the shadow of it—the unsettling kind that lives deeper than memory.

A phantom image flickered. A drawing maybe. Blue crayon on newsprint. Something from childhood, folded into the quiet corners of her mind.

Horse Island, a voice whispered across her memory—but the voice had no face, and the name left a cold trace down her spine.

She sat still. Listening. Not to the room, but to the way her body suddenly remembered what her mind didn't want to.

The Curve of the Earth

The Artist

She was circling now.

Not blindly. Not like before—those early weeks, fumbling through headlines and autopsy reports like they might form a constellation. No. Katherine was moving with intent. Precision. The right kind of desperation.

The kind I designed for.

She was starting to see it wasn't about the blood. Not really. Or the girls. Or even the fingers. It was about design. Message. Intimacy. The communion between artist and witness. And Katherine? She was always meant to be the witness.

The only one who could.

I stood at the edge of the inlet, the sky overhead black and bottomless. No stars tonight. Just the low sound of wind through pine and the slap of water against rock. The silence out here was different than the city's. Thicker. It filled the bones, not just the ears.

Katherine would hate it.

At first.

But she'd come. She had to. The final letter made sure of that. The way she clung to ritual—order—meant she'd follow the trail all the way to its end, even if it led her straight through herself.

Especially then.

I imagined her face when she read the last note, her fingers tightening on the page, her mouth going still. The way her eyes would narrow when the implications started to take root. She'd try to outpace it at first. Rationalize. Reroute. But it would pull at her—like gravity.

She would start to question everything.

The victims. The timeline. The meaning behind the artifacts. And eventually—*inevitably*—herself.

That was the true masterpiece. Not the bodies. Not the staging. But the reflection she would see when the canvas turned back on her.

I'd given her the shape of something unspeakable. And now, she would have to name it.

Nineteen shadows laid to rest. One left to step into the light.

But this one wouldn't be found in a church or alley or art gallery ruin. No. She'd have to come here—here—to the place she'd been carrying in her bones for decades without knowing its name.

I didn't need to send a location. I'd already sent something better: momentum.

The kind you can't fight.

She'd feel it in her marrow soon.

She'd feel *me*.

And when she finally arrived, breathless and ready, she'd understand that the end was never about solving a crime.

It was about surrendering to the truth she'd buried a lifetime ago.

And I will be waiting.

Not with blood.

But with revelation.

Proof of Possession

Katherine

She didn't want to open the email.

It was a stupid thing to hesitate over—a PDF attachment, subject line: *DNA Confirmation – Case #LRM2147*. But her hand hovered over the mouse like it might bite her. Her other hand clenched the coffee mug too tightly, forgotten and cold.

Katherine stared at the screen. Her chest was an emptied room, her pulse the knock she couldn't answer.

She had expected one of the victim's names, maybe Dayna. Needed it, even.

The ribbon had been tied too precisely, too gently. The hair itself was long, brown, slightly sun-bleached. It had smelled like dust and rosewater when she first unwrapped it. And the way it had been preserved, wrapped like a keepsake—not a trophy—that was the part that unnerved her most.

He had kept it.

She clicked.

DNA Result: 99.94% match. Subject: Katherine Poe.

For a second, she didn't understand the letters. She read it again. And again. And then—

The mug slipped from her hand—the porcelain split the way she suddenly felt—fractured, impossible to piece back together.

She didn't even flinch.

Her ears rang. Something high and sharp and constant. She didn't move. Couldn't. The cursor blinked at her like it knew what she didn't want to say out loud.

It was hers.

The hair.

Not another's.

Hers.

But that couldn't be right.

She didn't have that colored hair. Hadn't in years. Not like that. Not that short. Not that shade.

Unless—

A memory tore across the back of her skull, sharp and sudden. The sink. Rust-stained porcelain. The flicker of a buzzing light that made the whole room hum like a nerve about to snap.

She was twenty. Raw from the escape, shaking so hard the scissors slipped in her grip. They didn't cut clean—they chewed, catching strands and yanking until her scalp burned. The cheap dye stank of ammonia and plastic flowers, the kind that clung to skin no matter how many times she rinsed. Brown water swirled in the drain like something rotting.

She remembered shoving clumps of herself into a grocery bag, fingers sticky, flushing what she could. The rest sat there, damp and ugly, staring back at her from the bottom of the trash like proof. But not all of it.

He'd found a piece.

He had taken something from her then—quietly, without her knowing—and preserved it for years. And now... now he'd given it back.

The blue ribbon hadn't meant comfort.

It had meant possession.

Her stomach lurched. She stumbled into the kitchen, bracing herself against the counter as bile clawed up her throat. She didn't throw up. Just gasped. Shaking. Burning.

He hadn't just been watching her now.

He had been watching her then.

He had touched her before she even realized it.

The briefcase wasn't a breadcrumb trail. It was a mirror. Every piece tucked inside like a bone in a reliquary, whispering one single, unbearable truth:

You've always belonged to me.

Katherine slid to the floor. Hands over her mouth. Knees pulled tight to her chest. Didn't do anything but stare at the broken mug and the blood pooling beneath it from a small cut in her palm.

Then, slowly, she looked back at the screen.

Subject: Katherine Poe.

And that was when it hit her.

This was about her.

And she was next.

When the Quiet Turns

Katherine

She didn't want to be alone.

Not because of the case. Not because the walls of her apartment were closing in or the maps were screaming. It was something else tonight. A hollowness. A quiet that pressed too hard behind her ribs.

She missed him.

Not the idea of him. Not the distraction. Him.

His voice low in the dark. His hands warm where they rested. The steadiness he carried without ever needing to announce it. She missed the way he listened without interrupting her spirals. The way his presence made space instead of noise.

She found herself texting him without thinking.

You up?

The reply came so fast it made her throat tighten.

Always. Want me to come by?

She didn't overthink it. Didn't pretend it wasn't exactly what she needed.

Yes. Please.

Thirty minutes later, she was standing at her door when he knocked. Devin looked tired—creased shirt, sleeves pushed up, hair slightly mussed like he'd run a hand through it too many times. But when he saw her, the edges of him softened.

He stepped inside without a word, just opened his arms.

And she folded.

No explanations. No posturing. Just silence and skin and breath. Her head fit beneath his chin like it had always belonged there. His hands smoothed up her back, steady and slow, grounding her.

That fleeting thought about the risk of letting herself lean on someone scratched at her mind.

She didn't speak for a long time. Just stood there, letting the warmth of him melt some of the cold she hadn't realized was clinging so hard.

Eventually, they moved to the couch. He kicked off his shoes. She curled into him, knees drawn up, fingers twisted in the hem of his sleeve. Neither of them turned on the TV. The quiet wasn't dangerous now. Not with him in it.

His voice was the first thing to break it.

"You want to talk?"

She shook her head against his chest.

"Okay," he said gently, pressing a kiss into her hair. "Then we won't."

She didn't sleep, but she rested. For the first time in what felt like days, her body stopped bracing for impact. Her eyes didn't dart to the door. Her muscles didn't twitch with invisible alarms.

She just existed.

And somewhere between the soft cadence of his breathing and the steady weight of his arms, the world stopped clawing at her for answers.

For one night, she didn't need to solve anything.

She just needed him.

Nothing Held Back

Katherine

She hadn't planned on sleeping. But somewhere between his arms and the soft, rhythmic rise of his chest under her cheek, she gave in. And now… morning poured in like warm syrup, slow and golden across her apartment floor.

Devin was still there.

Still beside her. One leg tangled with hers. One hand low on her spine, fingers splayed like he didn't want to let go. His breath hit the back of her neck, steady, soft.

And for the first time in years, she *didn't* want to move.

She'd been with people before. A couple boyfriends, in high school, a couple in college, in the years before the worst things. But this—this wasn't that. Devin wasn't a break from the weight. *He was the reason she could breathe under it.*

And she wanted him.

Not slowly. Not delicately. Not after another date or two. Now.

She rolled toward him, her fingers trailing across his chest. He stirred with a groan, eyes still half-closed.

"Hey," he rasped.

"Stay," she whispered.

His hand cupped her jaw, thumb brushing her cheekbone like she was made of something rare. But the look in his eyes wasn't gentle. It was heat curled under restraint. It was everything she wanted to surrender to.

"Katherine, we don't have to—"

"I know," she said, pressing her mouth to his. "But I want to."

The kiss deepened. His breath hitched as she moved, as her body slid against his. She was all nerve endings—heat and hunger. And the way he touched her? *Like reverence lived in her skin.*

She didn't flinch when his hand slid under the hem of her sleep shirt. She arched into it.

"I want to feel everything," she said against his mouth.

Devin froze for half a second. Then leaned over, reaching for his jeans on the floor. The soft crinkle of foil unwrapping made her heart stutter. Prepared. Careful. He hadn't come here blind.

He kissed her again, slower now. His hands mapped her like they'd been waiting a lifetime. Shirt off. Legs parted. He looked at her like she wasn't a body, but a moment. One he wanted to remember in fragments and fire.

When he pushed into her, she gasped—tight, breathy, undone. It had been too long. Her body needed time to open. He gave it. She clutched his back, nails digging in. Not because of pain. Because of how it *started* to feel once it stopped hurting.

Like she was coming home to something she'd never had before.

He moved inside her like he was listening to her body more than her voice. Every thrust deliberate. Every roll of his hips like worship.

"Katherine," he breathed, burying his face in her neck. "You feel like, home, you feel like mine."

She didn't answer. Couldn't. Her body had already broken apart, her legs trembling, her voice caught somewhere in her throat. She kissed him instead—open-mouthed, gasping, hungry. She chased the next wave before she even realized it had started. And when it hit—oh—it shattered her from the inside out.

He followed a heartbeat later, voice guttural, body trembling against hers. He didn't pull away. Just held her tighter.

And for a moment, the silence that followed wasn't heavy.

Slick with Sin

Katherine

The shower steamed fast, heat fogging the mirror before her feet hit the tile.

She hadn't said a word since the bedroom. She didn't need to. Her body did the talking—every brush of skin, every glance, every ache still echoing low in her belly.

He followed her in like he'd always belonged there.

Katherine leaned into the wall, water cascading down her back in rivulets, and closed her eyes. Just long enough to stop thinking.

Devin's hands were on her hips.

Not rushed. Not fumbling. Steady. Claiming. He moved behind her, fingers smoothing the soap into her skin, sliding up her spine in slow, reverent strokes that had nothing to do with cleanliness and everything to do with memory.

"You don't have to—" she murmured.

"I want to," he said, voice lower than the water.

His palms traced her waist, gliding forward to her ribs, then higher, washing her like she was breakable—but sinful enough to handle. He kissed the back of her neck, then her shoulder, and she melted into the tile, warmth from the water replaced by something far more dangerous.

His touch dipped lower.

He slid a hand between her thighs, teasing, coaxing her apart until her breath came sharp and shallow.

"Devin," she whispered, voice shaking.

"Tell me to stop."

She didn't.

He turned her around slowly, water trailing down her chest, catching in the hollow of her collarbone, the curve of her breasts, his eyes following every drop. He sank to his knees. *Right there on the slick tile.*

Her legs nearly gave out.

His hands held her steady as his mouth pressed to her hip, then lower. She gasped, one hand bracing the wall, the other in his wet hair, her whole-body tightening, trembling, falling.

And when he stood again, water running in rivulets down both, she saw the truth in his eyes—no mask, no softness. *Just want.*

She wrapped her arms around his neck, pulled him down to her mouth, and kissed him like she'd drown if she didn't.

He lifted her effortlessly.

Her back hit the wall. Her legs wrapped around his waist. He fumbled for the packet near the towels. She helped tear it open, heart hammering, limbs shaking.

The second he entered her, everything else went silent.

There was no faucet. No breath. Just movement. Slick, raw, perfect movement.

Katherine cried out—high, helpless, overwhelmed.

The steam made it impossible to breathe. His name left her lips repeatedly, until it wasn't a word, just a sound.

He was deeper than before. Slower. Rougher. Water beading between them. Her thighs trembled. His grip tightened, grounding her in the rush.

"*Katie,*" he rasped against her throat, the word bitten out like a groan, like a prayer.

And when she came—it was with a full-body quake that didn't stop. He followed her into the heat, groaning against her skin, biting down just enough to anchor himself there.

Neither of them moved for a long time.

The water had long since gone cool.

Tangled in the Quiet

Katherine

The towel barely clung to her hips.

She stood at the bathroom sink, flushed and still dripping, her palms braced on either side of the counter as she stared at her reflection in the fogged mirror. Her lips were swollen. Her skin glowed with heat that hadn't come from the water. Her hair hung in damp, unruly waves around her shoulders.

Devin was behind her.

She could feel him before she saw him—moving with that same unhurried confidence, the one that somehow felt earned instead of arrogant. He leaned against the doorframe, towel slung low on his hips, eyes tracking her like she was a riddle he'd already solved but couldn't stop reading.

"You, okay?" he asked softly.

No.

Yes.

Not even close.

She met his eyes in the mirror and forced a breath through her lungs. "I think I forgot how to stand."

He smiled, but not smug. Something warmer. Protective. "I'd help, but I'm not sure I'm the steady one right now."

She laughed—quiet and surprised—and dropped her gaze to the sink to hide it. When he moved, it was slow and certain. His arms wrapped around her waist, chin resting on her shoulder. He smelled like her shampoo now. Like warmth and soap and sin.

"I could make you breakfast," he murmured. "Or just coffee. I know better than to come between you and caffeine."

She turned in his arms, towel shifting. "You cook?" She teased.

"I scramble eggs. I burn toast. I make excellent apologies."

She pressed her forehead to his chest and closed her eyes.

It was too much. And not enough.

"I've never let anyone stay past the night," she whispered.

"Breakfast?" he teased gently, but when she didn't smile, his hand slid up to her jaw, coaxing her face back to his. "Hey. Katherine. Look at me."

She did.

"I know," he said. "I figured. Doesn't change a thing."

The way he looked at her… it almost broke her.

"I don't usually let people stay," she said.

"I'll go, if you want."

She shook her head.

He kissed her—forehead first. Then cheek. Then her lips, soft and slow, like a promise instead of a possession.

"I'll make coffee," he said. "Burn some toast. You come when you're ready."

She watched him go—barefoot, towel clinging low, bare back disappearing into her kitchen—and told herself not to memorize it. She'd need the memory later.

The Hourglass Room

Katherine

By the time she made it back from the Marcellano, the sky had turned the bruised shade of late afternoon—4:07 p.m. according to the security panel by the door.

The chair squeaked when she shifted, too soft in the middle like someone else's weight had lived there longer than hers. She crossed her legs, then uncrossed them. The sun through the blinds left thin bars of light across the carpet like a prison diagram, and for a second, she imagined lying down between them just to see what she'd confess.

Somewhere in the back of her mind, the Marcellano file sat on her desk—open, unfinished, waiting for her to decide where the tip was smoke, fire, or just noise. She'd left it there on purpose. Today wasn't about them.

"Start wherever you want," said Dr. Delaney.

Her voice was calm. Always calm. Like nothing in the world could shake her. Like monsters didn't exist.

Katherine's fingernail dug into the seam of her jeans.

"I slept with someone," she said.

No preamble. No build. Just the sentence. Heavy and hot in her mouth.

Dr. Delaney didn't flinch. "Was it someone *safe?*"

Katherine blinked. "Define s*afe.*"

There was a pause. The kind where therapists leave silence like bait.

"I mean," she added before it could stretch too far, "he's not a stranger. We've… been spending time together. Dinner. Coffee. It's not reckless. Not really."

Dr. Delaney tilted her head. "You're explaining it like a report, Katherine. Not an experience."

"Maybe that's the only way I know how to talk about it."

Dr. Delaney folded her hands. "Okay. What does the report say?"

Katherine stared at the carpet again. The light. The dust floating in it. She felt like dust lately—suspended in something she couldn't name.

"The report says I let someone in," she said. "Against my better judgment. Despite every survival instinct I've honed since I was twenty. I let him in. And it felt... *good.*"

The last word cracked. She hated that. She hated that it mattered.

"I'm not stupid," she continued. "I know what intimacy can do. What it takes. I teach trauma response. I've seen the damage. The aftermath. I've *been* the aftermath."

"But you still chose it," said Dr. Delaney softly.

"I did." Her hands clenched. "I wanted something to feel good. Even if it wasn't smart. Even if it was temporary."

She didn't say Devin's name. She couldn't. Saying it would make it real. Naming him meant acknowledging the thing that had shifted inside her. That brittle little crack widening somewhere just beneath her ribs.

"It was just one night," she lied. *And already her body knew better.*

Dr. Delaney didn't call her on it.

Katherine picked at the edge of her thumbnail, peeling a strip of skin until it stung.

"I thought I could keep it compartmentalized. Him in one box. The case in another. But something's off. I can't sleep right. I keep checking the locks. And when I woke up this morning... I didn't want to get out of bed."

"Because you felt unsafe?"

"No. Because I felt—" she faltered "—happy. And that scared me more."

Dr. Delaney wrote something down.

Katherine swallowed. "I don't trust that feeling. Every time I think I've found solid ground, it turns out to be quicksand. And I keep—I *keep* thinking I'm past this. That I'm healed. That I'm fine."

"Are you?"

"No." The word landed like a blade dropped on stone.

The room got smaller. Or maybe her chest did.

"I don't know how to want something without trying to autopsy it first," she whispered. "I analyze people. That's what I do. But he makes me forget to do it. And that terrifies me."

Dr. Delaney closed her notebook. Not abruptly. Just… enough to signal they were out of time.

But not out of damage.

"Feelings aren't evidence," the doctor said gently. "You don't have to cross-examine them. You just have to feel them."

Katherine stood too fast. Her knees ached. Her heartbeat in her throat.

The sun had moved. The light bars were gone.

"How long," she asked, hand on the door, "can someone stay suspended before they fall?"

Dr. Delaney smile held steady. "It isn't falling. It's gravity. You're meant to feel it."

Katherine stepped into the hallway without replying.

She didn't know whether she was falling… or about to land.

Performance Art

The Artist

She laughed like she didn't know.

I watched her across the candlelit table, the low hum of the bistro softening the edges of her exhaustion. She curled her fingers around the wine glass, not to drink, but to anchor herself. *Always pasta. Always too polite to send it back when it arrived late.* She never wore perfume, but I knew her scent now—faint shampoo and skin warmed by subway air.

As Devin, I got to sit close enough to memorize the angle of her jaw when she tilted her head mid-thought. Close enough to catch the hesitation in her smile when she caught herself drifting. She didn't speak easily, not about herself. But she asked questions. Probing ones. The kind that would have gutted a lesser man.

I answered them with care. Devin always answered with care.

That was the role. The man who waited. The one who saw her clearly, but never too quickly. The version she could fall into without tipping her own alarms.

It wasn't difficult. I studied her better than any victim.

Not from childhood memories—I had none. But from the moment I laid eyes on her. Even before my first gallery frame. From the way she tucked her hair behind her ear with her non-dominant hand when she was too tired to think.

This morning, her hair was damp when she laughed into my chest. Her towel had slipped twice. Her lips were still swollen from the shower, her eyes soft with sleep and trust. I watched her make coffee barefoot, still humming something under her breath. I watched her memorize me.

She doesn't know she's already been archived. Every sigh. Every smile. Every tremble.

She was not a woman to be chased. She was a problem to be solved.

And I had given her Devin: the quiet man who let her breathe. Who never interrupted her spiraling thoughts. Who asked, gently, how she slept the night before, knowing full well she hadn't. Who made her laugh in small doses, because anything more would have felt like pressure.

She leaned into that fiction like it might save her.

And I let her.

Because when it ends—when the final truth blooms like ink dropped in water—I was pretending to be someone she could love.

And when the mask drops, when she sees me fully for the first time—not Devin, not a name, but what I am beneath the names—she'll feel it.

Recognition.

Not from memory.

But from design.

I've made her part of this gallery from the beginning. Left her every clue carved in horror and clarity. Laced everybody with riddles written in her dialect.

I am not the chaos.

I am the order that followed it.

And when she steps into the final display, she'll know:

Devin was never a lie.

He was the bridge.

And I, the one she's always been searching for, waiting on the other side.

The Face She Couldn't Forget

Katherine

The desk phone shrilled at 6:37 a.m.—an hour when the precinct still smelled more of floor wax than burnt coffee.

I hovered over my half empty mug, debating the odds of another false alarm, and answered anyway.

"Poe."

A breathless voice stabbed through the line. "She's here. The girl who—who got away. She won't stop crying. Says she remembers."

Madeline.

My chair scraped as I stood. "Keep her talking. I'm on my way."

Madeline sat curled on the plastic bench outside Interview Two, sleeves of an oversized hoodie swallowed almost to her knuckles. Her eyes—bloodshot, swollen—barely registered the fluorescent hum. Tears had crystalized to salt at the corners. Every exhale shuddered.

I knelt in front of her. "Madeline?"

She flinched, as if my name were a strike. Then recognition. Then relief that flickered and died.

"I was wrong," she whispered. "I see him every time I close my eyes now. I was wrong."

I'd seen survivors shatter before—adrenaline crashes, dissociative spirals—but this was different. This was haunted.

"Let's get you water," I said. "And space to breathe."

She shook her head hard enough that brunette strands—too clean, too soft—slapped her cheeks. "*No space. Only pictures. I must show you. I must fix what I broke.*"

Detective Cheryl cleared Interview Three, swapped out the interrogation desk for the sketch artist's easel, and dimmed half the overheads. Low light, fewer shadows. Psychological trick to coax memory without drowning it.

Madeline clutched a Styrofoam cup, knuckles bone white against the cheap foam. I sat adjacent, not opposite—ally, not examiner. The sketch artist, Ramon, perched at his pad, charcoal poised.

Ramon's voice always landed soft, almost coaxing. "We'll start with broad shapes. Gender?"

Madeline's gaze narrowed. "Male."

"Approximate age?"

"Thirty-ish. Maybe older. Eyes like—" She faltered, breath snagging. "*Like they're laughing at you even when the mouth isn't.*"

Ramon's charcoal swept.

I catalogued every tremor in Madeline's fingers, every half-swallowed sob, because trauma is a language of micro tells. She wasn't fabricating; her body was translating terror into motion.

"Hair?" Ramon asked.

"Dark brown, but when the streetlamp hit it, I saw threads of gold—like old varnish on wood."

Golden undertones. Devin's after-work curls flashed behind my eyes.

Coincidence. Maybe. Keep breathing.

"Length?"

"Longer on top, like he runs his hands through it. Sides neat. Not shaved—just disciplined."

Ramon sketched. A jawline emerged—sharp, but not gaunt.

"His jaw," Madeline said, voice cracking, "looked carved. And a scar. Here." She touched her own skin, just left of center—diagonal, maybe an inch.

My pulse stuttered. Devin had a shaved nick on that same path—barbershop mishap, he'd joked.

Ramon added the line.

Madeline's breathing quickened. "His mouth… it's soft until he smiles. Then it splits wrong. Like the smile gets there before his soul does."

My stomach turned.

"Teeth?" Ramon asked.

"Straight. Too straight. Like he replaced them to be perfect."

Ramon nodded.

Madeline's fingers clawed at the paper cup. "He smelled like cedar and lavender."

Ramon lifted his charcoal. "Eye shape?"

Madeline stared at the blank page. "Predator's eyes. Hooded. The light was dim, but I stared into them. Amber gold."

Devin's eyes—hazel gold when he leaned close.

I felt the room spin.

Ramon offered the pad for review; rough lines formed a near likeness. Madeline recoiled. "No. The chin is— thicker. He clenched it when I turned, and he saw me."

Ramon adjusted. Stroke, shade, erase.

"How tall?"

"Six feet? Maybe a little taller."

My heart crashed against my ribs. Devin stood at six foot two, posture rigid from marathon training.

Ramon's strokes darkened; the face came alive.

For one suspended second, I didn't see a suspect.

I saw him.

The towel slung low on his hips that morning. The curve of his smile when he offered burnt toast like it was fine cuisine. The warmth of his arms still ghosting around my waist as I rinsed shampoo from my hair.

Then Madeline recoiled, and the sketch—

No.

No, it was wrong.

Except it wasn't.

Madeline jerked back as if the sketch had breathed. "That's him."

I leaned in. And ice spread in my veins.

Devin.

Not suggestion. Not paranoia. Devin.

Madeline's shoulders caved. "I lied to you before because I was sure he'd kill me. But he's killing me anyway— in my dreams. I can't keep the wrong face in my head anymore."

Tears flooded fresh. I pulled tissues from the box, but she waved them off, fingers trembling.

Ramon dated the sketch: 07:14 a.m. He slid it toward me. The face stared back—handsome, kind, ruined by intention.

Madeline's statement took two more hours.

When she finally slept in the break room cot, I stood at the window and watched daylight smear across the East River. I felt the universe tilt.

I'd suspected. Whispered doubts in showers, in alleys, in the hush between heartbeats. But now the suspicion had skin, hair, a scar just left of center.

And a smile that split wrong.

Across the room, Ramon covered the sketch with a clear envelope. The charcoal smudged my glove as I lifted it. Devin stared back—alive only in fingerprints of dust.

I sealed the evidence bag. The weight felt like a verdict.

Madeline had been wrong, and then she'd been more right than any of us.

The next step would cost me.

Reflections

Dusty

While she studied the fresh lines of his face in an office across the city, he sat in his gallery and traced older ones—inked into journals, carved into memory.

The spine of the first book bent beneath his fingers. *2000–2009*. Pages soft, margin notes blurred by sweat and years. He didn't need to reread them; every line was already etched across his mind. But tonight, with the noose tightening and her breath close enough to feel, he wanted to remember how it began.

How she rose.

How he followed.

The Farmhouse, 2000–2002

Eleven days. No sleep. No trail. Just static voices on the trucker band and church bulletins thumbed thin. Then— Boone County. The old Poe farmhouse.

A porch light clicked off too early. A curtain snapped shut too tight. A sheriff's cruiser sat warm at midnight.

She was inside.

The house held its breath like it remembered the last time she bled.

He learned her rhythm. The blackout-curtained room upstairs never lit, but the living room bulb clicked on at 6:42 sharp and died at 11:10. Mosquitoes tore his arms; he let them. She never came out.

The diner filled in the blanks. *She won't touch a doorknob. Sleeps under her bed. Shoulda kept her locked up.*

They thought she was broken.

She was fermenting.

A storm gave him his first glimpse—her shadow at the up-stairs window, hair pulled back, spine bent over a flame that vanished before he could breathe her in.

Enough. She hadn't disappeared. She had congealed. Sharpening. Waiting.

For war.

And he would be the battlefield.

The College Years, 2003–2005

Her name surfaced in a course bulletin—Psychology, sophomore year, Marshall University. Just Katherine.

The smile was wrong, practiced, but he knew it.

Spring 2005, a car wreck. He reached the flashing lights in time to see blood at her temple; her hand braced around a stranger's. *You're okay. I've got you.* Even bruised, she held someone else together. That almost undid him.

Early CID, 2007–2009

He found her outside courthouses now, clipboard in hand, boots polished, hair knotted severe. Crime Scene Assistant. Forgettable to most.

Not to him.

He watched her scrape secrets from tire treads and dog hair, saw her lift death from dirt like an archaeologist of silence. They called her Katherine Poe. *The one with the dead-girl eyes.*

They thought she carried death.

But he knew—

She birthed it.

Echoes of the Ascent

Dusty

The second journal bore coffee stains and blurred fingerprints. *2009–2016*. The years she stepped from shadow into command. He hadn't needed to stalk every movement—her name spilled across newsprint often enough—but he still tracked her rhythms. Still waited for the moment she might look up and feel him, just beyond the frame.

Into the Field, 2009–2012

By 2009 she carried a full title: Crime Scene Investigator. She led now.

He memorized her tells—the flex of her hands, the murmured words no one else caught, the way she stole two minutes in hallways to collapse in silence before standing straight again.

He wanted to be that silence.

One night outside her office window, a crooked paper snowflake fluttered above her desk. Two mugs sat there, one forgotten. He left only because the urge to press his hand over hers was too loud. Louder than ever.

Preparing the Frame, 2012–2014

Her reputation hardened. *Run it through Poe before it hits court.* She didn't demand authority. Rooms bent around her.

He began sketching brides. Not bodies—silhouettes. Veils. Drafts of a masterpiece.

Not yet art.

Preparation.

The Catalyst, 2014–2016

The Kanawha River dismemberments. He read her report a dozen times, tracing where her brilliance had been edited down by lesser minds. It made him furious.

So, he wrote. Not letters. Scripts. An opening act: *Silent Invitation.*

Dayna Cookson wasn't perfect, which made her useful. Loud. Fragile. A fitting prologue. He posed her on courthouse steps, tiara crooked, ring finger missing.

Katherine crouched over the body like it meant nothing— until the moment she saw. Until recognition burned between them.

Artist to artist.

That was the moment the gallery opened.

That was the moment he stopped watching—

and began inviting.

Where Obsession Took Root

Dusty

He closed the final journal like sealing a love letter—slow, deliberate, aching with everything unsaid. His fingertips lingered on the worn leather, tracing sixteen years of devotion.

She had poured her light into a world that never deserved her. Now it was his turn.

Not just to show her his masterpiece.

To give her himself.

Devin. Dusty. The Artist.

It didn't matter what name she spoke when she reached the island.

Soon, she would understand they were one and the same.

One Step Behind

Katherine

The warrant paper crackled between my fingers like a live wire. Judge Morales's signature was still wet; ink barely set under the desk lamp. A single line of legal authority that should have felt like triumph—yet under my tongue it tasted like metal. Probable cause to shatter Devin Grayson's illusion. No guarantee I wasn't already too late.

"ESU is staged on Lafayette," Brandon said, voice low, steady. "You say go; they breach."

I nodded. The hallway buzzed fluorescent. My brain catalogued everything—sweat damp on the warrant sleeve, Brandon's swallow, the elevator ding like a countdown bell. Cheryl's warning rang in my skull: *No heroics. Secure, preserve, process.*

My Glock slid back into its holster. Madeline's sketch burned in my pocket, charcoal eyes smudging through plastic like infection. Devin's eyes—kind, until they split wrong.

"Let's go."

Devin's building was old brick dressed up in false charm—ivy, iron balcony, overpriced authenticity. ESU kicked the lobby door open over the doorman's protest. Marble cracked under boots. The elevator climbed in silence so heavy my ears rang.

Seventh floor. 7B.

The ram struck twice. The door folded.

"Police! Search warrant!"

We surged inside.

And found nothing.

Not emptiness—worse. Abandonment.

Furniture outlines on dust, couch divots, TV-shadowed wall. Kitchen shelves yawning clean. Refrigerator unplugged, door wedged to keep out mold. Closet stripped—no hangers, no shoe marks, only cedar and lemon polish.

Bathroom bare. Mirror spotless. Medicine cabinet empty, glass gleaming. Not a fingerprint. Not a speck. He'd even pulled the rug tacks.

"Clear!" ESU voices echoed hollow.

I gripped the windowsill. Outside, the city sprawled, indifferent. On the sill—a single pale hair. Blonde. I bagged it, though I knew it was mine now.

Ghost.

***

We moved fast. Devin's office: badge dead, servers gone, desks stripped to bone. Coffee machine left on, mocking, espresso bleeding into an overflowed cup until the reservoir hissed dry. Router ports unplugged. Files erased. On the glass wall—a sticky note in neat hand: *Perfection requires timing.*

Ramon would want the handwriting. I bagged it. Tasted failure anyway.

A shell-company unit turned up dust and concrete. Shelving scars on the wall. No boxes. Just a strip of painter's tape, fresh, rectangle large enough for a mannequin. Or a coffin.

I peeled it. Beneath—a bead of wax, faintly gardenia. Burned candle. Taken away.

A ritual. A goodbye.

Security footage, thirty-seven cameras. At 5:12 a.m., Devin walked out with two charcoal suitcases. Hoodie, cap, mask. Head low. But the gait was his. Gold strands in his hair caught the light. He slid into a rideshare registered to a stolen phone. Three blocks, switch. Classic shell game.

Brandon's voice cracked. "He played us."

Cheryl swore. "Traveling light. He'll kill again soon."

I studied his frozen frame—shoulders hunched, suitcases dragging like severed arms—and felt my pulse calm. The hunt reset to zero.

***

Night pressed close before we left the precinct. I sat at my desk, warrant limp, Devin's file open beside a missing-person report his landlord had filed. An envelope of cash. A note: *Thank you for the memories.*

I set Madeline's sketch over it. Charcoal eyes aligned with ink. My fingers pressed the paper's phantom features. Five seconds of rage. One. Two. Three. Four. Five.

Then I opened my notebook. Built a new timeline. Catalogued every absence as presence:

No toothbrush → traveling.

No logs → inside wipe.

Rug tacks gone → fiber paranoia.

Candle wax → fragrance signature.

Absence becomes evidence when arranged deliberately.

I wrote until pen grooves scarred my fingers. Sirens wailed outside, thin lullabies.

Devin Grayson had become a ghost. But ghosts always haunt where it matters. And I was what mattered.

***

At 3:02 a.m., I climbed the precinct roof. Sketch in hand. City lights trembled below.

I touched flame to the corner. Watched Devin's eyes blacken, curl, collapse into ash. Embers scattered upward like fireflies, vows carried over Manhattan.

My whisper followed them. Low, deliberate. A promise only he would hear.

You can't edit the truth forever.

And across the city, somewhere, I knew he was smiling. Frost settled in my lungs.

I turned toward the stairwell, new warrant requests already forming behind my eyes.

The hunt was reborn.

And ghosts can bleed. You only have to cut them in the right memory.

The Circle Narrows

Katherine

The precinct's Situation Room felt even smaller than usual—low ceiling, frayed carpet, and grainy stills of Devin's empty apartment looping on the wall.

"Twenty-four hours," Brandon said, hands on the table. "Three locations cleaned, four trails spoofed, no traffic cams. How?"

Cheryl's voice was flat. "We gave him the clock. The sketch started the countdown."

"This wasn't instinct," I said. "It was rehearsed."

"He couldn't have anticipated Madeline," Katherine said. Unless she was a plant, meant for distraction, misdirection and enough time for him to run.

The wax bead CSU analyzed—gardenia with a trace of vetiver—narrowed suppliers to eight small-batch shops. Patrols took Devin's photo to each. Brandon tapped his laptop. "Coordinates from the burner's digits. Ninety-six points."

"Over lay with old kill sites," I said.

Three hits landed in Queens. *Daydream Gardens*. Abandoned greenhouse.

Devin's kind of beauty.

We go tonight," Cheryl ordered.

***

Rain slicked the padlocked gate. ESU breached without a sound. Inside, moonlight bled across benches and feral ferns.

Section C—a glint. A cigar cutter. Fresh.

Then: the motion sensor tripped.

We stormed into a chamber. Strips of wedding gown swayed from wires overhead.

At the center: a dress form. Gloves stitched to its sides. Pinned to its chest: a Polaroid.

Me—on the precinct roof, hours ago.

My stomach dropped. He'd been watching.

Outside, a mannequin waited against the SWAT van, a veil draped over its face.

In its lap: a phone, screen ticking down.

"Device!" ESU barked. A blast blanket dropped, two men lifted the mannequin like a coffin and hustled it into the lot. The phone hit dirt, bounced once, intact.

We braced for the blast.

Silence—then tinny speakers blared Beethoven's *Ode to Joy*.

Static broke, then his voice, cool and close.

"I told you—perfection requires timing."

The line went dead.

***

Back at the precinct, dawn bled through the blinds. The Polaroid pinned dead center on the evidence board. Cheryl said, "This scene was for her eyes only. He's cutting her from the rest of us."

A possible lead: white box truck heading east from the greenhouse. It never appeared on the far side of the bridge. I marked an abandoned ferry pier.

Then—every light died. Phones, generators, all dead.

My phone buzzed anyway. A scheduled notification, pre-loaded hours ago.

SHE WAS ALWAYS GOING ALONE.

No signal to reply.

Flashlights cut through the dark—and froze.

The Polaroid of me was gone. In its place: a new one. The conference room. Us.

Something skittered in the vent above.

We raised our guns.

Blackness stared back.

Art of the Bride Cipher

Katherine

02:16 a.m.

The power returned in stages—emergency strips, fluorescents, the low hum of servers rebooting. My monitor blinked awake to a new email.

Subject line: *There is symmetry in violence.*

No body. No attachments. No IP trail. Just a familiar footer:

— 929 / 0142

Three years of silence. Now he was back—like he'd never left.

Brandon slipped in with two coffees. "He wrote you a love letter?"

I didn't smile. "Something like that."

The old burner logs still burned in my memory—four destroyed phones, every number starting with 929, ending with 0142. I'd chalked it up to noise. Not anymore.

"Time stamps," I said. "Every burner lived exactly nine minutes, twenty-nine seconds. Then silence. One minute forty-two seconds later, I got an email."

Brandon frowned. "You're saying he built a clock into the signal?"

"I'm saying he's been counting longer than I knew how to listen."

The scanner broke the email's numerals down at 3200 dpi. In the zero: a chess queen. In the nine: a blue ribbon.

Brandon leaned in. "That's you, isn't it?"

My chest tightened. "He's not sending me clues. He's sending me, *me*."

At the evidence board, I traced lines between kill sites and coordinates. A triangle emerged—deliberate, closing in.

"This isn't geography," I murmured. "It's obsession in co-ordinates. He's retracing me—every move, every memory."

Brandon's voice dropped. "Where's the endpoint?"

I kept my eyes on the center of the board. *Me.*

"Now," I said, turning back to the screen, "I bait him."

A burner Twitter handle. One message typed:

Numbers are names. Names bleed.

My finger hovered over Send.

Not yet. One more move.

She Was Always Going Alone

Katherine

Hours had passed since the blackout and the Polaroid, but the image still burned in Katherine's mind.

She didn't need sleep.

She needed answers.

The flickering light overhead matched the throb behind her eyes. The map blurred—not from exhaustion, but from something worse.

Recognition.

The black queen lay beside it. Heavy. Intentional.

The emerald—her eyes.

The ribbon—her contacts.

The coal scrip—not just West Virginia, but home. Sunday dinners with her grandfather, who always kept one in his pocket. She hadn't thought of that in decades. Who would?

Nausea coiled in her gut. This wasn't someone who studied her.

This was someone who had been there.

Before the blood.

The door creaked. Brandon's weighted footsteps.

"You're not sleeping again."

She didn't look up.

"You didn't check in after the scene," he said. "What's going on?"

"I've been working."

Cheryl's perfume cut through the stale air. "On what?"

"The map," Katherine said, steady but hollow. "It isn't just shapes. It's a funnel. Every line, every symbol—it all converges on Chincoteague Island."

Brandon frowned. "We already knew the island was connected."

Her hand pressed flat to the board. "Connected is noise. This is precision. He's been choreographing me there for years. It's not the island that matters—it's me, standing on it."

Brandon's jaw tightened. "So, he's waiting for you."

She nodded once. "Always has been."

Silence held.

"Then you can't go," Cheryl said quietly.

"I have to."

"It's a trap," Brandon warned.

"Of course it is. It's the only kind of gift he knows how to give."

"You're not going alone," Brandon said.

I always have been.

Cold air hit her like absolution as she walked out. She didn't look back.

He had always known her.

Now... she would know him.

The City That Chokes You First

Katherine

Before I pack. Before I board the plane. Before I face whatever waits on that island—I have to remember how this started.

Not the case. Not the bodies. Not even him.

The city.

The first time I stepped off the train at Penn Station, I nearly turned back. Not from the noise or the crush of bodies—though all of it pressed like punishment—but because the air felt wrong. Tight. Wet. Like the city had lungs, and I was already stealing its breath.

August heat clung to me like someone else's sweat. A carry-on on my shoulder, a manila folder under my arm, a badge clipped to my belt that meant nothing in New York. I was supposed to be a liaison—one, maybe two weeks. Share what we had on the bride cases, then go home.

Like grief knew schedules. Like monsters kept them.

The precinct was worse—phones shrieking, walls stained with voices. They gave me a fishbowl office: glass walls, metal table, one dusty computer. I hadn't even set the folder down when the door opened.

"You Katherine Poe?"

Tall, black blazer. Lipstick the color of dried blood.

"Yeah. You must be Cheryl."

"Word travels."

"Word sticks, when it's loud enough."

Her mouth twitched. Behind her, broad shoulders and a rolled-up shirt stained with coffee.

"Brandon Novak. Senior CSI. And designated pain in the ass."

Firm handshake. Honest eyes. The kind that see too much and sleep too little.

We didn't sit. Brandon spread photos across the table: Harper Singh, posed in a bakery window, wedding cake in her lap like a grotesque joke.

"Why call me now?" I asked.

"Because someone finally connected the ring fingers," Cheryl said.

Brandon pointed to the next timestamp. "Found at dawn. Public library. Eyes glued shut—with something that wasn't glue."

The details landed like body blows. Precise. Poetic. Revolting.

"You've got an escalation," I said.

"We've got a ghost," Cheryl countered. No prints. No DNA. Just an email: *A New Offering*.

The weeks blurred. Four hours' sleep in a mildew-stained hotel. Brandon brought coffee. Cheryl brought puzzles and sarcasm. I stopped answering my phone like I was out of state.

A florist gave us our first break—roses at Harper's door. No name. Gloves. A book under his arm. He said he was delivering something beautiful.

That night in the morgue, I stared at the delicate slice where Harper's ring finger used to be. Surgical. Reverent.

"He's staging them for someone," I whispered.

"You," Brandon said.

By month's end, I had a desk in the bullpen. A rhythm. And nightmares—veils stiff with rot, my own reflection in every victim. One night Cheryl found me in the evidence locker, staring at a cigar cutter.

"You should go home," she said.

"I don't have one here."

"Neither do I. But you've got something better—people who'll bleed with you if they have to."

That was the night I stopped pretending New York was temporary.

The last victim before I went full-time was the worst. Bride posed in a Windsor chair, hem fanned like petals, eyelids sealed. I didn't cry until after the scene cleared. Alone in a supply closet.

That was when I knew: this wasn't a spree.

It was a love letter. Addressed to me.

Even now I can hear Brandon's voice in the doorway:

"We're going to catch him, Katie. We are."

I thought I came to the city to stop him.

Maybe it was always about becoming the version of myself who could.

Now I just have to survive her.

Unplanned

Dusty

It wasn't planned.

No rope in the trunk. No duct tape in the glove box. Not trolling rest stops or tailing plates.

And then I saw them.

Beat-up blue sedan, windows down, music spilling out. Two girls—barely women—sun-browned arms, hair whipping wild. One singing off-key like the world was hers.

They missed their exit.

Brake lights. A slow shoulder pull. Front-right tire flat. The taller one—dark braid, tank top damp at the collar—got out, trunk open, jack ready. Calm.

The passenger door opened.

The other one—green-eyed brunette—blinked herself awake, slower to orient.

"What's going on?"

"Flat. Go back to sleep."

She didn't.

She stretched, glanced back, saw me.

And froze.

"Katie," she screamed. "Run."

The driver turned just in time to meet my eyes.

I didn't wait.

She fought—kicks, claws, wild panic with no aim. I had her halfway to my car before the other girl even moved.

The other brunette ran. Fast, but wrong.

I set the driver down. Followed. Twenty yards before I caught her—shirt yanked; elbow clipped my chin.

That made it worse.

Knee to her back. Elbow to her neck. Then the needle—sting, skin giving way, the chemical slip flooding in.

Her breath matched mine. Fast. Then slow.

Back to the driver.

Dead weight. Passenger in front, arms folded. Driver in back, head against the glass like she'd agreed to the trip.

Thirty miles north. Forgotten house. Found it last week—not for them. But it was ready.

I carried them in. Separate rooms, just enough space for fear to bloom. No windows. Generator humming.

They'd be safe here.

Safe for what came next.

Her Childhood, Rewritten

Katherine

The boat thudded against the dock, the sound echoing over still water. She stepped onto the warped planks, the wood slick with salt and rain, her legs unsteady after the crossing. The air smelled different here—damp pine, old rope, and something faintly metallic. The house rose ahead through the fog, its silhouette waiting like it had been expecting her.

She drew her gun and started toward the house.

Her childhood home.

Last time she'd seen it, flames had swallowed it whole. She and Elisabeth were fourteen, standing in the yard as the fire consumed everything.

Now she stood in the doorway, heart hammering, breath shallow.

It wasn't just a room.

It was a replica.

Not similar. Not inspired by.

An *exact* reconstruction of the kitchen from her childhood. She could picture Elisabeth sitting on the counter next to her when they were five years old and she had skinned her knee learning how to ride her bike.

Her throat burned. He'd rebuilt it. All of it. From memory? From surveillance? From photographs? Or had he been there?

A sick chill crawled through her chest. What had it cost him to build this? The time. The money. The precision. The obsession.

A part of her recoiled. A part of her wanted to run. But another part—the traitorous one—ached with something too close to understanding. To build this... he would have had to love her.

The kind of love that corrodes. That curates. That collects every broken piece and stitches it back together with wire.

Stepped farther in. Each detail felt louder than the last. The quilt folded on the couch. The handwriting on the fridge.

And by the door—shoes. Her size. Worn in just enough to suggest a life she never lived.

Her breath hitched. None of it was hers.

But it was meant to be.

At the threshold

Dusty

She was here.

Not just near—*here*. The weight of her steps vibrated through the floorboards he'd chosen, sanded, stained. Years of waiting, and now she was inside—not as a voice down a hallway, not as a blurred Polaroid, but alive, in the space he'd made for her.

From the second-floor railing, cloaked in silence, he watched. Katherine stood in the doorway like she didn't believe it was real—shoulders tight, pistol drawn. Her gaze swept the room, pausing at the ceramic bowl by the sink—peppermint candy, their mother's candy. She brushed it without noticing. He noticed.

Her eyes moved to the painting—a copy of the one from her grandparents' house. Recognition stirred in her bones. God, she was magnificent. Sharpened. Colder. Unbroken. No one else could have made it this far. No one else deserved this.

His fingers tightened around the velvet box in his coat. Inside: a black diamond carved into the shape of an anatomical heart. Not a gift. A seal. A lock. A vow she could not undo. His proposal wasn't flowers or sunsets. It was permanence. Elisabeth alive upstairs, hair brushed, waiting—proof of his devotion. A wedding gift no other man could offer.

When Katherine saw her sister, grief would dissolve, the gun lower. She would understand at last what he had built: a life, a family, a forever. Marriage wasn't a question. It was inevitability. Possession sanctified.

She moved toward the stairs. Purpose sharpened her posture.

He steadied his breath.
He was ready.

You Don't Get to Rot

Dusty/Katherine

The air around him thrummed with a sacred kind of anticipation. This was it. The final brushstroke. The crescendo. The moment the hunter laid down his weapon and opened his chest to the only woman who had ever seen him.

Their house hummed with warmth. Every beam, every scent... familiar. Designed for memory. For home. For her.

For them.

And she had seen him—that morning, in the shower, in the hush where she let herself need him. She loved him. Even if she didn't have the language for it yet.

The doorknob turned. He straightened.

Katherine stepped into the parlor. Gun drawn. Stance rigid. Her face carved from granite.

He didn't flinch.

"*Katie*," he whispered.

Her jaw trembled at the name, but the barrel never lowered.

"You came," he said.

Her voice cracked like a whip. "Who are you?"

"Dusty."

One step forward. Careful, reverent. "I was going to kill you," he admitted softly. "You and Elisabeth. That was the plan. Break you down, build you into something better. Mine."

The name split her in two. Dusty. It ricocheted off bone, burned through marrow. *The boy who ripped her world apart. The ghost she'd hunted from West Virginia to New York. The man who violated her, not just mind but body as well. The man who turned her twin into a grave-shaped question mark.*

Her chest tightened until every breath scalded. She wanted to lunge, to drive her fists into his face until it stopped being his face. To scream her sister's name in his ears until the weight of what he'd done shattered him the way he had shattered them.

But she didn't. Couldn't.

He wasn't allowed to see that kind of victory.

She forced the fury into a single word. "Stop."

"But I couldn't." His eyes burned with something that looked too much like devotion. "I studied you. And something shifted. You weren't just a girl anymore—you were fire wrapped in flesh. I fell in love with the way you survive."

Her hands shook, her body begged for violence, but she stayed still.

Because if she moved, she wasn't sure she'd stop.

"I thought if you just had enough time, you'd see me. Understand me—love me back."

A silence hung. Then—her arm dipped. Just barely. The gun lowered a fraction, enough to make his pulse surge.

"You want me to believe this is love?" she asked, voice trembling. "All the bodies. All the lies."

"I made them beautiful—for you. Each kill a sonnet. Each display a proposal."

She stepped closer, slow. Calm. Deadly.

"And all this time..." her tone sharpened, "you were right there. Devin. Dusty. Whatever name you think you deserve."

He flinched at his real name from her lips.

Still, she inched closer. Close enough that hope flickered—

"You should've told me sooner," she murmured. "You could've trusted me."

His throat bobbed. "I—"

Her hand lifted. Touched his cheek.

He leaned into it.

That was his mistake.

The barrel pressed against his sternum.

Her eyes changed.

"I hope it burns," she said, voice like ice. "Knowing the thing you wanted most is the one taking your life."

His mouth opened—

—but the shot rang before words could catch up.

He staggered. One shot to the chest. A second tore through his thigh. He dropped, gasping, blinking up at her like she was sunlight breaking through stained glass.

She moved above him, calm now. Ice instead of fire. Precision instead of rage.

"You don't get to rot in prison," she said. "No trials. No appeals. No podcasts. You vanish. Forgotten."

His chest stuttered.

He coughed blood.

"K-Katherine…"

She didn't flinch.

"…Elisabeth…" he rasped.

She froze.

"…alive."

Silence devoured the room.

His gaze locked to hers. Then slipped away. His chest stilled.

Nobody to No One

Katherine

The gun felt heavier now.

Her arm hung useless at her side, the metal dragging her down, still warm. The silence rushed in—thick, unnatural, like the walls themselves were holding their breath. Every tick of her pulse filled the room that should've been echoing with screams.

He wasn't breathing. Dusty.

Not Devin. Not The Artist. Just... *Dusty*.

A name that didn't mean anything anymore. No legacy. No brilliance. Just a boy who grew up to poison the world. Who thought obsession was love.

Her knees gave out. The floor met her hard, cold seeping straight through her jeans, into her bones. Her fingers clutched the boards, desperate for something solid—anything that didn't feel like collapse.

The quiet wasn't peace. It was after. The kind that followed hurricanes, sirens, screams already burned out.

"He's gone." Her voice cracked like old wood. Maybe the house heard. Maybe the ghosts—the women, the brides, mutilated and displayed like twisted icons. Maybe they were still here, listening. Waiting.

"Elisabeth..." Her throat burned. "I got him. For both of us."

The weight of it broke her open. No sobs—just a tremor that started in her shoulders and spread. She curled forward; forehead pressed to her knees. Her chest felt hollowed out. Like she'd screamed everything she had years ago, and this was what remained.

Dry, soundless grief.

Every display. Every ring. Every frozen, staged body flashed through her. "You mattered," she whispered to the floor. "He didn't. He thought he could shape you into something beautiful, but you already were. You were galaxies and storms and fire."

Her palms flattened to the floor. Her hands still shook, blood still racing, even though the monster was gone.

"I ended him here. No trial. No headlines. No podcasts.

No one gets to remember him."

But her breath caught.

What if it was true?

What if Elisabeth really was alive, and this was the one time he didn't lie?

Or worse—what if it was his last twist of the knife? One final game.

She forced herself to look at him again.

And there it was.

That smirk.

Faint. Crooked at the corners, like it had been stitched in place. Like he died smiling. Like he wanted her to wonder.

He hadn't begged. He hadn't raged. He'd spoken her sister's name like a promise and gone still with that look.

He knew she'd never stop questioning it.

Her stomach twisted. Acid climbed up her throat. She wanted to scream, to claw the expression off his face, but her arms wouldn't move. He had stolen years, her innocence, stolen futures, stolen breath—and even in death, he was still taking.

She pulled herself upright, every joint burning. Her spine un-coiled like a blade.

"He's nobody now," she said. A vow. A curse.

She turned. Finished.

One last glance—

He looked small. Just a body. Nothing of the legend, nothing of the shadow that had haunted her.

But the smirk lingered.

And then—

A scream.

High. Human.

Not her.

Her lungs seized. The air ripped away like a rug pulled from under her feet.

Again. Muffled. From deeper inside the house.

Real.

Her legs moved before thought did. Down the hallway, past the narrow staircase. The scream sliced through her like an electric wire.

Victim twenty. Someone alive. Not a display. Not another body. Alive.

Another door.

Locked.

"Hello?" she shouted, pounding. "Is someone there?"

A voice. Small, broken. "Katie?"

Her lungs froze.

Again, louder: "Katie—is that you?!"

Her heart shattered. Only one person had ever said it that way.

"Elisabeth?"

She slammed her shoulder into the door. Wood cracked. Gave.

And then—she was there.

Alive.

Not pale and broken, not the ghost Katherine had carried for so long. Flushed. Braided hair. Clean clothes. Tears shining on her face. Real. Whole.

Katherine rushed forward and Elisabeth collided with her, sobbing, arms clamped tight. Katherine held on as if she could press every piece of her back into place by force alone.

"Please," Elisabeth choked into her neck. "Please don't let this be a dream."

Katherine collapsed to her knees again, this time with her sister in her arms. Not for grief. Not for loss.

But for the truth.

She didn't have to mourn a ghost anymore.

She could hold her.

She could bring her home.

Elisabeth clung tighter, face buried against her neck. Her words trembled, almost too perfect, almost rehearsed.

"Please," she whispered again, softer this time. "Please don't let this be a dream."

Katherine shut her eyes, clutching her like she could stitch the years shut. She wanted to believe every word. She *had* to.

But for just a heartbeat, as Elisabeth's grip slackened, something hollow passed through her voice. A pause where love should have lived.

She felt the weight of her sister in her arms—alive, real, returned.

And beneath it, a silence that was waiting to bloom.

The World Didn't End

Katherine

They didn't stay on the island long.

The rental car turned down the gravel road like it remembered the way better than she did. Katherine gripped the wheel—not from fear, not even from rage, but to hold herself together.

Elisabeth slept in the passenger seat, curled toward the door like they were sixteen again on a road trip. Only now, her hands twitched in her lap, and Katherine didn't ask about her dreams.

The house came into view. Porch light broken. Wind chimes tangled. Steps still leaning left, like time hadn't touched them.

She braked slow, gravel crunching. This was where it ended-or began again.

"Hey," she whispered, touching Elisabeth's arm. "We're here."

Green eyes blinked open—familiar but dulled.

Katherine opened her door. October air smelled like wood smoke and damp leaves. She came around and offered her sister a hand. Elisabeth took it. Their fingers threaded like they'd never missed a day—though they had. Thousands.

The front door opened. Their mother stood frozen, hand to her mouth. Their father stepped up behind her, barefoot, staring like they both stepped out of a dream.

Katherine didn't speak. She brought her sister forward like an offering.

"Elisabeth?" her mother breathed, voice breaking.

Elisabeth fell into her mother's arms, clinging with a sob that tore through the doorway. Their father wrapped around them both, whispering her name like it might undo the years. Katherine stood just behind, breath trembling in her chest, watching the family knit itself back together in front of her eyes.

It was over. Dusty—no, not even his name—was gone. Erased.

"You're home," Katherine whispered into her sister's hair as she leaned into the embrace, adding her arms to the tangle. "We're safe. He's gone."

Elisabeth's face stayed buried in their mother's shoulder. A choked sound slipped out—half sob, half something else—but Katherine didn't question it. She only held tighter. For the first time in years, she believed it.

After the Fire

Katherine

The room was the same.

Yellow chair. Crooked vent. Tissue box with one already pulled like a dare.

But I wasn't the same.

The couch creaked under me. 4:17 p.m. I hadn't looked at clocks in days, but this one glared—proof time moved, even when you didn't.

Dr. Delaney sat opposite, legal pad balanced on her knee. Blue glasses. Gray curls. That same look—therapist and archaeologist, ready to dig through ash for bone.

"You came back," she said.

I nodded. "Took the long way."

Her pen scratched.

"It's over," I said.

"Is it?"

I thought of the gallery. The air stale with salt and dust. Each display dismantled in silence—no cameras, no press. Just us and what he thought would outlast him: rings, fingers, hair braided with ribbon. Names he's written with distinction.

I made the calls myself. Told mothers their daughters' things were recovered. Husbands-to-be that fiancés could be buried whole. Sisters got back necklaces they'd made together, brothers, graduation watches. We gave it all back— not to memorialize him, but to cut him out of every story.

My voice felt smaller when I finally said, "Yeah. It's over."

I stared at a crack in the baseboard. "I keep thinking I should feel relieved. Or angry. But it's like I left myself on that island and came back wearing someone else's skin."

Silence. Permission.

"I kissed him. Trusted him. Let my guard down, and he was waiting for me to blink."

"Do you think that's what made it happen?" She asked gently.

I shook my head. "No. It was always going to happen. He built it hoping I would."

"And now?" She asked.

Air didn't taste like smoke but still made me choke.

"I keep dreaming of the briefcase. The ribbon. The chess. Queen. The coal scrip. And what he didn't put in there—no photo of Elisabeth. No note. Just symbols." I answered.

I added. "That was the trap. Not the knives. Not the island. The need to understand him."

"And you still do?" she asked.

"I hate that I do." I answered quietly.

"You survived," she said.

"Yeah. But I don't know who did." I answered.

She leaned forward. "Maybe that's who we find in here."

Something shifted under my feet. New ground.

"Where do we start?" I challenged.

"With the part of you that wasn't built by him." She answered.

And for the first time, I wasn't afraid to find her.

October song

Katherine

The sky didn't owe me anything anymore.

It just stretched—quiet, wide, a pale October blue, the edges soft like frost melting off a windowpane

We walked slow along the trail behind the farmhouse, leaves breaking under our boots, the scent of wood smoke in the air. Elisabeth kept her coat buttoned despite the unseasonable warmth, one hand tucked deep in her pocket, the other brushing against the bark of trees as we passed.

Neither of us spoke. The world moved the way I thought healing should—never fast, never cruel, just forward.

At the edge of the clearing, she stopped. Pulled something from her pocket.

A ribbon. Blue. She tied it into a loose knot, stepped to the old stone fire pit and set it down inside. Not burned. Not buried. Just...surrendered.

She came back without a word. We sat on a fallen log, the cold seeping through our jeans. I passed her a thermos of cider. She drank slowly, like she had to remember to enjoy it.

We weren't whole. We weren't healed.

But we were here.

She looked toward the line of maples along the ridge. "Do you remember the song Mom used to sing in the car? The one about the boat?"

"Yeah."

After a while, she rose. "I'm going to walk a little further."

I didn't follow. I stayed, listening to the wind sift through the dried leaves, letting it carry away the footsteps.

Epilogue

Elisabeth

Six months since the leaves fell in silence behind us, since I pretended the trail meant freedom.

The farmhouse was small, the kind that held onto warmth even after the fire died. Katherine said she picked it because of the porch—east-facing, so the mornings would always start with light. She liked to sit out there with tea. I liked to sit beside her and let her think she'd saved me.

Tonight, the air was cool, carrying the smell of cut grass and wood smoke.

Bernie—my ridiculous little dachshund with the crooked teeth—curled at my feet, snoring like an old man. I could hear Katherine in the kitchen, the soft clink of a spoon against ceramic, the squeak of the screen door as she stepped outside.

She always asks less now. Less about the island. Less about him. She thinks it's because I'm healing. Maybe I am. Just…not the way she imagines.

I pick up my brush. The canvas in front of me is a mess of color—yellow bleeding into black, streaks of green curling like vines. I'm not painting for skill. I'm painting because it's loud enough to drown out the way my mind keeps going back to him.

To the sound of his voice when he said my name.

To the way he looked at her.

To the night he touched me like he thought I was her.

My fingers pause on the bristles. I press the brush to the jar of water, watch the yellow cloud drift and vanish.

I stand and step out onto the porch. Katherine is already there, curled on the swing, watching the stars like she's memorizing their positions. She smiles when she sees me, and for a moment I almost believe I can be the sister she remembers.

"Couldn't sleep," I say.

"Me either."

I sit beside her. The swing rocks. Bernie shifts and sighs at our feet.

She tilts her head toward the sky. "Do you think quiet like this ever lasts?"

I keep my eyes forward. "No," I say softly. "But it changes."

My hand drifts—just briefly—to rest on my stomach.

She doesn't notice.

She wouldn't understand.

We sit until the first light brushes the mountains.

And the world, impossibly, keeps turning.

Some things you bury. Others you keep.

Author's Note

He was always real.
Not by name.
But in the way the world teaches women to flinch before they speak.
To second-guess the monster when it smiles.
To call it love.
To carry the blame.
Silent Invitation is a story carved from silence.
It's about what happens when the past isn't buried deep enough.
When grief becomes currency.
When justice comes too late—or not at all.
Katherine Poe was never a hero by design.
She was made that way—through fire, through blood, through every breath no one believed she'd take again.
And like so many survivors, she didn't rise unscathed.
She rose unfinished. Unrelenting.
Alive.
To those who know what it's like to be hunted—and to those who fought their way back anyway—this book was for you.
Monsters die.
But memory doesn't.
And sometimes, survival *is* the story.
—Devona Burgess

ABOUT THE AUTHOR

Devona Burgess writes stories that live between beauty and brutality, truth and obsession. She began crafting *SILENT INVITATION* as an English assignment while pursuing her bachelor's in criminal justice– and what started as a classroom idea evolved into a haunting debut thriller.

She lives between three mountains with her husband Quincy, their four children, and two beloved dogs. She has two children from a previous marriage and two beautiful granddaughters. When she isn't writing, Devona can be found doing crafts, spending time with family, or making jewelry while chaos unfolds in the next room.

www.ingramcontent.com/pod-product-compliance
Lightning Source LLC
Chambersburg PA
CBHW030346120726
47901CB00007B/1928